# The Chair

## Daniel And The Twin Fountains Of Alcazar

JOE SIMONDS

# DEDICATION

To Daniel, who taught me that the only disability is a bad mindset...

# CONTENTS

# 1 TROUBLE BREWING

Vosco laughed.

He was staring at the zombie-like people on the sidewalk in front of him. After seeing how out of touch they were with everything around them, he felt a glimmer of hope. Trying to blend in wouldn't be as tough as he had initially thought. These humans were so glued to their phones he was sure they wouldn't notice anything out of the ordinary—not even a talking frog.

Vosco tried to swat away a pesky mosquito that continued to parade around his face. It was a blistering summer day in Florida. He wasn't used to this humidity. Nor was he used to the bugs and sticky pads on his feet, though he should have been by now. Another mosquito whizzed by. He unexpectedly had the impulse to roll out his tongue and make it his dinner. Gross. On second thought *save that for the real frogs...*

Usually Vosco was very tall—6'4" to be exact. He was muscular and intimidating. He was built with big broad shoulders, a thick bodybuilder neck, and powerful legs like an NFL wide receiver. He had a deep cleft on his chin, which further masculinized his rugged features. His sandy blonde hair was just beginning to show a few streaks of grey.

Today was different. Vosco and his friend Skylar had *shapeshifted* into animals in an effort to disguise themselves in this new world. His tall, masculine frame was exchanged for that of a plump, green frog with a horned back and webbed feet. His deep-set, brown eyes were now bulging on either side of his head. He was one ugly frog.

While Vosco continued to swat mosquitoes, his friend Skylar perched on a tree branch overhead trying to gather her bearings. Time was ticking and they had no idea in what direction they were headed. They only knew that they'd made it to the boy's neighborhood, but they had to find his home fast… even if that meant knocking on every door.

The trip to St. Augustine had been a long and dangerous one. After a brutal trek through three dangerous middle grounds they found themselves lost in a suburban Florida neighborhood. They had no map, no GPS, no smartphone, and no guide to get them to the house of a boy named Daniel. They were going on what little information their prophet friend, Maku, had given them. According to the all-knowing Maku the Magu, there was soon to be an attack on The United States of America—an attack so sizable it would devastate the nation beyond repair.

Skylar, in owl form, ruffled her feathers. Her large, yellow eyes did not miss a beat. "Hoo-hoo-hoooo!" her screech echoed across the sky as her sharp beak quivered. Normally she was an attractive girl in her mid-twenties. She had light brown, wavy hair that most women would die for. Her bright green eyes always seemed to sparkle, and her smile left an impression as big as the two dimples on her cheeks. She was 5'7" and built like a lean swimmer. Long legs, slender body, broad shoulders and back… muscular. She was neither plain nor elegant. She was normal. Normal Skylar. That's how she felt at least. She had never worn make-up before and she probably never would. She rarely went out of her way to look beautiful, yet most people would describe her this way. She was independent to an extreme; in fact, she had never dated anyone, never had a crush, or even considered love. This was mostly due to her fears of ending up like her mom... a control freak who found a way to worry about everything. It was a miracle she finally gave in and allowed her to go on this trip.

Skylar was certainly the youngest of her kind to ever set out on a mission like this. If her mom was here, she probably would have had a heart attack. Skylar, however, felt exhilarated to be here. She was a little scared, but mostly excited to finally be out of the house and part of this important assignment.

Skylar signaled down to Vosco to start moving west. Just as he was rounding the corner of a bush, he came face to face with a couple of second graders waiting for their summer camp bus to arrive.

One of the freckle-faced boys immediately saw the big, green frog. He dropped his backpack and Toy Story lunchbox with a clatter and ran towards him with outstretched hands. Vosco panicked. He looked to his right... then to his left. There was nowhere to hide. The boy cupped his hands in anticipation of his catch as his sneakers smacked against the pavement.

*No... I can't die today... not like this... not as a frog...* Before he could finish his thoughts there was a flash of brown feathers and a gust of air—he was gone. The freckle-faced kid looked down in disbelief. An owl had literally snatched the frog in a matter of seconds and vanished into the sky. He shrugged his shoulders and walked back over to his friends.

In the tree above Vosco was trying to regain his composure. He hadn't seen Skylar coming. She had literally knocked the breath out of him as she swooped him up in front of the boy's outstretched hands. By all means it appeared as if he had met an untimely fate as he was carried away with the owl's razor-sharp talons.

"Thanks for saving me back there," said Vosco. "After all we've been through to reach this world, who would have ever thought I'd almost be captured by a kid who can barely tie his shoes?"

Skylar chuckled.

"Perhaps it's just safer if I carry you until we find Daniel," she said.

The two of them watched the green patches of neatly manicured lawns move below them in silence. The oak trees slowly swayed in the gentle motion as the summer breeze drifted through the neighborhood.

"Think this Daniel is a huge warrior?" asked Skylar. "I wonder what kind of special magic his chair has? I've never met anyone who has a magical chair... have you? Do you think it can turn into a war machine with cannons and guns?"

Vosco remained quiet.

Skylar continued, "I bet he's incredibly strong and brave. That's what we could really use down there—someone who can lead us towards peace and end the fear..."

Vosco stiffened. He stared ahead and began to fidget with his tiny, webbed fingers. How did anyone reach peace through war? Was there such a fight as a "good fight"? These were the questions that tormented him after what happened under his own leadership many years ago. He caught his mind drifting off to the civil war that ruined their nation. With a deep breath he tried to turn his thoughts elsewhere.

Skyler changed the subject. She was looking at the people below. "Do you think they are scared? Do you think any of them know?"

"Know what?" he said.

"That they are just days away from losing almost everything?" she replied.

Skylar's question hung in the air in an uncomfortable silence. It was a simple question, but it reminded them both of the importance of their mission. While Skylar was excited to be a part of this, it was easy to forget what was at stake if they failed. The prospect of losing everything was sobering. Vosco couldn't find his words.

"Do you think they even know who Kore is?" she asked.

Vosco found his words.

"No. Definitely not. An evil terrorist megalomaniac like Kore would not have the power he does if the public knew his true identity..."

"Well..." Skylar started, "They'll certainly know who he is when he shuts down the entire U.S. power grid. Modern civilization can't function without electricity, digital money, Internet... it will be chaos."

"It *would* be chaos if it happens," Vosco corrected her. He was trying to instill hope even as his own mind began to doubt.

The two peered down at the people walking along the sidewalks and in the park below them. From above Vosco thought they looked like ants. Little, marching ants—unaware of what loomed around them.

Skylar seemed to be responding to his thoughts as she said, "Even if they did notice anything out of the ordinary, there's literally nothing they could do to stop it. According to Maku, there's only one person here on Earth who can save the world from what's to come... and that's Daniel."

"We don't have much time left. Let's find him," Vosco said, bringing the conversation to a halt.

# 2 THE SITUATION ROOM

**Washington D.C.**

*Why do I feel this nervous?*

This should have been a proud moment: his first Situation Room meeting.

Jay Woodward McFarland, a poor boy raised by a single mom in Florida, had somehow done the impossible. Looking back on his life, most people never would have guessed he would amount to much. His biological father had walked out on Jay and his mom when he was only five years old. Jay was too young to understand what was going on. But he was old enough to feel the pain of having the only important man in his life walk out on him. No visits. No letters. No child support. Nothing. He just disappeared—never to be heard from again. Jay watched from the sidelines as his mom worked multiple jobs and long hours to support the family. Her work ethic became the driving force for him to get to where he was today.

Jay didn't move a muscle. Despite the anxiety roaring inside of him, his exterior remained calm and collected. He'd learned this from Jack Fullerton, the man who'd been the closest thing to a father for him. Fullerton had been the mayor of St. Augustine back when Jay was young, and just as so many sons follow in their fathers' footsteps, he was the reason Jay had become a politician.

However, the Fullerton family held value for Jay beyond its patriarch. The mayor's son, Mark, was also his friend. Together they had earned the reputation of being the baseball all-stars of the city. Jay had led the entire league with his bat. Mark had led with his arm; he was the best pitcher St. Augustine had ever had. College coaches were scouting these two young men even when they were still pimple-faced teenagers who couldn't drive cars.

One summer the boys were selected to join the Florida AAU traveling team. Jay was ecstatic. This was his first opportunity to travel outside of St. Augustine. However, his mother refused the offer. She couldn't afford the upfront cost for traveling, lodging, uniforms, etc. Nor could she afford to take a day off of work. Jay was devastated.

A few days later everything changed. Jay's mom opened the front door of their tiny, one-bedroom apartment, and there stood Mayor Jack and his son. The mayor not only offered to pay for all of Jay's dues, but also agreed that he and his wife would watch the two boys for the summer. After that amazing summer, the two of them were inseparable. Jay spent almost every weekend over at their house swimming in their pool and feeling like he was a part of their family. His mother was grateful for this opportunity.

The boys remained friends throughout high school. Mayor Jack became a father figure to Jay. So much so that Mark became envious of him. By the end of their senior year, their friendship had dwindled. Both boys suffered major injuries playing baseball ruining any chances of a Division I scholarship. Even worse, the mayor helped Jay land an internship in his office, while Mark was left to mow lawns their senior summer.

Two years after high school graduation the boys hardly spoke. Jay was attending Flagler College in St. Augustine, while Mark attended a local community college. The mayor was grooming Jay to become a politician, while Mark struggled through college and eventually dropped out. The mayor's son then went on to marry a girl he had only recently met at a bar, which shocked the family. Rumors spread that he married her because she was pregnant.

Then the unimaginable happened. It was the biggest scandal to ever rock the area—a violent and strange murder. The mayor and his wife disappeared. Most people assumed he'd somehow had a hand in it. It didn't make sense to him. None of it did, but the truth was never uncovered.

Jay had lost another dad. To make things worse, his mom was diagnosed with brain cancer shortly after the mayor's disappearance. Jay watched her take her last breath in a cheap hospital bed. He had never felt more alone in his life. In moments like this in the Situation Room, his thoughts would bring him back to when his mother died—the moment he felt lonelier than he'd ever been. Still as a statue, but with a storm of emotion raging within him, Jay continued reflecting on that moment; on the story that brought him to where he was now.

With no siblings or real family, Jay put every ounce of energy into his career as a politician. He had a chip on his shoulder—a big one. All he cared about was proving to the world that he could be somebody important; important enough that he'd never be alone again. The world would love him. He didn't need a family in order to belong. He could do it on his own. He didn't need a father figure to groom him for greatness. He would become someone great.

He finally did. He was President of the United States of America. Even his critics were calling his win unprecedented. It was the ultimate underdog victory in American history. He was a Republican according to the system, but deep down he was just a conservative American who believed neither "side" was always right. He was sharp enough to focus his entire campaign on one big problem—the lack of unity in America.

It also helped that he was handsome. Many said he was the most handsome president since John F. Kennedy. Jay stood at 6"1, he had wavy brown hair, light blue eyes, and the physique of a runner. He was also one of the most persuasive and high-energy public debaters to ever stand behind a podium. He was such an amazing debater that even the other side enjoyed watching him verbally assault and humiliate his opponents. That's probably why so many delegates from both the Republican and Democratic parties privately urged him to run for president. He did, and he won. Now he wished it had never happened. No one told him being president was going to be like this...

It was too late. He was now the most powerful man in the world, whether he felt like it on the inside or not. The craziest part of his unprecedented climb to the top was that he barely won the election; barely won as in more people voted against him than for him. In fact, it was entirely possible more Americans disliked him than liked him right now. It was not a good feeling. It certainly didn't help that the media was painting him to be some ignorant goon, who would quickly run the country into the ground from his lack of business experience. He could only imagine what people would be saying about him when they heard about this current crisis.

From the minute he stepped foot in the White House just a month ago, nothing had gone well. Two top advisors sent in their resignation letters the day after he was inaugurated. The Speaker of the House decided to retire out of the blue. China announced they were going to back out of a trade agreement that negatively impacted almost every Fortune 500 business in America. The stock market was down over five percent in less than a month. However, none of this scared him like the news he had heard this morning: America was now under siege by the largest cyber-attack recorded in world history. Not only had a group of hackers found a way into the government's supposedly impenetrable servers, but they managed to steal billions of dollars. The hackers also downloaded thousands of classified documents, which would be an embarrassment for the country in the wrong hands. Interestingly nothing had been leaked thus far. Although this should have provided a sense of relief, it made Jay even more anxious.

Jay wondered, *Why would they just stop? Is it Russia? Will I go down as the fastest president to ever declare war?* He looked at his watch. Three more minutes until the staff meeting. Jay thought about the press; the talking heads, who live and breathe to make politicians look bad on their biased news stations. They loved to see politicians sweat it out in front of the public. Thankfully the press didn't know about this cyber-attack… yet.

He made his way into the Situation Room for the first time. The fear in the room was palpable as several sets of nervous eyes darted in his direction. The country had never experienced an attack like this before. The White House cyber unit, some of the most sophisticated hackers in the world, had never seen anything like it.

Something caught his eye on the table. His newly appointed assistant, Mary, was trying to get his attention. He glanced at the small plaque sitting on the thick mahogany table next to her. It read:

## President Jay McFarland

Before his rear end had even hit the leather on the oversized chair, he heard a voice pipe up from the back of the room.

"Sir, everyone is present. Are you ready to get started?" asked Bruce Cromwell, the Secretary of Defense.

Jay took his seat. He looked around the room and nodded. He wasn't sure what to say to start the meeting off. He knew he must have looked like a scared sheep about to get sheared for the first time.

Where were all of his aides to help him? Why wasn't there a handbook or something on what he was supposed to say and do? His thoughts were interrupted by Luke Christenson, the Chief of Staff.

"What's the latest on this hack? Any signs of them coming back?"

"No," replied Cromwell. "Our cyber-intelligence officers remain convinced that something scared them off. Perhaps they thought they were about to be traced."

He paused for a moment staring at his phone.

"Sorry," he continued, "I was just alerted that our team down on the main cyber-security floor uncovered some critical information on the hack."

"What is it?" asked Jay, more comfortable taking the lead on an emergent situation than leading a simple meeting.

Everyone in the room looked over at Bruce Cromwell, intrigued to know what he'd found out.

"They... can't tell me via text," he replied.

"Well, why in the world not?" yelled the impatient National Security Advisor to the president, Darren Daley. "Didn't the government pay a gazillion dollars of taxpayers' money to get us cell phones that were impossible to hack?"

"All I know is that he said he didn't want to send it through text. Paul's coming over here to tell us himself. He said we'll understand when he tells us."

The silence was deafening. They knew this wasn't a good sign if the head of cyber-intelligence was afraid to communicate inside of the White House. Were they being watched now? Had the hackers tapped into the Situation Room? Although no one said a word, they all felt it. Fear. Fear of the unknown.

"Perhaps it's the Mad Hackers." It was Anthony Clapper, the Director for Counterterrorism, whom everyone thought was a bit of a clown.

"Who the heck are the Mad Hackers?" asked Jay calmly, but already judging the name.

"Here he goes," whispered Audrey Marshall, assistant to Jay McFarland for counterterrorism. She rolled her eyes. Anthony didn't waste any time.

"Apparently a few detractors left the well-known hacking group Anonymous because they felt Anonymous wasn't monetizing their skills enough. They felt that they could be making a lot more money while giving some away to the poor."

"So they named themselves after the Mad Hatter in *Alice in Wonderland?*" Vice President Sam Hostler, perhaps the most introverted and inconspicuous vice president of all time, whispered from the back. "Seems like a missed opportunity to not call themselves something more *Robinhood* related…"

Anthony didn't even flinch at the comment. "They're known for stealing large sums of money from governments and mega banks and funneling it out to tons of different bank accounts through untraceable wires. After that, no one is really sure where the money goes."

"Here's the real question," howled Admiral Irving "Doc" Hardy. He was the oldest person in the room and had served America in the military since he was 18 years old. "How in the world does someone steal billions of dollars from the U.S. Treasury without getting caught? Is this some sort of joke?"

"It's got to be an inside job," said Luke.

"Sir, it doesn't appear to be," replied Bruce.

"It's got to be Russia then," the president replied.

"No sir. It doesn't appear to be Russia."

Vice President Sam Hostler chimed in, "Then who's behind it? China?"

Just then, a loud buzz from the conference table's main dashboard alerted them a guest was at the door. "Mr. President, Paul Glazer from cyber-intelligence is here for you.

"Send him in, please," the president said.

Paul, a middle-aged man who'd already gone fully grey perhaps ten years too early, walked in with a spring in his step. He stopped abruptly, catching himself mid-stride and adjusted his weight as he was met with stares around the room. Everyone was anxious to hear his news.

"Sir… you aren't going to believe this," Paul said, turning to face the president.

"Just tell us, will ya?" boomed Admiral Hardy.

"The attack is coming from…"

All eyes were on Paul.

"Yes, tell us," the president whispered softly.

"Underground."

Nobody moved. Nobody seemed to even breathe.

"Underground?" the confused National Intelligence Director asked. "You mean Australia? As in down under?" he asked.

"Impossible!" barked Colonel Hardy gruffly. "The Aussies would never hack the United States, not even if—"

He was cut off by Paul. "Listen, it's not Australia, and it's not New Zealand. It's not any country but ours—"

"Ours? Who in the heck are you talking about?" demanded Darren Daley, not letting Paul finish his sentence.

Everyone in the room fell silent. All eyes were on Paul.

"The signal is coming from underground."

"What in God's green earth are you talking about, son? Underground? Have you gone mad?" demanded Hardy.

He looked at each person in the room before replying. "Underground as in the attacks are coming in from under the earth's surface... literally."

"And if I were to ask under which part of Earth, I'm guessing you'd say under the very earth we're standing on?" President McFarland asked, his voice much quieter than everyone else's.

The room froze, waiting to hear Paul's answer.

"Yes, Mr. President. Under the United States of America."

As if all on the same swivel, a room full of heads turned in unison to face President McFarland once again. He stared down at his feet, his brow knit tightly over his eyes. He was silent for a moment before he spoke again, even more calmly.

"Anyone else's first day of work here look like this?"

# 3 THE HACKER

"They'll probably bury him there," she whispered with a hint of sadness.

The librarian with exceptionally thick hair and a light blue plaid dress was staring at the boy in the wheelchair. She was on break with her new summer intern. The intern was a shy, eleventh grade girl, who fit right in... well, fit right in at the library. She loved nothing more than reading books in quiet places. She slowly glanced over at the boy, who was currently the topic of conversation. He was over in the corner hunched behind a laptop, far too focused on the screen to ever notice anyone was talking about him.

"What's his story?" she whispered back.

"Oh dear, it's a sad one," the librarian said. She pushed in even closer to the young intern, their faces mere inches apart. "Did you ever hear the story of the woman they found in the downtown fountain, who was beaten to death?"

"No!" the intern whispered, curiosity spreading across her face. She couldn't believe she had somehow missed a story like this.

"Oh my, I can't believe you don't remember all of the controversy around what happened. Perhaps you were too young. Well, some tourists from Italy—or somewhere in Europe—had come here to St. Augustine to see the historic forts. On their hike back to their hotel they found a man, a woman, and a blood-covered newborn baby in a fountain outside of the old abandoned Alcazar hotel. The three of them were rushed to the hospital and the mother was declared dead upon arrival at the hospital. The medic was able to save the son, but he had been strangled by the umbilical cord during birth and was born with severe cerebral palsy. That's why he's in a wheelchair and can't walk or talk."

"That's horrible. What about his dad?" she asked.

She peeked back over to make sure he couldn't hear her.

"Well, the autopsy revealed his wife had drowned in the hotel fountain."

"In a shallow fountain?"

"Precisely. Which didn't make any sense at all. Someone had to have held her under the water, right? Since the cops had no leads whatsoever, they considered her husband a suspect who'd also been badly injured and found at the scene of the crime."

"Oh… I'd assumed the attacker had just attacked the whole family, including him."

"That's what he claimed. But he was unable to provide any details whatsoever about who *had* attacked them. He said they'd been drugged and blindfolded. He only had a guess: his own father."

"Huh?"

"They couldn't find a valid motive for why his father would be behind such a thing. Even his wife's parents didn't believe him. In fact, they actually sued him for the death of their daughter."

The eleventh-grader's eyes grew wider.

"Then what?" she asked.

"The court couldn't prove that he killed her. In fact, he actually passed the lie detector test saying he didn't commit murder."

"Wow. Was he really guilty?"

"No one really knows. Eventually, all of the publicity from the case drove him mad. He lost his job and his friends. He turned into a pretty nasty drunk from what I hear."

"Bet his son doesn't care much for being home with him then…" The intern's gaze wandered back to the boy in the wheelchair. "He was here twenty minutes before the library even opened. Is that a daily routine?"

"Yep. For as long as I can remember. He has the special needs school bus drop him off here every day. But don't let that wheelchair fool you—he's one smart cookie. He can't walk or talk but his brain is working on overdrive. Rumor has it that the school made him retake the IQ test because they didn't believe his first score. It was one of the highest in the state."

"What's his name?" the girl asked.

"Daniel. And he's a little whiz behind that computer. Many years ago, my husband was down at Scores sports bar watching Sunday NFL football when Daniel's dad came in to drink some beer. He brought Daniel with him. The game was down to the last couple of minutes. Daniel hacked into the bar's media system and changed all of TVs to the Disney channel right before the final play of the game. My husband said he had never seen so many grown men screaming in his life. People were cursing out the management. They had no idea it was the little kid in the wheelchair until later. It was the last time his dad ever took him to the bar again."

The intern smiled.

Daniel shifted in his wheelchair and glanced up from his screen. It was the first time he'd raised his head in probably twenty-five minutes. His eyes found the pair of young women hunched over in deep conversation with their eyes all on Daniel. As soon as they came into focus, they quickly turned away. Daniel smiled. He was used to this— people talking about him. His dramatic entrance into this world made him somewhat of a small-town celebrity. Having cerebral palsy was an unnecessary cherry on top, escalating his story to soap-opera-level drama; a guarantee that he would *never* quite escape the limelight.

Daniel had been going to the library every day for years. As a young seventeen-year-old confined to a wheelchair with no ability to walk or talk, he had no real friends. It didn't help that his dad was a drunk and also had no real friends—minus the bartender at the local pub, which was his father's second home.

The library was Daniel's escape from the real world. In the library he could dive head first into any adventure he desired. One day he could engulf himself in a Clive Cussler adventure book... scuba diving and finding buried treasure with Clive's main hero, Dirk Pitt. The next day he could join Harry Potter, casting magic spells and winning Quidditch matches with the crowd cheering him on...

Then Daniel discovered something that would take his life to the next level: coding. Computer coding was like getting lost in some fantasy fiction novel, but the difference was, *Daniel* was the protagonist. He was living the adventure in real life. He liked to envision himself as a hacker, but a hacker devoted to serving the greater good. Where did he learn everything he needed to know about coding? The library. He read every book he could on computer coding, development, and hacking. He downloaded every PDF, eBook, online course, and hack sheet that he could find on the web. He joined every hacking forum and spent hours each day chatting with other cyberpunks. He wasn't just a kid going to the library because he had nowhere else to go. He went to the library because he was on a mission.

Hacking had given Daniel a sense of power and purpose for the first time in his life. It was the first thing he had ever been remotely good at. When he was behind a computer writing code, he didn't feel scared or self-conscious. He was in his element. It was the one thing that he could do from his chair… the chair that somehow both made his life possible but also so limited… the chair that caused everyone in his path to stare at him… the embarrassing chair.

When he was younger the chair didn't embarrass him much. That all changed on his eighth birthday. All of the other kids in class were having birthday parties that year. Although Daniel rarely got invited to the other kids' parties, he wanted one of his own. His dad had urged him not to do it, but against his wishes, he spent a week making flyers for his Star Wars themed birthday party. He created custom Star Wars party masks for every kid in his class—over twenty. He personally hand-delivered the invitations at school one day. Not a single person showed up to his party. Not one. Daniel waited at the front door all day. The invitation said from 1-4 pm. Daniel still sat there at 5pm praying someone would show. He had all twenty-two hand-made masks sitting on the kitchen table. His dad had already started eating the cake and cookies while he drank his fifth beer of the day. Daniel had never cried so hard in his life. Neither the numerous surgeries to straighten his back nor the painful rashes that made his skin bleed from sitting in his wheelchair too long could compare to this pain; the pain of having no friends… of never being loved by anyone. Even his dad was more attentive to the beer can in his hand than his son crying at the front door.

Daniel blamed it all on his chair. *If I wasn't in this chair, they would have come.* It was a story he began to tell himself day in and day out. It was the story that seemed to define the rest of his life. That chair—the source of his anger and frustration in life—was what he sat on every waking hour of his life. The chair was inseparable from him yet also his greatest enemy.

"Hey Daniel."

The librarian's voice broke his train of thought. Daniel didn't respond. He just stared ahead at his screen through his wire-rimmed glasses. They were cheap with numerous finger smudges on both lenses. It was a miracle he could see anything out of them.

She waited awkwardly for him to respond, her eyes tracing his features for any sign of acknowledgment.

"What are you working on today, Daniel?" she drove the conversation onward, trying to be nice.

Daniel still didn't respond. He couldn't. He had never said a word in his life. Cerebral palsy meant that all of his muscles were incredibly weak. Every muscle in his legs, arms, abdomen, and yes… even his tongue.

However, he did have his own way of communicating. He spoke through an app on his phone, Apple iPad, or his laptop. The app was a voice synthesizer that could say anything he wanted to say; single words, full sentences, popular phrases, questions. The app came with a ton of pre-programmed voice commands to make it easy for a disabled person to use. Though designed to make his life easier, it still managed to frustrate Daniel. He kept finding flaws in the code. A year earlier he sent the app developer completely new code with a note that read:

*Just because you sell your app to disabled people doesn't mean we don't recognize sloppy code. I made some major improvements for you. Feel free to use them. Just give me credit in the code.*

*Sincerely,*
*Dan, The Man*

A month later the app company sent out a nationwide update to all users with Daniel's exact code. The company even offered him money. He declined it. He just wanted credit for the code. He did the same with numerous other apps, which he used and improved. His only goal was to become the best hacker. Plus, if he made more than $500 in a month, he would lose his Social Security disability benefits that pay for all of his computers and accessories. The government entitlements trumped the risk of getting a job. It just wasn't worth it.

Daniel stared at the librarian for one second longer before making a few slow strokes on his iPad keyboard. The librarian patiently waited for his response.

"Just hacking away," his app replied in a funny, machine-like, robot voice.

"Well, I hate to tell you this, but you've got to find somewhere else to hack away. We're closing the library in five minutes." She frowned slightly with something that resembled pity in her eyes. "See you tomorrow, Daniel."

It was nightfall when he arrived at the trailer he called home. Daniel waited for the wheelchair lift on the city bus to hit the pavement before he slowly unbuckled the protective strap and turned on his electric wheelchair. He zoomed off the bus and up to the front step of his house. There was a screeching, metal-crunching noise as he directed his heavy wheelchair up the hodgepodge ramp his dad had "built" for Daniel to get up the stairs. The sound reminded him of a 72-ton army tank going up a metal ramp that was made for a kid's Barbie car. He thought it might break at any second.

You'd think that after living with a handicapped son, his father would make their home more wheelchair friendly. However, his dad wasn't around much to do anything—not even that. He was either working his construction job or drinking at the bar. In fact, Daniel couldn't recall the two of them ever having a conversation beyond logistical chats to get them through the day.

As he approached his front door his eyes fell upon something unusual in his path and his wheels came to a sudden halt. A big green frog was sitting in his path, and it appeared to be staring directly at him. Daniel had never seen a frog in his yard in his life. Daniel nudged his wheelchair closer to the frog. It didn't budge. In fact, it seemed to completely lack the natural fear animals often (rightly) display around humans.

*What a weird frog*, thought Daniel.

Daniel briefly wondered if the frog could be trying to tell him something.

*That's idiotic*, Daniel told himself.

Without warning the frog finally hopped off to the side. Daniel was halfway through the entrance of his front door, when he stopped. He could have sworn he heard something behind him.

"Follow me," came a strange whisper from the darkness outside.

Daniel turned his wheelchair around as fast as he could. There was no one there except for that frog, still staring at him blankly, now from the grass just off the side of the porch. Either he was losing his mind or he was hearing things... or both.

*Man, I must really need some sleep*, thought Daniel.

He wheeled back around to go through the doorway when he heard it again.

"Follow me..." the eerie whisper echoed again from the dark night.

Daniel reached over to the light switch on the wall. He flipped on the outdoor flood lights so he could get a full glimpse of the front yard, assuming he'd see someone from school playing a prank on him. After looking around, there wasn't a person to be found.

*I'm really losing my mind*, thought Daniel.

He was starting to feel a little freaked out. His heart began to race and he began to sweat. He shut the front door, locked both locks, and practically jumped out of his wheelchair when he heard it one more time...

"Follow me."

He heard it faintly through the front door.

*How?!* Daniel knew someone must be playing a prank on him. He looked around the house. Everything seemed normal inside. Like most trailer homes, theirs was long and thin with a room on each side; one room for Daniel and one for his dad. The rest of the 900 square foot trailer was open with the middle area featuring a kitchen, small dining table, couch, and TV. Daniel could hear his dad snoring. He must have passed out early from drinking too much.

A brochure on the kitchen table caught his eye. Daniel picked it up, his hand a bit shakier than usual as adrenaline rushed through is body. He began reading. It was an ad; an offer to enroll in a new advanced computer programming summer camp. He quickly combed through the first few pages of the ten-page brochure with growing excitement. Then suddenly he stopped reading, and his heart sank. His dad would never let him go. They couldn't afford it. His dad was always broke. Daniel placed it gently back on the counter, as if the brochure itself was the precious dream it described. But as he laid it down, he noticed the tip of a white envelope sticking out of its back pages. He thought it might be part of the summer camp invitation but quickly realized the envelope must have accidentally lodged inside of the brochure.

It was addressed to his dad from some health group he had never heard of. It had already been opened. Daniel's curiosity consumed him. He unfolded it and scanned the first page. Nothing important. Page two... nothing but more medical jargon. Page three... there it was.

Short and sweet. It didn't need any explanation or footnotes. Its meaning was clear enough to stand on its own:

## Patient Name: Max Ruhlin
## Diagnosis: Stage 4 Lung Cancer

Daniel read the words again. And again. And again. Lung cancer… stage 4. The meaning didn't change. For the first time in his life he felt like he couldn't think clearly. His thoughts came in fragments. Time was stopping and starting. He was paralyzed in one moment and then lurching into existence in the next, unable to process this new information.

He had noticed that his dad had a persistent cough recently, which appeared to bother him. He had also his lost a ton of weight. Daniel just assumed it was due to his horrible diet of peanut butter sandwiches and beer; it was only a matter of time before malnutrition would catch up to him.

Daniel didn't know how he should feel… Mad? Sad? Remorseful? He didn't have a relationship with his dad. His dad had never once told him that he loved him. Not once. Everything related to his dad revolved around working and drinking. He tried to think of times when he and his dad did anything meaningful together—even just sitting and talking, *really* talking. Nothing.

His dad's entire past had been erased. It was like he was trying to hide from something. He would never talk about it. Daniel didn't know anything about his deceased mom or any other family members. It was as if they'd never existed. The only evidence Daniel even had of his mother was one single photograph. She was beautiful. He wished he could see more of her, hear more about her, but he never dared to ask his dad. That was a sore subject. Daniel knew his dad blamed him for his mother's death. There had been many times when his dad walked in the door drunk, yelling at Daniel and blaming him for all of his problems in the past. Occasionally he would apologize and make wild promises for the future that he would never keep. Over and over again, Daniel lived within the vicious cycle of drunken threats, fights, and then empty promises for a better life.

Still, this was his father. He was his only family member still alive. He had no one else; no known grandparents, aunts, or uncles anywhere. What would happen to him if his dad died? Where would he live? Who would take care of him? He was a seventeen-year-old disabled kid who couldn't walk, talk, or live independently.

Daniel's thoughts were interrupted by a notification on his phone. He tried to ignore it. It vibrated a second time... then a third... then a fourth. Something was up. It was a string of app notifications from his private hacker group. He couldn't believe his eyes.

**Breaking News: White House security system hacked. Billions of dollars stolen along with thousands of classified documents. Hackers not identified.**

Daniel's mind was toast. This was officially the most emotional day of his life. An unprecedented hack on the White House, his dad's cancer diagnosis, and that strange frog... *Was* it a prank? Or did that small amphibian actually speak? Unable to face anything more Daniel put himself to bed. He'd worry about everything in the morning. Exhausted, Daniel fell into a deep sleep within minutes.

# 4 THE DREAM

There was a loud knock at the front door. Daniel jolted out of bed.

His first thought was that his dad had woken up from a drunken stupor and accidentally locked himself outside. Maybe it was just his imagination. Daniel tried to fall back asleep, but he was startled by another knock. *It must be someone else—someone dad is expecting*, he thought.

Another knock, this time a bit heavier.

Daniel wished he could talk. He reached over to check the time on his phone. 3:11am. Who could possibly be knocking on his door at this time? He listened for his dad's footsteps.

Nothing.

Another hard knock on the front door.

Daniel's eyes shifted across the room and came to rest on a poster. It was a poster that had been on his wall for years. Stephen Hawking. Daniel's hero. *What would Stephen do?* Daniel thought. He found himself asking that question anytime he needed courage. He knew right then that he had to get out of bed.

He glanced up at the ceiling. Directly above his head was a wide metal bar dangling twenty inches from his chest. It was actually an old steel bar from a lat pull down machine. The steel bar had patches of rust from being left outside too long. The rubber grips on each handle had almost completely disintegrated. Daniel's hands had become used to it after years of using it to get out of bed. His dad had found the old weight lifting machine on the side of the road one day. He took it apart and loaded it into his truck. That evening he worked for hours building

21

Daniel a homemade pulley system, which would help him get out of
bed by himself. It was the first time Daniel saw his dad do any kind of
work outside of his normal job. He usually just drank and complained.
It was also the nicest thing he ever did for Daniel. Maybe his father
did love him, or maybe it was self-serving. After all, creating a way for
Daniel to get out of bed by himself meant he wouldn't have to do it.

Daniel used every ounce of energy to get his back off the bed. He
lunged for the bar. He missed. He reached it on the second try. Daniel
pulled himself up slowly. He slid his thin, frail legs and torso onto his
wheelchair, which sat directly next to his bed. He buckled himself in
and turned on his iPad. Daniel never went anywhere without his iPad.
Next, he wheeled over to his dad's room staring anxiously at the front
door as he passed it.

He could see the silhouette of a body in the bed. His dad's snoring
rumbled through the still night air. He was out cold. Whoever was
knocking had to be one of his drinking buddies. 3:11 am. That was late
even by their standards. Perhaps his dad had told a friend the bad news
about his cancer and they were coming over to check on him.

There was another knock at the front door. This time it was so loud
it startled him in his wheelchair. He hit two buttons on his iPad.

"Who's there?" came the words from Daniel's iPad.

Silence. Daniel turned the chair to see if his dad had budged.
Nothing. He turned his electric wheelchair around quickly with his
joystick. He then slowly approached the door and stopped. His index
finger pressed the same button again.

"Who's there?"

Silence. He hit the button again.

"Who's there?"

Silence.

Then there was a loud thud… followed by another one… followed
by a third one. Each one was louder than the preceding.

He pulled up next to the door. He glanced up at the peephole. It
was too high, so he quietly eased his wheelchair over to the front
window. His trembling hand grabbed one of the cheap blinds, carefully
pulled it downwards, and peered through the slit he'd just created.

To his surprise there was nobody standing there.

Knock, knock, knock! The front door rattled. It felt more urgent—
perhaps even a little annoyed at the lack of response.

Daniel couldn't stand the suspense anymore. With a sudden rush of courage, he unlocked the deadbolt, twisted the door knob, and flung open the door.

No one on the doorstep except for one... lone... frog.

Daniel froze. The *same* frog from earlier was back on his doorstep? Daniel's fingers glided across the keyboard as quickly as they could go. The frog continued to stare at him with his beady eyes.

"What kind of joke is this?" Daniel's iPad called out into the darkness. He couldn't make out anybody's shadow. No voices. No laughter. The frog turned toward his yard.

"It's okay to come out now," the frog said to what appeared to be nobody.

Daniel couldn't move. His mouth gaped open.

An owl emerged, flying out of the shadows and landing next to the frog on the doorstep.

Daniel's eyes continued to bulge. He feverishly typed on his iPad. "Did you just talk?" asked his iPad as he pointed at the frog.

The frog turned to face him. Its expression appeared somewhat coy. Was that even possible?

"Yep, I'm one heck of a talker... for a frog," bellowed a man's voice from the frog's mouth.

*Oh no! The frog is talking... the frog is talking* Daniel thought to himself. *I'm really losing my mind. This has to be some sort of crazy dream...*

Daniel looked towards the doorway imagining that if he peered into his own bedroom, he'd find himself still asleep in bed. Perhaps he could wake himself up from this dream.

The frog just smiled.

The massive owl flapped its wings up into the air, circled once around the yard, and then swooped down on Daniel. Its sharp talons tore into his shirt and nearly lifted him out of his wheelchair. Daniel's arms flailed wildly as he tried to bat it away. The owl continued to pull him up, but Daniel's arm caught its right wing. The owl lost its grip as Daniel's shirt ripped, and the owl flew up into the darkness.

What was going on? He brushed away the tattered pieces of his shirt. His left fist remained clenched in anticipation, while he tried to type with his other hand.

The man's voice rang out into the night once more. "We need your help."

It came from above. Daniel looked up. The frog was peering down at him. He was now riding on top of the owl's back as it sailed across the porch and landed on the railing in front of him.

"We need you to help us save the world," the frog continued.

Daniel looked puzzled. He began typing. The owl and frog glanced at each other, unsure of what was happening.

"You need me to do what?! To help you *save the world*? That's hilarious," Daniel replied via iPad.

Daniel's mind was still racing. He couldn't seem to wake himself up from this dream. He started typing away again, his crooked fingers punching buttons at a turtle's pace. He looked up at them while he hit enter on his keyboard.

"I realize you are a frog and an owl, so perhaps you are not too familiar with the human body. Have you noticed that I can't even walk? How is someone like me supposed to help you do… *anything*? You certainly must have the wrong person."

"Unstrap yourself from the chair," demanded the frog.

Daniel looked confused, and then slowly shook his head from side to side.

"*Please* unstrap yourself from the chair," the frog said again, trying not to lose his patience.

Daniel shook his head *no* once more.

The frog leaped off the owl's back and landed on Daniel's face. Daniel yelled. He hated anyone or anything touching his face. The frog's sticky green arms gripped his cheeks, forming a suction around Daniel's entire mouth and nose. He could barely breathe. Daniel attempted to hit the frog with his right arm, but accidentally hit the wheelchair joystick instead, sending his chair right into the metal wheelchair ramp. The sound of metal scraping across brick became louder and louder until the ramp jolted to a stop. The wheelchair couldn't move any further.

"STOP!" thundered a woman's voice. It belonged to the owl. "You two are going to wake up the entire neighborhood!"

The frog jumped off of Daniel's face leaving behind a sticky residue.

"You *are* Daniel, right?" she asked.

He nodded. He didn't see the point in lying. The truth should be more than enough to deter them.

"Daniel, my name is Skylar. This is my friend, Vosco. We've come a long way to show you something very important. But you've got to trust us."

There was something about her voice. It reminded him of what he dreamed his mom would sound like. It sounded familiar somehow. It seemed bizarre coming from the mouth of an owl, but he wanted to trust her.

"Okay. Here's what we need you to do," she continued. "Unbuckle your wheelchair strap and put your arms out to your sides. I'm going to pick you up. I promise I won't drop you. Trust me, okay?"

That feeling of trust began to give way as fear and confusion began to creep across Daniel's face. *Was he dreaming? Did an owl just ask him to trust her?* Before he could answer in his mind, he felt some unseen force begin to move his hands towards the seat belt, which was strapped snuggly across his lap. He watched as his hands unbuckled the belt, faster than normal. It was almost as if he was watching himself in a movie—someone else was in control of his body. The next thing he knew he was being pushed forward. He felt helpless as his body lurched forward out of the wheelchair towards the concrete.

He tried to use his hands to break the fall, but they were caught on something. Mere seconds before his face could feel the impact of cold concrete, he felt his stomach drop. He was breathless. Then he was flying.

Daniel was being pulled higher and higher. He could see the glowing screen on his iPad, which still lay on his wheelchair below. It was getting smaller and smaller as he rose into the air. He could see his entire neighborhood; the small porch lights appearing like fireflies across the night sky.

Without his iPad he couldn't talk. He had no way to communicate. He wondered where the owl and frog were taking him. He felt somewhat helpless, while at the same time invigorated by a sense of adventure. This was freedom. Daniel had never left the city of St. Augustine.

He could feel the owl veer off to the left. That's when he saw it. Smoke was billowing up into the air for what seemed like miles. A massive fire burned below and he could hear what sounded like gunshots echoing off the buildings surrounding it. He immediately recognized where they were: downtown St. Augustine. City Hall was on fire. The streets were in chaos. Daniel was incredibly confused. *What was going on?*

The owl dipped down. Daniel's body was dangling in mid-air. He overheard the frog talking to the owl, but Daniel couldn't make out the words. The chaos on the streets below was drowning out everything.

As they swooped down lower and lower, mobs of angry people came into focus. They were throwing bottles, which appeared to be on fire. He could see police lights, but there were too few of them and they were too far away. He saw some groups throwing rocks and heavy items at the City Hall. Others were breaking into local stores. Another group was lighting a church on fire.

"Daniel, can you see what's happening below?" the owl asked.

He nodded.

"This is the future of America. This will be the scene in every city across the nation within the next few days if we don't stop Kore and his evil army. Violence, theft, murder, and fear will rule the nation. This is just the beginning. The cyber-attacks will create fear and panic. It will also lead to an internal war between the rich and the poor. It will get worse… much worse. There is an underground empire, which wants to wreak havoc in America. They want to take over. They want to create a new world order where they have all the power… a new world order where nobody has freedom. This is why we need your help."

Daniel stared below, the bright flames glistening in his eyes as they glazed over. He had so many questions. *Was this already happening here, right now, in downtown St. Augustine? Who was Kore and why would he do this?*

Daniel tried flapping his arms to get the owl's attention. He felt the owl make a sharp turn away from the riots. He flailed his arms harder, hoping they'd circle back so he could piece things together.

The frog and owl ignored him. They appeared to be looking for something down below. All Daniel could see were a few street lights in the distance, but it was mostly darkness.

"Get ready to hold your breath," said the frog. "We're almost there."

*Almost where?* Daniel thought, dying to know.

Before he could finish his next thought, the owl plummeted down to the earth at breakneck speed. Daniel could see the ground approaching quickly. The owl continued to nosedive.

With air rushing into his mouth like a firehose, Daniel considered the possibility that this was not, in fact, a dream. His stomach was up in his throat. This felt far too real. He couldn't tell how close they were to the ground at this point, but he did notice a reflection below. As they came closer, he realized it was a small fountain.

"Hold your breath now!" screamed the frog as loud as he could seconds before the water engulfed them.

Daniel held his breath. He was submerged underwater... getting pulled down deeper by the owl. He didn't know how long he could hold his breath. He'd never timed it before. He felt his glasses sliding off of his face, but they were moving through the water with such force that he was not strong enough to raise a hand to push them back up his nose. Then as if a switch had been flipped, he came to the realization that he was running out of air. *I can't breathe.* He was becoming disoriented.

All of a sudden, the owl yanked him sideways. The three of them shot through a small tunnel. Seconds later Daniel felt himself falling in midair and gasping for air as he fell.

Boom! He was lying on his back with the air completely knocked out of him. He gasped a second time, wheezing now, as his lungs were worked overtime. After a moment he glanced up and noticed the tree tops gently swaying above him. The ground was cold and damp. He was in a forest.

He raised his head to look around him. The owl and the frog had vanished. However, in their places stood two people: a tall, burly man and a young, attractive woman. They appeared human, yet there was something unhuman about their energy. Daniel instinctively knew they were different from him.

The man was tall and built like a freight train. He was dressed in black tactical pants, a light green short sleeve t-shirt, and black boots. He had an air of strength and wisdom about him. Daniel immediately felt he was someone to trust to get the job done, no matter what it was.

To his left stood a young woman. She looked to be only slightly older than Daniel. Her long, brown hair was still dripping wet from the pond. Her face was bare yet wildly beautiful. She appeared confident, brave, focused; the complete opposite of Daniel.

St. Augustine was gone. They were now in a jungle-like forest with trees, which grew straight up into the sky with no end in sight. Vines hung down in their direction and swung with the breeze. There was just enough light peeking through the tree canopy to aid the naked eye, but much of the forest still remained in darkness. Shadows moved in the distance, as if the trees were trading places with each other. It felt eerie. He reached up for his glasses, but they were gone. Maybe that's why his eyes were playing tricks on him. He could only see the three of them, but he felt that they were not alone. He could sense a large presence out there—it wasn't welcoming.

Daniel turned around to examine the water pipe, but all that was there was a red brick wall. It was approximately 15 feet wide, 6 feet tall, and free standing. It looked odd. Why was it there? It was as if someone had started to build, finished one wall, and then gave up. The strangest part was the hole in the middle. It was three feet in diameter and filled with water—though nothing was holding the water in. Tiny beads of water trickled down the bricks below. Was that hole what he came out of? *How? How did— How was—*

"How are you feeling?" asked the man. Daniel immediately recognized the deep voice—it was the frog's voice. Had the frog turned into this man? He helped Daniel sit up so he could see what was going on.

"I'm Vosco. This is Skylar." he said pointing to the young woman. "Welcome to the enchanted forest. It's the first of three levels we must pass through before we get to Alcazar—the place where we all live… where we desperately need your help."

Daniel tried to take all of this in, but this adventure was only becoming more and more unbelievable. He wanted to talk, but he couldn't. His iPad was back at home. How would he speak to these people?

He thought, *Enchanted forests, talking frogs, owls strong enough to carry people, shape-shifters, and a brick wall… portal?*

"Daniel," said Skylar. "Our world is in dire trouble." She paused. "And so is yours. There is an evil force below the Earth's surface that has taken over and is gaining strength every day. It's led by an evil man named Kore."

*Here we go talking about this Kore again*, Daniel thought, praying he'd get more details this time around. Skylar continued talking.

"He and his corrupt army plan on shutting down America's power grid, creating chaos and fear across the land, and stealing money from the banks by hacking computers. Anyone who opposes him will be imprisoned, or worse, killed."

"The first thing Kore plans on doing is dividing America in two…" Vosco jumped in, nodding. "The rich and the poor… to create hatred and fear. He'll start a civil war in your country. He'll support the poor with money and weapons because they are the majority—but only so he can use them to take down the wealthy. Then when he has enough power, he'll turn on the poor and force everyone to either join his evil army or perish."

Daniel looked confused.

Since he couldn't speak Skylar continued, "We have reason to believe that he's about to create a dangerous riot that will spark murders, vandalism, and hate crimes across the entire country of America—to a level that has never been seen before. If you thought your country was divided and full of hatred already, you haven't seen anything yet."

Daniel tried to make sense of this, but he couldn't. It was unimaginable. A villain, who literally lives underground, trying to hack America's power grid to create a civil war. He started reconsidering the possibility that he was still dreaming. *But what does this have to do me?* Daniel thought.

"Daniel," Vosco interrupted his thoughts. "I'm sure this is a lot to take in. Trust me, if these evil forces get their way, you won't exist— and neither will anyone else up in your world."

If only he could speak. He looked down at his legs, sprawled motionless on the forest floor. He wished he had his chair—the embarrassing chair. He needed it—perhaps now, more than ever.

Suddenly, a loud rumbling sound echoed in the distance.

"Is that getting closer?" Skylar asked, turning to Vosco.

The three of them froze trying to decipher in what direction it was coming. It sounded like the entire forest was shaking—like a herd of elephants was stampeding towards them from all sides. It was getting closer.

In an instant a black cloud engulfed the forest and that black cloud was headed right at them at full speed.

"BATS!" screamed Vosco. It was too late.

Before he could say, "Get down," the three of them completely disappeared in a swarm of what seemed like never-ending bats. Vosco and Skylar knew from experience to lie flat against the forest floor. Daniel couldn't move as the bats pummeled him from all directions. It felt as though their wings were beating him everywhere at once; his face, his ribs, his arms, his legs. He even felt one biting his neck. A small trickle of blood ran down his shoulder. It felt intentional. The bats were largely leaving Skylar and Vosco alone. He felt his body go limp as it was hit with such force that he flew backwards. His head slammed against the ground. Everything went black. Just as suddenly as they appeared, the bats lifted up in an angry cloud and flew back in the direction from which they came.

Skylar and Vosco were shaken. Catching their breath, they looked over at Daniel's body. He wasn't moving at all. He looked like some sort of contortionist; while his legs remained crossed, his upper body was twisted onto its side and his face was flat against the ground.

"Is he still breathing?" asked Vosco. "Please don't tell me that we killed the chosen one."

"He's breathing. He hit his head on a tree root. It knocked him out cold."

"He must have broken some bones though…" Vosco said, eyeing his strange position.

Skylar quickly assessed Daniel. He appeared okay except for the bat bite on his neck.

"Perhaps an able-bodied person would have broken some bones… but Daniel seems to be more flexible than most," she replied, hesitant whether to label this a good or bad thing. "It's strange…"

"Let's get him back home so he can get some rest."

Skylar and Vosco exchanged looks. Skylar decided to acknowledge the elephant in the room—er, forest.

"Is it possible we grabbed the wrong guy?" she asked. "We haven't even made it past the first level of the middle grounds and he's already out cold. We've still got two more levels ahead of us before we get to—"

Vosco cut her off mid-sentence. "No, he's the one. I'm certain of it. He's exactly who Maku told us to get."

He seemed to be saying this to convince himself just as much as to convince her.

"I'm still not sure," Skylar said quietly. "He doesn't look like the chosen one to me. Plus, do you plan on carrying him through all three levels? How's that clunky wheelchair going to make it down here?" said Skylar while looking down at the young, unconscious boy.

"Do you really think what we need is a kid with one exceptionally strong *body* to defeat Kore?" Vosco asked, his voice dripping with sarcasm. "No. What we need is one exceptionally strong *mind*. It's the strategy we're missing. It's the brains we're missing. We have a fair amount of muscle, but we don't have enough knowledge."

Skylar paused in silence for a moment.

"That's true. But… he hasn't proven himself much in that

department either."

"Ok, I'll admit it," he said, "We've got our work cut out for us with him—that's for sure. I'm certain we can teach him quickly. Now he needs rest. We'll test him again soon."

Minutes later Daniel awoke. He was in his own bed and his sheets and clothes were completely soaked. He breathed an unexpected sigh of relief. *It had been a dream after all…*

# 5 LIES

Jay was locked inside his presidential office. He was alone, afraid, and unsure of what to do next. His mind was racing a million miles per hour. He tried to focus. He couldn't. He was furious at everyone in that meeting. He wondered how this could be happening. How could he be asked to lie in front of his country? He felt like it wasn't really a choice, but an expectation. The words of his staff kept ringing in his ears...

*"That's the way it's always been done... the public is better off not knowing the truth... if you tell them the truth your career is done... there will be rioting in the streets... they'll blame you... they'll impeach you... we'll impeach you..."*

His mind raced back to his mother. She was the voice of reason. She taught him right from wrong. He thought about his mentor, Jack. He knew what they'd both instruct him to do. Tell the truth. *The truth shall set you free.* That was what he'd always said, but it wasn't that easy this time. Apparently the further you made it in politics, the more you were forced to lie. As many of his fellow politicians liked to say, *to bend the truth until the public is ready to know it.*

His thoughts were interrupted by an abrupt knock on the door.

"Mr. President, the live press conference starts in twenty minutes," chimed his personal assistant, Mary. "The reporters are already out on the lawn—they are demanding some answers. Rumors are already starting to spread about a cyber-attack. The secretary of defense and the head of White House security need to speak with you in the green room before you head outside."

"Tell them I'll be there in a couple minutes," he replied.

There was desperation in his voice. Could he betray the same Americans who just voted him in by not telling them the truth about this cyber-attack? Would they even believe the truth? Would they panic if they knew that these untraceable hackers had stolen billions of dollars from right from under their noses?

***

## St. Augustine, Florida

Daniel rolled into the kitchen after having just woken up. The dream from last night was still fresh in his mind. It had seemed so real. He remembered the talking frog and owl, the forest, the bats... nearly drowning. He didn't particularly want to remember these things, and he wished he remembered less. Glancing up, he saw his dad over on their small couch in the living room. He was so focused on the TV that he hadn't noticed him come into the room. Daniel hit the joystick on his wheelchair. He stopped a foot behind the couch. His dad turned around.

"Shouldn't you be at the library or something?" his dad asked in an irritated tone.

Daniel ignored him. He too was focused in on the TV. He watched as the headline flashed across the bottom of the screen.

## President McFarland To Address White House Cyber-Attack (LIVE)

"Our lousy president is about to come on," his dad said, his voice still rough and scratchy from heaving drinking the night before. "It's some emergency press conference. Hackers took billions of dollars or something."

*Hackers?* Daniel suddenly felt his stomach in his chest. Had his dream been a premonition? Talking frogs and owls aside, perhaps it had been a real warning. Were there already riots in the streets like he saw in his dream? His hands were shaking as he checked his phone to see if there were any new notifications from his hacker group. Nothing. Over thirteen updates but no one had claimed ownership of the hack job.

He drew his attention back to the TV. The nation's new president was just stepping up to the podium. He was holding some note cards in his left hand. He didn't look like the same confident man who inspired everyone with his debate skills a few months ago. He looked nervous. He made a weak attempt to smile at the camera. The camera immediately panned away from him to show the White House lawn. It was jam-packed with news reporters and cameras. A female news anchor came on.

"In just a minute the president of the United States will come on to address what we believe is a cyber-attack on the White House. There have been rumors circulating about who's behind the attack, including what was stolen and how the hackers pulled it off." She paused and put her right hand to her ear. "Okay folks, I'm being told the president is ready to speak. Here he is."

In a flash the female reporter was gone. The president was live. Daniel and his father watched in silent anticipation. He fumbled with his notecards at the podium and brushed his right hand across the front of his suit in an attempt to smooth out invisible wrinkles. What would he say? Would this be a declaration of the first cyber-war in history? The president glanced at his notecards and began to speak.

"Good afternoon. I regret to report to the American people, and to the world, that the United States has been the target of a malicious and illegal cyber-attack. Over the last ten years, thanks to the tireless and heroic work of our military and our counterterrorism professionals, we've made great strides in the effort to ensure we never suffer an attack like this. We've disrupted countless cyber-terrorist attacks and we have done everything in our power to strengthen our homeland security.

"Unfortunately, in the last twenty-four hours a group of hackers were somehow able to penetrate our security system. Due to the sensitive nature of this attack and our ongoing investigation, I cannot divulge all of the details at this time. However, I can update you on the following:

"First, this attack wasn't as serious as some news outlets are making it out to be. The hackers, in the brief time they were behind our security firewall, were not able to get away with much. The only files they were able to download were not highly classified and provide no threat to our nation whatsoever.

"Secondly, the hack appears to be all about money. Unfortunately, billions of dollars were stolen from White House bank accounts. We are already tracing the funds in order to get every penny of your tax-paying dollars back.

"The good news is we've identified where the attack came from along with who they are. It is still a very active and ongoing investigation. You can rest assured that your country, money, and lives are safe. My top priority is to protect this country and to ensure that we never suffer an attack like this again. We will continue our broader efforts to disrupt, dismantle, and defeat any future cyber-attacks. You have my word that these attackers will be caught and dealt with accordingly. Thank you."

The president grabbed his cards, waved to the crowd, and was escorted back inside. He was sick to his stomach. Secretary of Defense Bruce Cromwell whispered something in his ear and patted him on the back.

"He's lying!" Daniel's dad yelled at the TV. "That back-stabbing McFarland is lying through his teeth. I know it."

Daniel had never seen his dad so upset. He watched his face turn bright red. He was fuming. He started cursing under his breath just loud enough for Daniel to hear. This didn't make any sense. Daniel was pretty sure his dad had never even voted. Why did he care so much about what a politician had to say about a cyber-attack?

"Hey dad," a robotic voice echoed from his iPad.

"What?" his dad snapped back at Daniel.

"Is everything okay?"

"What's that supposed to mean?" Max yelled. "Of course I'm okay. I just can't stand that lying president of ours. And—"

His dad stopped talking rather abruptly. Daniel thought he heard him cursing under his breath again, but he then quickly realized he was crying. Daniel sat in his chair, not sure what to do or say. This was the first time he'd ever seen his father cry.

Max wiped away a tear as it came down his nose. Seconds later, the tears turned into small coughs. Then coughs grew louder and then became violent. He covered his mouth with his hands as the coughing continued. Daniel sat there, again not sure what to do. He finally stopped coughing. That's when Daniel saw it. A small amount of blood was splattered across his hands. He was coughing up blood.

Daniel instantly remembered the letter. He had almost forgotten about it after the crazy dream from last night—or perhaps he wanted to believe the cancer letter was a dream too. He started typing. Max got up and quickly moved to the sink to wash his hands.

"Dad, can I ask you one more question?"

Max ignored him. He coughed into his hand again. More blood splattered across his callouses.

"How are you feeling?" Daniel was hoping his dad might open up about the letter.

He wiped his hands off on a thin white paper towel. "What, a man can't cough now?" Max replied sarcastically.

He was too proud and stubborn to ever admit he was sick or weak. His right hand held the corner of the sink to prop him up. His left hand was now holding his side just below his rib cage. Daniel felt as though he was watching his dad die.

He tried to process this possibility. Max might not be dying in this exact moment, but he could be in the not so distant future. Daniel felt a wave of guilt. His initial reaction to his dad's cancer diagnosis had been fear for himself. *Who would look after him with his dad gone? How would he survive without someone paying the rent and bills? Who would he live with?* There was no family that Daniel was aware of. *Besides, who would want to inherit a teenager in a wheelchair who can't walk or talk*, he wondered.

That's when it hit him. He still didn't know what had happened to Max's parents—his grandparents. He knew that his mother had died giving birth to him, but every time he had asked about his grandparents his dad would become angry and storm out of the room. He had to know the truth before it became buried with his dad.

"Whatever happened to your mom and dad?" Daniel's iPad asked bluntly.

This time, Max didn't react immediately with anger. He was too tired. Instead he pretended to ignore the question. Daniel watched him walk to the fridge. He yanked open the fridge door, grabbed a cold Busch Light, cracked open the can, and drank half of it in one sip. He looked back at Daniel, his still watery from a combination of crying, coughing, and chugging half a cold beer. He responded with ice in his voice.

"They died after I was born. I never knew them."

# 6 THE MESSENGER

The creepy old man with the white beard wouldn't stop staring at him.

Daniel was headed to the library. It was just the two of them at the bus stop. He looked around to confirm his suspicion. Yep, the old man definitely wasn't looking at anyone else. He was casually dressed in jeans and a short-sleeve, white, fishing shirt. He wore an Atlanta Braves baseball cap. There was something intriguing about him. Perhaps it was his eyes. They seemed to almost glitter in the sun. Maybe it was the gigantic bald eagle tattoo spanning the length of his bicep. Clearly the man was a patriot.

Daniel turned away from his gaze. He waited a few minutes and then glanced back over his shoulder again. He was still there. The man gave Daniel a warm smile. His white teeth looked like pure ivory against his weathered, tan face. He didn't say anything. He just kept smiling. Daniel wished he had the courage to go up to him and ask him if this was his first time seeing someone in a wheelchair. Of course, that would take courage—something Daniel lacked.

The bus turned the corner. Daniel was relieved. It also meant he could keep an eye on the old man because the city bus had a rear-entrance wheelchair lift—the back seat belonged to Daniel. He was even more relieved to see the bus already had a dozen passengers on board. Once they boarded, the old man sat three rows in front of him. Although he could no longer see the man's face, he could feel his presence. It was palpable.

As the bus started to pull away, Daniel checked his phone. He was curious if his hacking app had any updates. He swiped over to the app's main news feed. He read through the headlines. No one had claimed credit for government hack yet. It was strange that nobody was taking credit. Usually hackers find it hard to keep quiet. *Why wouldn't someone own up to it? They always did. It was part of the hacker code. Who could be behind it?*

Daniel stared out the window. He got lost in the hustle of workers, students, and tourists walking around downtown St. Augustine. His thoughts wandered back to his dad. His heart sank. It was strange to feel empathy for his father—someone who seemed to care so little about him. Perhaps he was just grieving the fantasy of what could have been… a real relationship with his father.

A voice on the bus suddenly interrupted his thoughts. *Was this someone familiar?* Daniel tried to listen closely. It sounded like there was a second person—yes, two men talking. Daniel looked around the bus. Nobody appeared to be engaged in conversation. Nobody's mouth was moving. Others turned their heads. They had heard the voices too. The old man looked at him with concern on his face.

The two voices continued. Daniel couldn't make out what they were saying. They were speaking in English, but the words sounded strange. It was like listening to a radio station that just went out of range. He tried to pinpoint where the conversation was coming from. The speakers… it was coming from the speakers on the bus.

He looked up at the bus driver. He was a balding man with what appeared to be a perpetual frown plastered on his face. He most certainly wasn't speaking. In fact, his brows were knit together more tightly than usual… he was just as confused as everyone else on the bus. The voices stopped abruptly followed by complete silence. The passengers exchanged bewildered glances as the vehicle paused at a traffic light in downtown St. Augustine. They were only a few blocks from the library.

Daniel glanced at his phone and noticed the entire screen was white. He wondered if he had accidentally reset it. He attempted to turn it back on. Nothing. Then he tried swiping, but nothing worked. His phone was frozen. He pulled out his iPad. Same thing. White screen. Nothing was working.

"Hello citizens of America," suddenly echoed a much louder voice throughout the bus. Daniel looked down at his phone. It was glowing… almost phosphorescent. He glanced up. Everyone on the bus was staring at their phone screens.

"My name is Kore," the voice continued. "I want to start off by apologizing for this unannounced interruption. I have an extremely important and somewhat alarming message that you need to hear. I attempted to share this with your government, but they didn't want you to hear this. They seem to believe that only politicians and wealthy businessmen deserve to know the truth."

"You see, there is a lot that they are hiding from you. Since you don't know me well just yet, I realize I will have to show you. Here's a quick glimpse into the conversations that are going on behind your back every single day."

Daniel's white iPad screen went black, as did every other phone screen, tablet, and computer in America. Seconds later a video appeared and began to play. It was from a hidden camera. The clip began with a room full of government officials, including the president. He was in the middle of speaking.

"Are you asking me to lie to the public?" the president asked his staff.

"Listen," said the chief of staff. "The public isn't as smart as you think they are. Heck, most of them can hardly read at a third-grade level. They really just want someone to tell them everything is going to be okay. We've been doing this since the early 1920s, and it has served us well. If you want to succeed as president and have a shot at getting re-elected, you're going to have to learn the difference between what we say in this room and what we share with the American people."

Daniel couldn't believe what he was seeing. He looked up. The entire bus was quiet. Some people's mouths were open in a look of surprise. Others appeared angry as if this video was a call to arms and they were already ready to fight. The driver brought the bus to a complete stop.

Another elected official entered the frame. Only the back of his head was visible. He slowly handed the president a manila folder.

"Sir, here is the speech we've written for you to deliver to the public regarding the hack. Your only job is to read it word for word. Play by our rules and everything will be just fine. You do your quick dog and pony show, make a few waves to the cameras, and head back inside. Do you understand?"

Every wrinkle in the president's forehead was visible as he paused before responding. The entire country waited to see what the president would say. He looked down at the manila folder and sifted through the speech that had been written for him. He glanced around the room one last time before he spoke.

"Okay. I'll tell them what they want to hear."

The video stopped abruptly. All screens went white again. Daniel could feel the anger building up in the bus. The voice of the mysterious Kore returned.

"The footage you just witnessed was taken from a White House camera yesterday afternoon—minutes before the president went live on TV. He lied to you. Let me say that I'm sorry you had to see this. I truly am."

"Well here's the truth my friends. It's time for change. There is so much hatred, animosity, division, and lack of trust among yourselves. It's no wonder the poor resent the rich. It's no wonder there is still so much racial tension. It's no wonder that most Americans are in debt. The system is deliberately structured to keep these things from ever *really* changing. You're stuck playing a losing game, while being told you might win. But you can't a win a game that was never designed to be won."

Kore's voice became louder. Sharper. The bus became quieter. Daniel could feel the hairs on his arms prickling.

"If there was ever a moment in the history of America where fear and downfall was not an option, this is that time. If there was ever a moment to stop letting those political and social forces hold you back, this is that time. Now is the time to stand up and fight against the political leaders and the top 1%, who are stealing your well-deserved success and happiness."

There was a pause. Daniel wasn't sure if the speech was over or not. A few people on the bus started clapping. He could hear others shouting in the streets. There were shouts of affirmation and agreement. The voice of Kore boomed again.

"It's time for a *new world order* where you are in control. You deserve to have a voice and be heard. You deserve to know the truth. You deserve to receive more money and benefits from the government. You don't deserve to be bullied by the rich, who only want to hold you back."

The bus erupted into cheers and applause. Horns were honking. People were shouting. Daniel wondered if he was witnessing a revolution.

"Friends, tonight nearly fifty million Americans will sleep in the streets, under bridges, or in shelters that aren't fit for a dog let alone a human. Eighty percent of the country lives paycheck to paycheck, while wealthy business owners and politicians live in gluttony. The middle class is almost gone, and the wealthy continue to steal your hard-earned money. The rich are getting richer. It's time to put an end to this as a nation... it's time to stand up for what is right... for what is *your* right as a citizen of the United States of America..."

More noise erupted from the streets. Daniel jumped in his chair.

"That is why today I am coming to you with plans for a new world order. I believe you are entitled to your share of the nation's wealth. It's your right. Do you recall the billions of dollars which were recently taken from the government's greedy hands? That money is now yours. I took it, and I'm giving 100% of it to you—the American people. That's just the beginning. There is more to come!"

The city erupted in defiant screams, cheering, and chanting. There was an energy in the air. He felt himself seduced by this new America. Who was Kore?

"Friends, friends!" the voice shouted. "I need one more minute of your time. There's one thing I need from you if I'm going to help you. Although you don't know me, I'm a lot like you. I was taken advantage of for the majority of my life. I was teased because I was different. I was made fun of because I didn't look like everyone else. I was told I was ugly. I was told my entire life that I was inferior—that I'd never amount to anything. I lived in a constant state of fear; fear of being alone, being made fun of, not being good enough, being poor, dying alone. I never thought that I'd amount to anything great.

The cheers died down. Everyone's eyes were glued to their phones again. The old woman next to him wiped away a tear.

"Then one day I decided I'd had enough. I wasn't going to be a second-class citizen any longer. I wasn't going to let unethical leaders and aristocrats tell me how to live my life. I wasn't going to live in fear and poverty anymore."

Everyone leaned closer into their phones. The old lady next to him grabbed the edge of her seat.

"My goal is to empower those who need it most; the blue-collar workers, the poor, the hungry, the single moms and dads working two jobs just to make ends meet.... people like you... like me."

The bus exploded with cheers. The noise outside the bus was

equally thunderous. Daniel felt his heart skip a beat. Free money sounded... well... great. He felt himself swept up in the excitement. It felt so natural. It was as though the voice was speaking to him.

"So you're probably wondering, how do we create change—a change today? Here's how. Here's the one thing I need you to do. Stop working. Yes, you heard me. Stop working. Don't go back to your jobs this afternoon, tomorrow, or ever again until they give us what we deserve. If you go back to work, the people at the top will know they've won. If they know they've won, change will never happen."

Daniel glanced up for a second. Nobody was moving. It was almost as if they were hypnotized.

Kore continued, "So instead, we'll show them how important we are. We'll show them that we have the power. If we don't do their dirty work then nothing gets done. We'll show them that they need us more than we need them. So instead of working, march up to your local city hall, the mayor's office, and every big business and corporation. Tell them you aren't working for them anymore. Tell them you're sick and tired of struggling, while politicians and business owners sit behind the desks and make rules that serve their own purposes. Tell them you deserve better. Demand better. If you do that, I'll take care of the rest."

The bus remained silent. The city stayed silent. Everyone in America stayed silent. Many citizens were wondering the same thing: was this treason? Was he right?

One man in the middle of the bus jumped up and yelled, "The courthouse is this way. Let's go!"

The passengers began to leave their seats and exit the bus into the chaos. Daniel gazed out of the window as the streets began to fill. People filed out of office buildings still in uniforms, some sporting name tags, and gathered outside the courthouse. The bus driver turned around. Daniel and the creepy old man were the only passengers left. The driver shrugged his shoulders.

"In all my years of driving a public bus, this is the craziest thing I've ever—"

Before he could finish his sentence, a gunshot rang out. Then there were two more. The driver and the old man ducked down. They were definitely gunshots—and they were close by. Daniel was stuck in his chair. A few more shots echoed down the street followed by the sound of breaking glass. People were throwing bricks and rocks through shop windows. A police car was being attacked by dozens of people.

The bus driver, still on his knees, looked back at Daniel and said, "Sorry kid. We're sitting ducks here. It seems like these people have gone mad. They're attacking anything run by the government. I'm not going to sit around and wait for them to figure out public transportation is paid for by their tax money. I'm out."

Daniel watched him slip out of the bus and dart off into an alley. Great, now he was stuck on a deserted bus in the middle of a riot with the creepy old man.

"Are you Daniel?"

Daniel looked up at the old man, making no attempt to hide the fear on his face. *How does he know my name?* His heart began to race. Should he lie? Was he in danger? He was too overwhelmed to come up with anything other than the truth. He nodded.

"I'm here to help you. Any idea on how to work this wheelchair lift?"

Daniel's muscles relaxed. The man seemed genuine… and suddenly far less creepy. He watched him immediately fiddle around with the levers to no avail. Daniel made a few keystrokes and hit enter.

"I thought you said you were here to help."

It was the first time Daniel had smiled in days, even with all of the chaos and uncertainty around him. Something about the old man made him feel comfortable suddenly.

"Real funny," the old man replied.

A rock smashed through the front window of the bus. Daniel and old man jerked their heads to follow the sound of the shattering glass.

"We've got to get you out of here before they torch the bus," the man said. The smirk faded from his wrinkled face.

# 7 DEAD END

"Hey! You, in the wheelchair! Stop!"

Daniel could hear footsteps closing in on the pavement behind him. It sounded like multiple people. The old man started walking faster next to him. Daniel sped up to keep pace with him. The voice behind them yelled again.

"Dead end ahead, little man. Where are you going in such a hurry?"

Daniel saw the wall about two hundred feet in front of them. It was indeed a dead end. He and the old man had turned down the wrong alley. He stopped his wheelchair and spun it around to face the voices. The old man was already staring at the three young punks now blocking off the only passage out of the alley.

Two of the men were white. The third was Latino. The three of them appeared to be in their mid-twenties. One held a baseball bat in his right hand. Daniel noticed the guy in the middle was holding something as well, but he couldn't see what it was. The man in the middle stepped forward.

"Didn't you two hear the message from the Kore dude? Everyone is supposed to head towards downtown, not away from it. Why are you running away so fast? You with the government?"

"No," the old man spoke up. "We were stranded on a bus. I'm trying to get this young man home and out of harm's way. That's all."

They looked down at Daniel in his wheelchair, their energy softening. Daniel eyed them carefully—were they about to let them go? Then suddenly the guy with bat spoke up.

"Hey, where did you get that?" he asked, pointing to Daniel's iPad.

Daniel moved his thin fingers across the top of the iPad and slowly pulled it closer to his chest. He was hoping they hadn't noticed his phone too. The man with the bat stepped in closer.

"Is that a new iPhone? Pretty fancy equipment for a poor boy in a wheelchair."

His two friends chuckled.

"Look, gentlemen, please leave us alone," said the old man. "He's just an innocent kid in a wheelchair. Just let us get out of here and you have my word we'll never be back."

"How do we know you didn't steal it?" replied the guy with a long red and black snake tattoo wrapped around his forearm. "There's been lots of reports of stolen goods around here, and we don't take kindly to others stealing things on our turf."

"Does it look like he could get away with stealing an iPad from... where? An *Apple store*?" the old man asked, his voice suddenly dripping with anger.

The guy with the snake tattoo poked his head closer to Daniel's face.

"I was asking *him*. What do you say, boy? The cat got your tongue or are you too handicapped to speak?"

The men laughed again. Daniel's iPad was glued to his chest. His heart was beating a million miles per hour.

"Since your little friend here can't seem to talk," the man said, "We'll let you communicate this to him. You guys have two options. One, he can hand over his iPad and phone and you guys can get out of here safely. Or two, we can beat it out of him and you guys walk out of here with broken bones and nothing else. Either way, the two of you ain't leaving this alley without paying your dues."

The Latino man reached down to swipe Daniel's iPad. Daniel closed his eyes and held onto it with every ounce of strength he had. Nothing happened. The next thing Daniel heard was a thud. He opened his eyes. The Latino man was on the ground. The other men stared in disbelief as the old man stared down at the opponent he had just knocked off his feet.

The man who had been concealing something in his hand made a quick motion with his wrist, revealing a serrated switchblade. The man who had been pushed down pulled out brass knuckles from his cargo pants and placed them on his right hand. The third man with the bat slapped it gently across his other hand, signaling a fight.

"You picked a bad day to push someone old man. The cops are too busy to help you tonight," one man threatened.

The old man took a step back. He put his hand on Daniel's chest, motioning him to back up quickly. Daniel threw his wheelchair in reverse and started closing in on the brick wall behind him. Pretty soon he wouldn't be able to go any farther.

Daniel's wheelchair collided with the wall in a dull thud. The back two wheels just kept spinning. He couldn't go any farther. The old man stopped a few feet in front of him. The three men continued to approach.

"Any final last words, old man?"

The old man just stood there with his arms at his sides. Daniel noticed his fists slowly clenching. The guy with the bat laughed.

"This is easy… a weak old man and a teenager in a wheelchair, who can't even talk or yell for help? It's like stealing candy from a baby."

He took a step forward as the other two chuckled. He was slowly tossing the bat back and forth between his two hands. Before he could take another step forward, his friend to the right threw his arm in front of him to stop him.

"I've got this one, Drake."

They both smiled. Drake, who seemed to be the leader with the bat, nodded in agreement. His friend walked up to the old man.

Daniel was whimpering in his wheelchair. He was ducking down in order to avoid eye contact. The young tattooed man spoke up.

"This is your last chance to hand over the iPad, both your phones, and any cash you have on you. You can walk out of here safely if you give them to me now. Well… one of you can *walk* out," he snickered.

Daniel picked up his iPad and poked the old man in the back with it. He motioned for him to hand it over. He didn't want any more trouble with these guys. The old man grabbed it and then handed it right back to Daniel with a wink. He turned back around to face the men.

"Sorry guys, but you'll have to come get it yourselves if you want it that bad."

"You crazy old geezer. You're going to wish you hadn't said that after we're done with you!"

He planted his foot and threw a right punch to his temple, but the old man ducked the punch. The other two street punks burst into laughter. They weren't going to let their boy live this one down.

"You're losing your touch, Bobby. Old Man River here is showing you up," snorted Drake.

They continued to laugh as the old man just stood there with his hands down by his side. He was showing no intention of fighting back. Daniel feared for his life. He wished the old man would hand over the devices so they could walk away.

Bobby faked a left hook, hoping to see the old man duck again so he could get a cheap shot. The old man didn't budge. Bobby went in again confidently, with a real right hook to the side of his head. As his fist cut through the air, the old man leaned back, his nose missing knuckles by mere inches. Daniel watched as the old man used his right hand to punch his opponent in the ribs. The young street fighter quickly recovered and threw another punch. This time, the old man blocked the punch and grabbed his wrist. A loud pop ensued as he snapped his wrist in half. The young man dropped to his knees in pain. His hand was dangling awkwardly from his wrist. The old man kicked him in the chest, throwing him back into the side of a steel dumpster. He was out cold. Drake stepped in.

"Let's see how you do against a baseball bat, old man!"

The intensity of his gaze made him think twice about swinging the bat. For the first time in years, Drake wasn't confident that he was going to win the fight. He took a step towards the old man and swung the bat with everything he had. The old man ducked just in time, but the tip of the bat grazed the back of his head knocking off his hat.

"It will be your head rolling off next," threatened Drake.

As he cocked the bat the old man lunged forward, grabbed the handle of the bat just above Drake's hands, and used his knee to kick him in the groin. He instantly released the bat as his hands moved to clutch between his legs. He was down on both knees screaming in pain. He looked up to see the old man holding the bat just inches from his face.

Drake quickly grabbed the barrel of the bat with his right hand, but the old man pulled Drake in closer. In an instant, he shifted his upper body to the left with his legs sweeping fast behind him. The impact hit Drake right above his calves, knocking him off the ground and onto his side. The wooden bat bounced on the ground and then rolled to a stop, inches from Drake. The old man snatched it up. He grabbed the barrel and slammed the bat handle on Drake's back as hard as he could. Drake screamed and grabbed his back.

"Now get out of here and leave us alone or *you'll* be needing a wheelchair," the old man sneered.

The third man was already running down the alley before the old man could finish his sentence. Drake still lay there rolling around in pain. Daniel was speechless, and not for lack of an iPad.

"Let's go, Daniel." He motioned to Daniel and slowly walked out of the alley towards the main road. Daniel swerved around Drake, but made a point to run over his left foot, which happened to be sticking out. Drake groaned. The old man grinned. He threw the bat away in the dumpster and they started making their way out of downtown St. Augustine.

"Do you know how to get home from here?" he asked Daniel.

Daniel typed.

"Yes. Where did you learn to do that?" chimed the robotic voice that Daniel had adopted as his own.

The old man just smiled.

Once they made out of the downtown area, the rest of the trip was easy. No one was in sight except an occasional police car, fire truck, or ambulance. Fear of the unknown had paralyzed everyone who didn't want to take part in the riots. They stayed in their homes and monitored the news.

An hour later they arrived at Daniel's home. The two had not spoken since the alley attack. The old man wasn't much of a talker and Daniel could only talk if he wasn't moving. He had so many questions. Who was this strange man who had saved his life? How did he manage to beat up those guys back there? How did he know Daniel's name? *Why* was he there? It was as if he had known what was going to happen.

Daniel wheeled up the sidewalk to the front steps of his house. The old man followed alongside. He looked up at the mobile home trailer, which stood in front of him.

"Is this your house?" he asked.

Daniel nodded. The old man shook his head. It almost seemed as though he was disappointed.

"Do you mind if I come in for a moment?" he asked gently.

Daniel agreed enthusiastically. He had never brought home a guest in his entire life. He couldn't wait to tell his dad about how this man had saved his life.

Inside the old man looked around. It smelled like someone had been smoking. The TV was on with the volume turned up. Some reporter was talking about the riots, which were breaking out across the country. The old man stepped closer to the TV, picked up the remote, and lowered the volume to a reasonable level. He noticed someone fast asleep on the couch. A robotic voice from behind him piped up.

"That's my dad."

The old man turned around to face Daniel. He nodded that he understood. He gently grabbed Daniel's father's shoulder and tried to wake him. His dad was holding a mostly full Busch Light can in one hand while an unlit cigarette dangled in-between two fingers in his other hand. He slowly became aware that someone was shaking him awake.

He looked up at the old man now hovering above him. He squinted his eyes and propped himself up on his elbow. Daniel watched his dad's face turn from red to scarlet. He assumed he was embarrassed. The blanket slid off of him as he sat up, revealing dark blood stains all over his white t-shirt. Daniel gasped.

Max didn't seem at all bothered by it. He looked the old man up and down. He looked at Daniel and then back at the old man.

"Why are *you* here?" he screamed, accidentally spilling beer on himself. The blood stain spread further across his shirt.

Daniel didn't know what to think. Did his dad *know* this man? What exactly was happening right now? He moved to type on his iPad, but the old man spoke up first.

"Perhaps you are too drunk to remember, but you were the one who called me out of the blue and asked me to show up after not returning a single call or letter for almost twenty years." He paused to take a deep breath. "I know you might not believe me, but it's really good to see you again, son."

*Son?*

Daniel wished he could scream the words he was thinking. Instead, his mouth just opened and closed without a sound.

"It was a mistake," Max spat. "I never should have called you. I didn't realize how much I still hated you until I saw your face in my house. I think it's best if you leave now."

The two grown men, completely caught up in the drama, had forgotten about Daniel behind them. Daniel tapped on his iPad. He wasn't typing out words this time, just tapping his index finger as if to say: *Hello???*

The old man turned around to face him. Daniel had a look of bewilderment.

"Daniel, you deserve an explanation. I'm sorry I didn't get to tell you earlier. I didn't anticipate it going like this. I don't know how else to tell you this but... I'm your grandfather."

Daniel started typing feverishly. He looked up at his dad, his t-shirt still drenched in warm beer and blood stains. He slammed the button.

"You knew he was alive this whole time?"

Daniel's grandfather, Jack Fullerton, disgraced mayor of St. Augustine, spun around to face his son.

"You never told him I was alive?" he asked incredulously, anger clouding his face like a storm moving in quickly. "You've been hiding the truth from him his entire life? I assumed you'd tell him everything that happened once he was old enough to understand."

"Understand?" Max screamed. "What did you want me to tell him? What exactly did you want him to understand? That you walked out on us? That you disappeared? That you were responsible for the death of mom? That you were responsible for the death of my wife? That you were the reason Daniel is in a wheelchair—that it's because of you that I'm dying of cancer right now?"

Daniel's grandfather stared at Max. The anger had evaporated as quickly as it had materialized. He thought he saw a glimmer in Jack's eyes as if they were watering ever so slightly. There was a long pause as if everyone was holding their breath.

"I told you… you can fight this," he encouraged softly.

Max threw his body back on the couch and let out a grunt. He then stole a quick glance at Daniel.

"Look, son," Jack continued quietly, "I know I've made a lot of mistakes—"

"Save it," Max barked.

Jack stopped speaking abruptly, torn between the yearning he felt to rekindle his relationship with his son and the responsibility he felt to respect his space. He'd never imagined his son would shut him out of his life for so many years. He'd always told himself he'd be able to make up for the mistakes he'd made, for the time he neglected Max during his teenage years. He wanted nothing more than that; to repair their relationship. Now knowing that his son had cancer, he was at a loss of what to say or do. The silence was deafening.

It hit Daniel like a wall. Max knew he was about to die so he called his only other living relative... his father. It was probably the only reason he would have ever called his father; Daniel needed someone to care for him. Now it seemed he was doubting his decision. Max pointed to the door.

"Get out. Get out now. It was a mistake calling you. You're right— I'll fight this and be fine," he yelled with venom in his voice. Daniel wondered if he actually believed that. "Daniel doesn't need you. Leave us alone and never come back, ya hear? GO!"

Max was coughing up blood. Daniel watched his grandfather reluctantly give him one last look before he walked out of the door. Daniel wanted to yell, "Wait!" but he couldn't type quickly enough. He put his electric wheelchair in gear and followed his grandfather out the door.

"Stay here, Daniel," Max ordered. "Don't follow him. He's crazy. He'll end up getting you killed."

Daniel ignored his dad. He had too many questions to ask his grandfather. He was certain his dad wouldn't tell him the truth.

"Fine! Neither of you come back! Ya hear me?!" Daniel's dad yelled loud enough for every neighbor to hear. "Stay away and go bother someone else. The two of you have ruined my life. Now leave... I hope I never see you again."

Daniel spun around after hitting the bottom of the small wheelchair ramp only to see his dad slam the door shut. He hadn't planned on abandoning his father at that moment, but that exchange confirmed for him everything he had feared. His dad had blamed him for all the pain in his life, and he always would. Perhaps the kindest thing would be to relieve him of the responsibility of caring for him... especially in his final days. Maybe he could have a chance at something different with his grandfather. A tear rolled down his cheek. Then another.

"Daniel," a warm hand touched his shoulder. "I'm sorry... I'm sorry you had to witness that. Your dad didn't mean what he said. I hurt him many years ago and he was just lashing out at me. Let's take a walk. Let's give your dad get some much-needed rest. He's going through a tough time. You deserve to know the truth about our family once and for all..."

# 8 REUNION

They weren't even three blocks away from the trailer home when they heard it...

"INCOMING!"

It was a man's voice coming from above. Daniel and his grandfather looked up just in time to see an owl drop a frog right onto Daniel's shoulder. *An owl and a frog.* Was he dreaming again? No, of course not. Daniel's head began to spin as he realized this was really happening. It had not been a dream after all.

The frog made a quick leap and landed right in the middle of his iPad. Daniel, irritated at the slime on his device, pushed the frog away with his hand.

"I see the two of you have met," said Vosco.

Daniel was now utterly confused. He looked up at his grandfather expectantly.

"Hello, Vosco," said Jack. "I see you're still scaring kids."

Vosco didn't laugh. He pointed his webbed hand over to the owl who had just landed next to them.

"This is Skylar. She's actually the daughter of Captain Teddy. You remember—from down below."

Jack gave her a warm smile.

"It's nice to meet you, Skylar. I'm sorry for the loss of your dad. He was a friend of mine. One of the best soldiers I've ever met."

"Thank you," Skylar replied meekly, struggling to look at Jack in the eyes. She hadn't talked about her father in quite some time. It was forbidden in her household.

The three of them continued to talk for a few minutes before Daniel interrupted.

"Will someone please explain what's going on here?"

"Daniel," his grandfather replied. "Vosco and I served in a war together many years ago. It was Skylar's father who saved my life. He's the reason I'm still alive today."

"What war?" Daniel asked. Was this when Jack had been mayor? The timing didn't seem to add up.

"It wasn't a war involving the United States. It was a war which happened very far away in a place called Alcazar," Jack explained.

Daniel had always been quite good with geography. He couldn't recall a place called Alcazar.

"How far away?" he asked.

"You might say... worlds away," his grandfather replied.

Daniel shrugged his shoulders as Jack turned his attention elsewhere, pointing to an old abandoned van across the street. It had been partially destroyed. Metal seats rusted the torn and weathered canopy.

"Let's head over there so I can sit down and tell the story. It might take a while."

The three of them watched as Jack whipped out a pocket knife, popped the lock, and slid open the doors to the van. He then took a seat in one of the rusty chairs, while Vosco and Skylar shared the other. Daniel stared intently from his wheelchair.

"Daniel, many years ago I was the mayor of this city. Our entire family was loved and admired by pretty much all of St. Augustine. Your grandmother was a stay-at-home mom, who did her best with our only son, Mark."

"What?" Daniel asked immediately confused. "Mark? Fullerton? But our last name has always been Ruhlin."

"Yes and no. Your dad's real name is Mark Fullerton."

"What?" Daniel sputtered again through his iPad.

"He changed his name shortly after you were born to make sure he had no association with our family. He didn't want anyone to know that he was related to me. He didn't want you growing up knowing you were related to the biggest scandal in St. Augustine. He legally changed his own name and your last name the day you were born."

Daniel found it hard to swallow as Jack continued.

"Anyway, your dad was quite a good student and one heck of a baseball player. As he got older, I became busier with my role as mayor. In fact, the state of Florida was grooming me to become governor."

Daniel listened eagerly, unsure of what was to come.

"I still remember coming home late one evening after missing one of Mark's baseball games. It wasn't an incredibly important game, but it was one of many that I promised him I'd attend. I got carried away at work and completely forgot about it. He wouldn't speak to me for days. The third night he ran away from home. But I knew where he was… his favorite hiding spot… the old Alcazar hotel."

Daniel straightened up at the mention of the Alcazar. How peculiar that the war he'd mentioned earlier occurred in a place called Alcazar.

"The Alcazar was an extraordinary hotel built by Henry Flagler back in 1888, which eventually closed down after the Great Depression. It was also a common place for teenagers to visit at night because the hotel was said to be haunted. I found him sitting on an old bench near a fountain. We made some small talk and all of a sudden it hit me. Mark and I had never done anything together. Here I was mayor, with so much power, and I had never given him any opportunities. I told your dad that I would approach the city about rebuilding the historic Alcazar hotel. He could be my assistant. It would be our little project. He could help make decisions and recommendations every step of the way. Your dad was excited. So was I."

Jack paused for a moment. A tear rolled down his thin-bridged nose. The memories were bringing back emotions he hadn't experienced in a long time. Daniel wasn't sure what to do, so he remained quiet, listening in anticipation for the rest of the story.

"It wasn't long before we had the money for a full rebuild of the hotel. Your dad came straight over to the Alcazar every day after school. He'd even skip baseball practice on numerous occasions. I fell in love with the hotel too. One evening I couldn't sleep a wink. All I could think about was the hotel. After rolling around in bed for what seemed like hours, I snuck out of the house and drove down to the hotel. I walked the perimeter, admiring what we had accomplished in such little time. I unlocked the door and strolled the corridors envisioning what it must have been like when the likes of Henry Flagler, John D. Rockefeller, and Andrew Carnegie walked the halls. I was on the second floor when I saw it. The entire fountain in the middle of the courtyard was…"

Jack furrowed his brow and swallowed hard. His eyes darted to the side as he searched for the right words.

"I know this sounds crazy, but the fountain was glowing. It was glowing bright green. It looked like something out of a movie. At first, I thought I was dreaming. I continued to stare at it through the window pane as I quickly made my way to the closest stairwell. It seemed to glow brighter and brighter as I came closer."

Daniel was on the edge of his seat. Vosco and Skylar were leaning in as well. Skylar had never heard this story before.

"By the time I made it to the courtyard the green fountain was glowing so brightly I wondered if someone was playing a joke on me. Surely someone must be shining a green light on the fountain to make it look this way. I looked around but saw no one. It was a quiet night. I reached down to touch the water. The second my index finger touched it, I felt this pull... like some unseen force had grabbed my forearm and was yanking me into the fountain. Suddenly, I was completely submerged in the water—being pulled down farther and farther. I remember the panic I felt in that moment like it was yesterday. I was certain I was going to die. I couldn't hold my breath a second longer, so I opened my mouth and water flooded into my lungs. Moments later I felt as though I was going through a pipe, and the next thing I knew I was lying on the ground— but not the ground I'd just left.

"When I came to, I was coughing up water. My head ached and my back was killing me. I had no idea where I was, but I was certain it wasn't St. Augustine. It looked like a forest."

Daniel's eyes darted to Skylar and Vosco. *Forest?* Was this the same forest he had been in the other evening?

"I looked around the forest. It was... well, it felt like a place I'd never been before. The air smelled different. The forest colors were slightly off. It was like I was experiencing the world in another dimension. I knew I couldn't comfortably explore it without first knowing I could get back home safely... so I swam back through the water pipe to see if I could return. Sure enough, I ended up in the fountain. I was afraid to tell anyone about what had happened. For countless nights I would sneak out of the house with food, water, and weapons, and venture further and further into the woods. I even had to fend off a wolf once. After that they left me alone. I would take trips down there for years. It was my reprieve from the real world. I never ventured too far though for fear of getting lost. Then one trip I made it all the way through the forest, only to find an entirely new dimension. Unlike the forest, this one was mostly water. There was no land. Giant lily pads floated on the water's surface. There were crocodiles too. I'm still not sure why, but for me it was the tipping point. I decided it was time to tell my family.

"Of course, they all thought I was crazy. My wife was relieved that I wasn't having an affair. However, she still wasn't buying my story. I begged her, Mark, and Mark's new wife to come with me. At first, they were hesitant. It certainly didn't help that your mom was pregnant with you, Daniel. She was still a few months away from her due date and we assumed this would only be a short adventure. After begging them, they all agreed to come with me to see this hidden world for themselves. The fountain wasn't green at first, but at the stroke of midnight, it turned from its normal murky brown color to a bright, neon green. My family was shocked. They were also suddenly much more curious. Before we knew it, we had made it through three wildly different and dangerous terrains. At the end of that journey, we found ourselves in a magnificent new world... Alcazar."

Jack smiled, his mind taking him back to the first day he saw the lush and untarnished lands.

Skylar interrupted. "How did you make it through the middle grounds safely? Those three lands are incredibly dangerous. They're designed that way specifically to keep newcomers out."

"It was beginners' luck I presume. I had the advantage of knowing the forest like the back of my hand. The wolves were scared to death of me because of my gun. We almost lost Mark's wife to a crocodile and I nearly got impaled by an angry scorpion, but we made it there nonetheless."

"Yep. Those were the good days," said Vosco. "That was back when Alcazar was a utopia; when it was truly magical. Many have said Alcazar was the world God built before he made the rest of the Earth. He called us *The Mogans*. The fables say he started his first creation in the center of the planet, thinking the sun might be too strong. He thought Earth would be more protective with its crust surrounding us rather than underneath us. He gave Earth its own sun at its core. The molten lava served as a sun of sorts for Alcazar. It was a land of light. We never experienced darkness. There was no night. All beings in Alcazar recharged by sunlight. There was no need for sleep whatsoever. It was a peaceful place. We lived in love. There was no greed, unhappiness, or disease. We Mogans had unlimited fruit and vegetables growing year-round. We had plenty of food and most Mogans lived to the ripe age of three hundred years. No one fought with each other like they do today. There were no wars, no murders, no violence. It was close to perfect."

Skylar interjected, "Every Mogan had one unique special power, which they could use to help out a neighbor or friend. It made everyone inherently valuable to one another. Now we are killed on the spot if we use our powers—even to help a friend. The entire community lives in fear... thanks to Kore."

"*Kore?*" asked Daniel. "The hacker, who seems to have won over the entire country?"

"Yes, that Kore," Skylar replied.

"He is from Alcazar?"

"Yes."

"How? Why? What happened?" Daniel couldn't type quickly enough and the robotic voice certainly wasn't *speaking* quickly enough.

"Many years ago, the very first human entered Alcazar," Vosco piped up. "He was an adventurer; a pirate. He was leading a group in a search for the fountain of youth. He discovered the fountain where the hotel now sits, and he was the first to make it all the way through the three middle grounds. However, the entire group lost their lives in the process. He entered Alcazar barely alive, belligerent, hungry, and angry. He came into our peaceful village swinging his sword at anything that moved, knocking down our fruit trees, scaring children, and demanding food and rum from each home."

"Even though we are very peaceful and loving people, no one really wanted to take him in. Maybe it was *because* we are so peaceful and loving we could sense he was neither of those things. His eye patch didn't help. His other eye darted around like a fruit fly. It's hard to trust someone who won't make eye contact with you."

"Our leader, Hathor, held a council meeting late that evening to decide what we should do with him. A couple village leaders offered to transport him back through the middle grounds and send him back through the fountain. We knew he'd be back—probably with more people next time. No one could agree on what to do with him. Finally, one couple offered to take him in. They were an odd couple, who lived on the outskirts of town. They were always testing out new and radical magic. They were the wizards of Alcazar. They were constantly conducting experiments and blending realities. They searched for ways to harness the laws of the universe, but in the context of *magic*. Perhaps they needed a new guinea pig.

"After much debate, everyone in town agreed under two conditions. One, the couple must keep him hidden in their home away from the village. Two, after one year everyone would re-evaluate whether he should continue to live in Alcazar."

"By the end of the year, it was too late," interrupted Skylar. "This pirate, called Slick, was a greedy man. He also happened to be a very persuasive man. He had all but brainwashed the couple to believe that they were the rightful rulers of Alcazar. He convinced them that their magic was power—that the villagers were holding them back. He also convinced them to teach him their magic, but he was unsuccessful. He couldn't make magic.

"Eventually Slick married their beautiful daughter, Gwen. He told them he could provide them with grandchildren, and they would harness their magic together and take over the land one day. A year later Gwen gave birth to a son. They named him Kore."

"In the ancient Mogan tongue, Kore means 'the void'. His name fit him perfectly. He was void of love, emotion, empathy; he did not embody the values of Alcazar. His family bred hatred in him. They cultivated contempt. They nurtured discord."

"When Kore became a teenager, it was obvious that he didn't fit in. He was shorter than all of the other boys his age. He wasn't attractive. He was half human and half Mogan, and thus he had no special power. Everyone saw him as being different, not normal... less than."

Daniel, who'd been spellbound by the story, suddenly scrambled for his iPad.

"So... disabled?"

Everyone turned to look at him. He kept typing.

"They saw Kore as disabled, essentially. Right?"

Jack's expression melted into something Daniel had never seen or experienced: pride.

"Yeah," Skylar said quietly. "Yeah, I guess so, Daniel."

Daniel leaned back in his wheelchair, realizing it was never as simple as labeling people good or bad. He'd made his point. He waited patiently for Skylar to continue, but she didn't. She seemed distracted.

"Kore was laughed at every time he came into town," Vosco chimed in. He realized this part of the story might impact Daniel in a different way. "Sadly, he was teased until he no longer wanted to leave the house. His parents put him in their dark basement and left him there to hack away on the computer all day. For years he spent long days in his parent's basement, worked on his computers, and plotted how he would take over Alcazar one day. He longed for respect and control; two things he had never had in life."

"Then the unthinkable happened. His parents and grandparents were murdered. It was the first time anyone had been murdered in all of Alcazar. Since we had no police, lawyers, or judges, no one really knew what to do. The only suspect was Kore, but nobody could *prove* it was him. It was months after the murders before anyone knew of them. Kore blamed their deaths on a failed experiment—something about an electric gun that backfired. Nobody really bought that story. Kore had a clear a motive."

Daniel was sitting on the edge of his wheelchair. He now felt conflicted regarding his strange connection with Kore. Was he really that similar to a *murderer?* Daniel's eyes were glued on Vosco as he continued.

"With Kore on his own, it didn't take long for him to recruit a few friends… especially the young men who were computer geeks like him. This was around the time that Alcazar was first exposed to the concept of the Internet. Pretty quickly, Alcazar was connected like never before. Kore also saw the opportunity the Internet offered: a place where he could have a voice and be heard. This is where his movement began. He had an entire band of outcasts, who would scheme to exact their revenge on the rest of the community. Some of it was innocent hacking. Some of it was more malevolent. They were so brainwashed that they actually started believing that *we* were evil. They believed that they were missionaries called on by God to take over the land and rule it. After multiple petty thefts, break-ins, vandalism, and scare tactics, Kore and his small army staged their biggest attack yet. Shortly after midnight one evening they broke into our leader Hathor's home and murdered him."

"At this point, the people of Alcazar had seen enough. We weren't going to sit by and watch this malicious man and his tribe of bandits spread fear and hatred throughout our peaceful land. We formed an army to fight them and end their evil ways once and for all. Of course, Kore got wind of this and recruited harder than ever. He promised anyone who followed him that they would never have to work again and they would receive a portion of the money they stole. Their families would have full protection for life. Guess what? He recruited half of Alcazar, if not more."

Daniel looked down at his feet. His mind wandered back to the bus and Kore's promises. He was so persuasive. It had struck a chord in everyone around him. People were afraid of not having enough; of not being safe. He had felt it just like everyone else.

Jack started speaking, his eyes fixed on Daniel.

"We arrived in Alcazar during Kore's movement. The next thing you know they were asking us to help them fight this civil war. Your dad really wanted to leave and go back to America. It wasn't a safe place for your pregnant mother. After a long debate, your grandmother and I decided to stay and fight. We sent Mark and your mom back through the middle grounds to safety. It was a risky move, but Mark was armed very well.

"Somehow Kore found out about your mother and father leaving. He assumed they were sent to get more help from up above. Kore sent his men to chase them down. Your mother was struck by a steel club and your dad managed to injure the rest of the men with his gun. It was too late. Your mother was losing too much blood too quickly. You weren't due for another two months, but your mother went into labor. She used every last ounce of energy she had to get you into this world."

Daniel gripped the top of his shirt collar with his fingers. He wiped away a tear, which was rolling down his cheek. His parents had loved him after all. The tears kept coming.

Vosco and Skylar were silent. They both knew how the rest of the story played out. The events, emotions, and fears from the Alcazar civil war, which had plagued them for decades, came rushing back. Jack continued.

"While your mother and father tried to sneak away, I stayed back in Alcazar to help fight the war with my wife and the rest of the community. Over the next few days I watched Kore and his evil army murder women, children, and anyone else who refused to join him. He murdered Skylar's father. He murdered Vosco's wife. I was captured and forced to watch as Kore took my wife's life. I eventually escaped the prison where I was held. I no longer wanted to be in Alcazar. I ventured back through the dangerous three middle grounds only to discover that everything I had on Earth was gone too. I'd been stripped of my position as mayor due to my unexplained and sudden absence.

Even worse, Mark had told reporters that I'd killed my wife and that I was responsible for the death of your mother. I went into hiding until one day I decided I had to meet you—my first grandson. I'd heard that you'd been named Daniel. You and your father were living in my old home. I snuck in hoping we could all start a new life...

Daniel hadn't known he was a Fullerton. He hadn't known his true identity his entire life.

"When I arrived at my old house, I was met with a gun in my face and told to never come near either of you again. Your dad said... well, he said a lot of things I don't need to repeat. I walked away that evening in complete despair. It was at that point I realized money, power, fame, and material things didn't matter. All I wanted was to be a part of your lives, but I couldn't. I relinquished my life as I knew it and hitchhiked my way to California doing odd jobs along the way. There I have resided as a hermit near the beach all of these years."

Jack paused to wipe a few tears from his own eyes. Even Skylar had tears running down her feathers. Kore had ruined the lives of so many families since he won the war. Now he wanted to take over America.

Vosco looked up at Daniel. "You might be wondering how you fit in here?"

Daniel nodded.

"Kore is planning on using the same tactics he used to divide Alcazar in order to conquer the world. This time he's going to do it all through hacking. He's got an entire world connected by the Internet... billions of people. He's got financial markets to wipe out and fear to spread."

Daniel let that sink in. The country was already facing a time of uncertainty. In fact, so was the entire world. People would panic easily. He typed.

"I'm still wondering how I fit into all of this... aside from being born in the fountain that connects these worlds."

"Well, that's exactly it," said Vosco. "You came into the world... *between* worlds. You're not completely of one world or the other. Though both your parents are from here, you were born in this in-between place. We think... you might be like Kore: half human, half Mogan. His hacking skills can only be matched by yours. You are the only one who can outsmart him and stop him."

Daniel just sat there, trying to process this.

"Listen Daniel," said Skylar. "I'm having trouble believing this as well. Maku the Magu, the all-knowing prophet of Alcazar, told us you are the only person who can defeat Kore. He's never wrong. He will explain the rest to you when you meet him."

Daniel thought about it for a second. He replied with this iPad.

"I'm not going."

"What do you mean you're not going?" asked Vosco, his jaw tightening. "Don't you understand? You are the chosen one!"

"I'm sorry," Daniel said via iPad. "You've made a mistake. I'm just a scared kid in a wheelchair. My dad is very sick. I need to be there for him."

Daniel spun the wheelchair around. He darted out of the used car lot gate and veered right towards his home. Vosco and Skylar looked at Jack, but he just shrugged.

"Sounds like he's not ready yet," Jack said. "He's afraid. I'll speak to him this evening and find out what he's afraid of." Jack paused. "Is he really that good of a hacker?"

Vosco smiled. "According to Maku, your grandson once hacked into the government's missile system. He was just minutes away from being able to deploy a missile. It caused a massive panic in the White House, which was immediately buried."

Jack smiled.

"Will you come with us and help fight?" Skylar asked.

"No. Alcazar holds nothing but painful memories for me. Daniel's going to need me here… whether it's someone to help him right now or it's someone to come back to. I'll swing by his house tomorrow morning and we'll see if he's changed his mind. Don't expect any miracles."

He started walking back towards his son's house.

"Hey Jack," Vosco said in a warning tone. Jack turned back around. "If you thought what you witnessed with Kore was bad, you haven't seen anything yet. He's been plotting this attack on America since you left. It's about to get really ugly fast. He's going to try every trick in the book to divide this country and have them eating out of his hands. Once he gets enough of them to join his army, there will be no stopping him."

"Well," Jack replied, "If Daniel really is the only one who can stop this, let's hope he does, huh?"

He turned back around. The thought of Kore ruling America was frightening, but he had personal matters to attend to first. He had to find a way to apologize to his son.

Daniel had beaten him to the house by the time Jack walked up the steps. Something was wrong. The door was wide open. He ran up the steps into the house and found Daniel frozen. Mark's body was strewn across the floor. He was covered in blood and didn't appear to be breathing. Daniel's eyes filled with tears. Jack bent down and placed two fingers on his son's neck. He tried another spot... then another. Nothing.

"Mark," Jack said. "Mark! No... I need you to be here to hear this." Tears were running down his face.

"I love you, Mark. I love you, son. I love you. I love you," he said, repeating the last bit over and over again as his voice cracked. He had waited almost twenty years to say it, and now he was too late.

Jack's eyes found Daniel's. He cradled his Mark's head in his right hand and kissed him on the forehead.

"I'm sorry for everything I put you through—"

The tears flooded his eyes and he stopped talking. He lost himself for a moment. Then he looked back at Daniel.

"He's dead."

# 9 RIOTS

"Are you crazy?" screamed Bruce Cromwell, the secretary of defense. He was yelling directly at the president, who sat on the other side of the thick mahogany table. "You can't issue an apology statement the day after the entire nation just found out you were a fraud. You told them that you had this whole cyber-attack under control and now they know you lied. These riots aren't just going to resolve because you apologize."

The other leaders in the Situation Room looked over at the president and nodded in agreement with the secretary of defense. Even the vice president didn't have his back. The entire group had spent the night at the White House. The place was surrounded by angry protestors. The entire country was up in arms. None of them had any idea when they'd be able to safely leave the White House.

"First of all," replied the irritated and sleep deprived president, "If my memory serves me correctly, it was your speech script which got us into this mess. Had we just told the truth from the get-go that video never would have surfaced. How in the world did they hack into our security cameras? Are we sure this room isn't being recorded right now?"

President McFarland looked over to the head of security.

"It's safe now, sir. They found an unforeseen loophole in our security camera system. We're 100% sure they don't have access any longer."

The president continued, "Regarding your question on a press announcement, how about we just tell them the truth? We messed up.

We want to work together on this… to unite—"

He was cut off by Darren Daley, the national security advisor. "It's too late for the truth. Do you really think anyone is going to believe you after what they just saw? That video is being replayed on every social media site on the web. Besides, anything you possibly say right now could create even more panic across the country. You've seen how fearful everyone is these days. It could be the tipping point that pushes these rioters into a real civil war…"

There was a knock on the door. Nobody moved. They were all paralyzed. All eyes went to Jay.

"Who's there?" Jay asked.

"Anthony Clapper, sir." It was the director for counterterrorism.

The president's assistant Mary unlocked the door.

"Where have you been?" asked the president as Anthony walked in.

He had been missing for hours. A few disapproving glances were thrown across the room by some individuals, who were certain they'd seen Anthony sleeping on the job.

"Don't worry about that—you've got to see what's happening out there. Turn on the TV!" Clapper said with an almost boyish excitement.

The TV in the Situation Room lit up. The news channel was already on. A female reporter was live. She appeared to be in downtown New York City. There was smoke all around her.

"Hey folks, I'm here in downtown Manhattan, just a block away from Wall Street. It's almost been a full day since the riots broke out and things are really heating up. We've yet to hear a single message from the president and the police across the country have all but given up. It seems they just don't stand a chance against the sheer volume of angry citizens."

The reporter turned around and signaled the camera to pan behind her.

"The smoke you see behind me is actually from the stock market exchange building. Rioters not only flipped over the iconic bull in protest of the bankers, but they have now lit the building on fire. According to the authorities, no one was hurt because the stock market floor was vacant due to the temporary shutdown of the financial markets. However, there have been numerous reported fatalities from the small bombs and fires on the streets."

The president watched in dismay as rioters threw everything from small home-made bombs, hammers, and rocks at the stores behind the reporter. The reporter suddenly jumped, startled by a small explosion behind her. She grabbed her head and ducked down out of the frame. A moment later, she was back—shaken but attempting to remain professional.

"As you can see behind me, looters are everywhere—breaking into empty shops and stealing everything they can get their hands on. The police were holding back most of the mob this morning, but they were quickly overtaken by the sheer masses. At the moment, I need to take shelter, but there will be more updates coming soon. Back to you in the studio."

The head anchor from the studio came back on. He showed clips of the chaos occurring across America. Destruction, vandalism, theft, fire, and even deaths were reported in Chicago, Los Angeles, Boston, Atlanta, San Francisco, Phoenix, New Orleans, Charlotte, Cleveland, Philadelphia, and every other major city in America.

The president's face fell into the palm of his hands. He couldn't watch anymore. How did this happen? How long would it last? How many more lives would be lost? How could he fix this? He had never felt so lost, scared, and helpless in his life.

The staff was silent as they watched the drama unfold on TV. The news camera zoomed in on a tall white man, who was about to throw a Molotov cocktail at the Detroit mayor's office. The TV screen suddenly went blank. Then… it turned white. It was eerily familiar. The staff members looked at each other; fear in their eyes. The president raised his head.

The voice was back. It was Kore. There were still no visuals. Just a white screen. Everyone knew whom the voice belonged to. Kore had hijacked the Internet and every TV station once again.

"Hello friends. It's me, Kore. I'm here with good news. While your political leaders and wealthy business owners are hunkered down in their mansions hoping and praying you just go away, I've been busy getting money for you—well-deserved money. The government has been stealing from you *by taxing you* to pay for their huge salaries, pensions, and extravagant lifestyles. Well, I'm pleased to announce that we just moved another three hundred billion dollars out of their corrupt hands and into an account, which will serve us all in our new world order."

The president's face turned pale. *Three hundred billion dollars gone?* He looked around the room. Everyone was stone-faced.

Kore continued, "Here's what I will do with this money. It will be the first installment for our new world order. We will overthrow the current government and create a fair system, which is run by the people—not by a few wealthy aristocrats. Everyone will have equal rights and an equal voice. There will be no poor or rich. You will all have the same amount of money. You are entitled to this money. You are entitled to being taken care of. This is only fair."

Admiral Hardy banged his fist on the table. "He's lost his mind. Our citizens won't believe this hogwash. They don't want handouts; they want a fair chance to make an honest living, right?"

The president shook his head. He wondered how this old man couldn't see the shift which had been happening gradually over the last couple of decades in America.

"Admiral, you came from a generation who worked hard and took pride in rising up to the top. The majority of Americans aren't like that anymore. They want entitlements. They want to be told that the government is going to take care of them. They don't want to worry about money. This terrorist is telling them exactly what they want to hear. The masses are eating out of his hand."

Hardy watched as everyone in the room nodded in agreement. They turned their eyes back to the TV screen.

"Here's what to expect next," Kore continued. "Your president should be receiving a special notice, which spells out exactly what he needs to do in order to step down and make this transition as smooth as possible. He'll have forty-eight hours from tomorrow morning to take action. All I need you to do is to continue voicing your opinion. Take a stand in front of your state capitals and local government buildings. Picket in front of large corporations, who suck the soul out of their workers. Don't show up for work. Let the rich feel how painful it is without their work force showing up. Let the world know how important you are. Without you their lavish lifestyles cannot exist."

Kore paused to let this sink in.

"Finally, if they don't respond to our demands, I'll be forced to shut down the entire power grid. And I'll keep the power grid down until they agree to these demands. Every American eighteen and older will have a salary, free health care, free college, and there will be no more class separation. You'll have the choice to work or not. Most importantly, the wealthy and the poor will merge together into a unified America. We will be ONE."

The TV flickered on and off. The white screen disappeared. The news reporter was back on the screen. It was obvious he didn't know he was live. He was still looking down at his phone. He had obviously been listening to the same message from Kore. He looked abruptly looked back at the camera.

"Are we back on? Are we live?" He asked, nodding to someone off camera. "Folks, we're very sorry for the unscheduled interruption, but we are back, and boy, what a message... a unified America. We'll continue to monitor this evolving situation. You'll be the first to know when we have news. In the meantime, we'd love to know your thoughts about the new pay raise. Shoot us a text or tag us on social media and let us know your thoughts on this new world order. This is Jake Rodgers, signing off from Channel 4 News."

You could have heard a pin drop in the Situation Room. No one said a word.

The conference room intercom made a loud buzzing noise. The president looked around the table. His staff appeared to be frozen. No one moved. The president slowly leaned forward, stretched out his arm, and hit the talk button.

"Yes?" he asked the security operator, who kept tabs on the entire White House.

"Sir, the head of housekeeping just came downstairs with a mysterious small box. She said it was thrown through one of the windows in the west wing. Among the shattered glass on the ground was this small metal box."

"I assume the guards captured the person who did it?" the president asked, wondering how a metal box could shatter the supposedly bullet-proof glass windows of the White House.

"No sir, there was actually no one to be found," the operator hesitated. "However, she did mention a large black crow near the window. It's—I'm not sure it's relevant... but she seemed to think it was... important to mention. She claimed the crow was looking at her. It finally flew off when she picked up the box."

"A black crow?" the president asked, wondering if his staff were losing their minds too. "You're telling me someone slipped through the front gate of the White House completely undetected, managed to launch a metal box through our window in broad daylight, and the only suspect is a large black crow?!"

He was screaming into the conference table microphone box. His staff had never seen him lose his temper like this. They stared at the microphone in the middle of the table awaiting a reply.

"Sir, I'm sincerely sorry. The secret service has the grounds on lockdown. No one is getting in or out for any reason. I'll let you know as soon as we have a suspect."

The president placed his forehead into his hands again. He looked over at the vice president, hoping for some reassurance from his right-hand man. Nothing. Was this some sort of nightmare? How could this be happening? How did one man turn the entire country against him? And who the heck was Kore? He lifted his head back up.

"Where's the box?" he asked. His tone was now quiet and despondent.

"It's almost out of forensics. They've been instructed to bring it to you personally once they confirm it is not an explosive or a virus. It should be here very soon, sir."

The president didn't even bother to thank him. He simply clicked off the talk button. Shortly after, there was a knock at the door. The forensics officer handed him a memory chip. There was a small note attached to it that simply read:

## To: The President
## From: Kore

They plugged the chip into the side of the TV monitor. A white screen appeared. It was the same white screen they had all seen twice in the past twenty-four hours. The clip began to play. There was nothing but a pure white background with black caption text, which slowly appeared as a voice spoke:

"Mr. President, it is with much regret that our first encounter is on these terms. The people have spoken. They want change. They want a new world order. They want to be treated as equals. They want to be guaranteed a salary regardless of their position in life. I aim to give it to them. There are two ways we can do this. One, you have forty-eight hours from tomorrow morning to appoint me as president, giving me full control of the government. If you do so, you and your entire staff will be given new identities and flown in private jets to the international destination of your choice. I will personally see to it that whatever sum of money you need to live a comfortable life will be wired into an offshore account of your choosing. You'll be taken care of for the rest of your life and can live out your retirement dream without ever having to work another day."

The staff all looked at each other with conflicted curiosity. The video continued.

"Two, you can choose to ignore my warnings... and shortly after the forty-eight hours are up, you'll witness the entire power grid shut down. Complete chaos and fear will overtake your country. Your access to money and the Internet will be gone... every single device, app, and piece of technology Americans rely upon on a daily basis will be useless. You will take all of the blame. If your own people don't kill you themselves, then I will personally send my army in to eliminate everyone in the White House. It's your choice. You've got a little more than forty-eight hours to decide. The clock starts ticking at 6 am tomorrow. Oh, and don't worry about how to get in touch with me. I'll be watching you. Sleep well tonight. Sincerely, Kore."

The TV screen went blank. Jay ejected the chip and threw it in the trash. He looked over at the vice president and Admiral Hardy.

"Get our entire military ready for war."

Sam Hostler's eyes nearly bulged right out of his head. He was an ex-attorney who looked like he belonged in a cubicle crunching numbers. He had probably never killed a fly, let alone been in a fight.

"War? With whom? We don't even know where this Kore guy is. Where would we send troops? Underground?"

"I don't care. We've got forty-eight hours to find him and get rid of him. Use every soldier and reserve officer we've got to find him. We're not going to let some underground terrorist hijack our country."

"Sir?" asked Admiral Hardy.

"Yes?" the president responded impatiently.

"I hope you know what you're doing. If we declare war, this is going to get a whole lot worse before it gets better..."

"Not worse than a civil war."

# 10 THE MIDDLE GROUNDS

"Are you guys okay?" Vosco asked.

Daniel was quiet for a moment in-between coughs as he spit out some of the water he had swallowed. He had opened his mouth a couple seconds too soon while passing through the fountain. Vosco and Skylar had changed back to their human forms again. The three of them were soaking wet. Daniel had miraculously made it through the fountain still strapped into his wheelchair. He frantically reached for his backpack.

Vosco had tried to assure him that the fountain water wouldn't hurt his iPad, phone, or any of his other gadgets. Daniel wasn't risking it. He had placed everything in a heavy black trash bag in order to be safe.

Other than Daniel doubting the security of his electronic devices, there really wasn't much holding him back from returning to Alcazar. There was nothing left for him in St. Augustine. His dad was dead. No one would miss him, except maybe the librarian. Was he scared? Yes. However, for once in his life he felt like he had a purpose, and he was excited about that. He didn't believe that he was the hero they were looking for, but he was too tired to convince them otherwise. He knew he could hack, and if they needed a hacker, then he was volunteering his services.

Once Daniel had inspected his devices for any water damage, he immediately began searching for a WiFi signal on his iPad. *Was* there even WiFi down here? He scrolled and scrolled. Nothing. He tried a special hack to ping some government satellites, which were used for emergencies only. Still no signal. *How far underground were they?* Vosco and Skylar appeared to be busy surveying the area.

"Any ideas on how I'm going to cross through this forest in an electric wheelchair without drawing attention to us?" Daniel asked.

Neither Vosco nor Skylar turned around. In fact, it was as if they were ignoring him. Vosco was staring out into the forest.

"We've got to get moving now," he said. "This forest has ears. It already knows we are here."

Seconds later a strange looking animal dropped down from the trees. The hideous creature landed only a few feet in front of them. Daniel had never seen anything like it before. It had the wings of a flying squirrel, the body of a chipmunk, the head of a weasel, and the two front teeth of a beaver. It was covered in a shiny oil-like substance.

"What do you want?" demanded Skylar. She waved a big stick she had picked up from the ground.

The animal ignored Skylar. It looked directly at Daniel.

"You're not welcome here," it said in a hissing voice. "Go back home where you belong. There is trouble ahead for you. You won't make it out of here alive. All that will be left of you is that chair..."

"Get out of our way," said Vosco, dismissing the animal and walking around it.

"Consider this your final warning. There is danger ahead for the boy. Turn around now while you can."

The animal scurried off while Daniel remained speechless. There was probably just as much danger waiting for him back at St. Augustine. For once the uncertainty didn't bother him. In fact, he was choosing it.

Vosco and Skylar forged onward. The three of them moved in uneventful silence deeper into the dark and eerie forest. Just like last time, Daniel felt like the trees were moving in strange ways. It almost seemed as if everything was closing in on them. Was his mind playing tricks on him? *Maybe that animal was right*, he thought. *I probably don't have any business here. Perhaps we should turn around before—*

Before he could finish his thought, a large tree branch smacked him in the back of the head. Another branch slammed down on his joystick jolting the wheelchair forward and knocking him into Skylar. The front of his wheelchair hit her left leg. Daniel reversed the chair as quickly as he could. Skylar collapsed onto the ground while holding the back of her calf.

"Are you okay?" Vosco asked, picking her up.

Daniel looked down at her leg. It was now bleeding where the metal foot plate had dug into the back of her leg. It didn't appear broken.

"I'll be fine. Just a bad cut. Let's get out of here," she winced, trying to hide her pain.

"It was that tree," said Vosco. "It looks like they aren't too happy we're here."

Another tree branch took a shot at Daniel. He ducked out of the way as the branch came within inches of his head.

"Go away," came an eerie echo from the forest.

Were these the voices of... the trees? Daniel was shaken. He felt the need to escape, but didn't know which way to go. The echoes from the trees seemed to come from all directions. He looked up. Another tree was bearing down on him from above.

"Duck Daniel!" yelled Skylar.

All of a sudden, the tree stopped. Its branches were so close to his face Daniel could feel the leaves tickling the back of his ear. The tree straightened back up. The forest stopped moving. It was as if someone had flipped the off switch.

"What happened?" Daniel asked, his robotic voice echoing.

"I'm not exactly sure," replied Vosco. "It could mean something else is just around the corner. Let's hurry up and go before these trees change their minds."

The three of them continued on through the forest. Small branches cracked, crunched, and snapped under the weight of Daniel's wheelchair. For Vosco and Skylar, it was like traveling with a trainload of clowns honking their horns. They were announcing their presence to everyone and everything. Skylar gave Vosco a look as if to say, *this is the chosen one?*

Luckily, they didn't seem to attract more trouble. In fact, there was hardly any sign of life. The wind had died down, and the trees continued to be motionless. Vosco and Skylar had passed through the forest many times and had never seen it like this. It made them uneasy. Daniel could sense that something was wrong.

Skylar heard it first.

"Stop moving. Don't say a word," she whispered as she looked out through the dense forest ahead.

They all heard it now. It sounded like a train was coming through the forest. The noise and vibrations were getting closer by the second. The three of them didn't know whether they should run or hide. It was hard to know in what direction it was coming. One thing was for certain: it was closing in on them fast.

"RUN!" shouted Skylar. "Let's go back to the fountain entrance as fast as we can! It's not safe here, and I don't think…" she huffed as she ran. "I don't think I can run to the next middle ground with my leg like this!"

They had only made it twenty yards when Vosco stopped in his tracks.

"STOP!" His face went from frightened to terrified. "Wolves. Hundreds of them," he breathed heavily. "There's no way to get past them if we head back to the fountain. Our *only* option is to head towards the next middle ground. NOW!"

They turned around and headed back. Daniel had only put his wheelchair in turbo drive once in his life. It was the day he first took it for a demo ride. The pushy salesman made him do it. It had scared him to death. He could still see the salesman and his father laughing at him in the parking lot that day. Daniel liked things slow, but this was the first time he had ever been chased by a pack of wolves.

He jammed the joystick down as far as it would go. He blew past Skylar and caught up with Vosco in seconds. He was cutting through the forest at breakneck speed. He felt a sudden rush. The adrenaline was like nothing he had ever experienced in his life.

Moments later, his exhilaration morphed into a fear. He saw it a second too late—a big tree root right in the middle of his path. His front tires hit it, launching the entire chair into the air. The four-hundred-pound piece of machinery was not meant for this. It crash-landed, almost flipping over. Somehow it managed to land upright. He looked down and was relieved to see all four tires still had air in them. Behind him came Skylar. She was sprinting as fast as she could—blood covering the bottom of her leg and shoe from earlier.

"Move, kid! The wolves are closing in!"

Daniel hit the joystick, but nothing happened. The wheelchair didn't move an inch. Skylar and Vosco kept going. They had no idea that Daniel was stuck. He didn't have time to type. All he could think about was getting his wheelchair moving. He could hear the sound of the wolves growing closer. He fidgeted with the joystick, moving it in every direction. Nothing. He checked to see if he had power. He did. The green lights were all on. He needed to do a reboot. There was no other option. He hit the kill switch and waited for what felt like an eternity.

Vosco became worried when he couldn't hear Daniel's chair behind him. He quickly turned around. He saw Daniel forty yards behind him. He was a sitting duck. The sea of wolves was closing in on him.

"Daniel!!!" he screamed. "Move! Now! They're right behind you."

Daniel was waiting for the four red lights to turn green, indicating the wheelchair was ready for use. Three of the lights were green. He had his hand on the joystick in eager anticipation, ready to throw it into full gear the second the fourth light turned green.

Skylar and Vosco had stopped running. They knew it was too late.

"Vosco, let's keep going. He's not worth dying for. I'm still not sure this disabled boy in a wheelchair is really the one. If he is 'the chosen one,' won't he find his way out of this?" Skylar grumbled.

After he'd almost broken her leg, Skylar wasn't very fond of Daniel. Based on the odds against him, she couldn't imagine he was going to make it through the three middle grounds in that big clunky wheelchair. As their adventure unfolded, Skylar was starting to believe they'd grabbed the wrong guy—either that, or Maku the Magu was wrong.

"We can't just let him die," he replied.

Vosco's face tightened. He closed his eyes for a moment. He recalled watching Skylar's father get torched by Kore's men. It was a nightmare he would never forget.

Vosco spoke in a low voice, "I watched too many of my men die during the war. I don't intend to let it happen again. We're getting him."

Daniel continued to flick every switch on his wheelchair, praying one of them might make the difference. The fourth light still burned red. He wasn't sure if it was the heat of the forest or his anxiety, but he was sweating profusely. He looked up to a sea of wolves. They had begun to form a circle around him. He was surrounded. Daniel continued to hit a small panel of switches, which controlled his wheelchair lights, alarm, and horn. Nothing.

One of the wolves approached Daniel. The rest of the pack continued to circle. He was the biggest one in the pack by far. His head was slightly taller than Daniel's, and the white fur around his chin and neck were stained red. Daniel caught a glimpse of his blood red eyes before he turned to face his pack. He started speaking.

"Looks like we've got ourselves dinner tonight, boys."

The massive pack howled and laughed. One wolf snuck up behind Daniel and made hissing noises in his ear. Another slithered up from the side and nipped at Daniel's foot. He watched as a small blood stain formed on his faded Nike shoes.

For as far as he could see, there were wolves. He could no longer see Vosco or Skylar. He didn't quite know how to feel. He still held onto a glimmer of hope that Vosco, Skylar, or his grandfather would rescue him.

His train of thought was broken as another wolf sunk its teeth deep into Daniel's calf. It was strange—he hardly felt any pain whatsoever. Another wolf lunged at him, tearing into his knee. Daniel stared—frozen—one eye still on that fourth light. Another wolf bit into his foot and another. Daniel felt the blood dripping from his calf down his leg, and at that moment pain shot up through his body. Then he heard something odd. There was a heavy grunt behind him. Daniel looked back only to see a wolf lying motionless on the ground. There was another thud, and one of the wolves ran off whimpering into the forest.

"What's going on?" yelled the leader of the pack.

"It's coming from over there!" yelled one of the wolves.

Two people came from behind the trees up ahead. They were holding rocks in their hands.

Vosco reared back like a baseball pitcher on the mound and launched a rock with full force at Natas, the leader of the pack. Vosco knew that if he could injure him, the rest of the pack would flee. Natas ducked. The rock nailed Daniel's wheelchair, barely missing his right hand.

Natas spoke quickly to his pack before any more rocks could be thrown. "Let's split up. You three come with me—we'll take down these rock slingers. The rest of you—kill the boy."

Daniel looked down at the light on his chair. It had finally turned green! The impact of the rock must have done something. However, before he could reach his joystick, the forest lit up like the fourth of July.

Daniel's wheelchair had come with a custom emergency package, which included red, white, and blue lights bright enough to guide a large ship into a harbor on the darkest of nights. The package also came with a built-in police siren, which was nothing short of ear-piercing. He must have accidently clicked the emergency switch because the siren and the lights were now screaming and flashing.

The wolves began to scatter. The siren blared as the bright lights bounced off the tree canopies. Daniel wasted no time. He jammed the joystick down and headed towards Vosco and Skylar. They both had their hands over their ears. They all took off for the next middle ground. Daniel noticed that Skylar's limp was getting worse as he zoomed by her in his chair. He caught up to Vosco, who pointed up ahead.

"Wow, that chair is moving Daniel!" he exclaimed in-between breaths. "Keep going straight. You'll see a cloud layer. Don't be afraid to go through it. It won't hurt you. But be prepared to stop quickly after you pass through it."

"What about you?" Daniel asked.

"Don't worry—we'll be right behind you."

Meanwhile, the wolves realized they had been duped by a wheelchair light show. Daniel's head whipped around as he heard Natas scream...

"ATTACK!"

Dozens of wolves were now back in pursuit. Skylar looked to be an easy victim as she trailed behind the two of them.

Vosco glanced behind him. His stomach dropped as he saw her lagging.

"Hurry, Skylar! We're almost there. The wolves are closing in!"

Daniel was far ahead of them at this point, but something inside of him told him to go back and help Skylar. He slammed the joystick into neutral. The chair skidded to a halt on the leaves, which blanketed ground. He whipped around and bolted past Vosco in the wrong direction.

"What are you doing?" Vosco screamed as Daniel blew by him. "Turn back around! Get to safety, Daniel!"

Vosco watched helplessly as Daniel headed straight for Skylar. The wolf pack was not far behind. Daniel slammed the wheelchair to the left, almost tipping it over as it spun one-hundred and eighty degrees. He pointed to his lap. Skylar understood. She jumped on. He slammed down the joystick. The wolves were just ten feet behind them.

With her extra weight, the chair wasn't as fast. It was barely faster than the wolves, but it was fast enough. Part of the pack dropped off completely. They had given up. A handful of wolves including Natas, continued the chase.

"We're not out of the woods yet," yelled Vosco. "Keep your legs up. They're coming up on your left."

Seconds later, Skylar felt a wolf brush up against the side of her left foot. She moved it just in time. Then there was a tug on her right shoe. A different wolf had latched onto her foot and was shaking its head from side to side. It was Natas. The wheelchair veered slightly off course. They were mere inches from the rest of the pack.

Skylar could feel the wolf's razor-sharp teeth as they entered her foot. Daniel steered the wheelchair over to the right to compensate for the extra drag, but Natas' extra weight made it impossible to drive straight.

Skylar screamed.

She looked down at her leg. His mouth locked down on her foot.

"Almost there!" shouted Vosco. "That's the end ahead. The wolves can't make it through!"

Daniel could see a wall of clouds, where the forest ended abruptly. The cloud layer stretched from left to right into eternity. It was perfectly vertical, like a screen which had been lowered from the heavens to touch the forest floor. It went up into the sky as far as his eyes could see. Daniel watched as Vosco evaporated into the clouds. In an instant, his body was no longer visible.

Daniel jammed the joystick down harder. He heard another wolf coming up to his right. Skylar suddenly laid flat on Daniel's lap. She threw a punch with her right hand. It landed squarely on the wolf's jaws. All he heard was a whimper and a thud as his wheelchair cut through the clouds.

"STOP THE CHAIR!!!" cried Skylar.

# 11 THE SWAMP

The forest floor ended in front of them.

Daniel had hit the brakes just in time. Another two inches and they would have been off the cliff. His wheels were teetering on the edge. It was pitch black below. It was like being on the edge of an elevator shaft—but there was no elevator or bottom in sight.

"Back it up slowly," Vosco said.

Skylar was gripping Daniel's neck tightly. She knew where this drop-off led, but she had no idea how Daniel was going to safely get down in a wheelchair.

He slowly inched the chair away from the edge. Skylar jumped off his lap. Pain shot through her foot as she landed. The bottom of her pants were completely shredded. Blood started pooling around her shoe. She tried to brush it off like it was ok, but Vosco knew she needed to get back to Alcazar fast. He walked over to inspect her leg and whipped out a small first aid kit. While Vosco attended to Skylar's leg, Daniel took out his iPad. He had a million questions.

"What now?" he asked.

Vosco spoke to Daniel while wrapping Skylar's injured leg with white tape. "We move on to the second middle ground."

"Where?"

Skylar pointed at the deep, dark shaft. "Down there."

"Uh… can we really call that a middle *ground*?" Daniel asked. "I don't see *any* ground."

Skylar glared at Daniel.

"I already answered your question," she spat.

"Skylar, come on," Vosco said. "Daniel saved you back there. You could give him a thank you, you know."

Skylar pursed her lips together and looked down into the darkness.

"Thanks," she said barely audible. "I would have been able to run just fine if that chair hadn't injured me in the first place."

"The next middle ground is below," Vosco said patiently, ending Skylar's rant. "Each level goes deeper into the Earth until we hit Alcazar, which is at the center. The only way to get to the second middle ground is down that hole."

Daniel looked at the deep, dark shaft again.

"I don't understand," he replied.

Vosco spoke up. "Daniel, in front of you is what's known as the Fall of Faith. Every level of the middle grounds is a test. This one is about the crucial role trust plays in overcoming fear. It was designed this way to prevent others from passing through. For the Fall of Faith, you must walk off the edge with faith that the floor will catch you—even though you can't see it."

Daniel started shaking his head. There was no way he was going to drive his chair off that ledge. He started typing.

"Has anyone ever gone down in a four-hundred-pound electric wheelchair?"

Vosco looked at Skylar. They all knew the answer. Skylar was skeptical it was going to work at all.

"Daniel, if you have faith, you'll be fine." It was all Vosco could think to say, though to be honest, he wasn't sure.

Panic flooded Daniel's body. Faith? The last thing he had right now was faith. What if he was too heavy? What if—

"Stop second guessing yourself," Vosco said sternly, as if he could read his thoughts. "Just *believe* beyond a shadow of a doubt that you will be protected, and you will."

"How does it work though?" Daniel asked.

"If I gave you a play-by-play of what is going to happen, it wouldn't require much faith on your part, would it? These middle grounds have eyes and ears and they would know you were jumping with *knowledge* instead of faith."

Daniel did not respond.

"Sometimes though…" Vosco continued, "Seeing is believing."

Vosco finished up Skylar's leg and slowly approached the edge. Daniel looked on—panic-stricken as he watched. Vosco moved his right foot out and lunged forward with his left. His body went into a complete free fall into the darkness. Daniel and Skylar rushed to the edge as he dropped. There was no thud when Vosco hit the invisible floor. Although it was dark, Daniel was certain he couldn't anything beneath his feet. Vosco looked up and smiled at Daniel. He appeared to glide downwards as though he were on an escalator into the depths of the Earth. He vanished. Daniel looked over at Skylar. His pupils were dilated in fear.

"Do you want to go next?" she asked sarcastically. He shook his head.

"See you at the bottom," Skylar said as she confidently walked off the edge. Daniel watched as she too glided down into the darkness out of sight.

*I can't do this*, Daniel thought to himself.

His palms weren't just sweaty, they were dripping. His entire shirt was soaked. His mind had been racing ever since Vosco told him they had to go down this shaft.

He paused. The only opportunity one has to demonstrate faith is when they are afraid. Faith does not exist without fear. If the person is not afraid then there is no risk. Faith, by definition, involves risk. It is a leap. This was his opportunity to have faith.

His sweaty right hand moved the joystick towards the edge. He took a deep breath before looking down. For the first time since he'd been down in the middle grounds he thought about his father. His dad had spent his entire adult life not taking action. He never ventured out or took risks. His dad lived a miserable and unfulfilled life. He had no faith in anything. He didn't want to be like his dad.

His wheelchair sat on the ledge. He kept repeating, *I'm not my dad*, in his head. He was ready. He pushed the joystick forward again. His front wheels went over the edge and the front of his chair began to nosedive. He was in a complete freefall. All he could see was darkness. The sensation of falling took his breath away. He tried to scream. Nothing came out. Instead, the air swept in, choking him. He panicked. Then he remembered what he was doing: *The Fall of Faith*. Daniel closed his eyes. He did something he had only done on one other occasion. He prayed.

The fall stopped. No thud. No jolt. It was unlike any landing Daniel had ever experienced in his life. He wasn't sure how or why, but he was no longer facing down. He and his chair were upright. He peeked down towards his feet. There was nothing but darkness. There was no floor or anything for that matter. Whatever was holding him there was taking him down slowly. He closed his eyes again and said a thank you prayer.

He wondered where he was now. It felt like he had been sinking lower and lower for an eternity. Suddenly, an intense odor wafted through the air. It smelled like a petting zoo. Geez, *what a stench*, he thought to himself.

His chair hit the ground softly. The bright light nearly blinded him. He squinted as his eyes acclimated once again to daylight.

"Welcome to the swamp," came a voice from nearby. It was Vosco. "This is the second middle ground. It is home to some of the smelliest and hungriest animals around…"

Daniel was finally adjusting to the light. The blurry images in front of him came into focus. He looked out over an array of giant lily pads, reeds, wildflowers, and a few monster cypress trees, which were scattered throughout the area. There was a winding stone path, which spiraled across the swamp. Unlike the forest, Daniel could see the other end of this middle ground clearly. On the other side of the swamp he recognized the wall of clouds, which stretched from the water's surface into the sky. It looked too simple. Daniel typed away on his iPad.

"Is this the entire level? All we have to do is make it across this path to the other side?" he asked.

"Don't let this one fool you," replied Vosco. "The length of something does not determine the degree of challenge."

Skylar interjected with a big smile, "Yeah, last time Vosco left this middle ground crying like a baby!"

"The croc spewed saliva all over my face!" he replied. "Those things must eat onions all day. I'm telling you it was terrible!"

She rolled her eyes. "Anyhow… the entire swamp is filled with crocodiles. These aren't just any crocodiles. They're massive. They can grow as tall as a house and as wide as a two-car garage. The good news is that these crocs are blind and deaf—so they can't see or hear a thing."

"Okay…" Daniel said slowly, still confused.

Crocodiles, who were blind and deaf—albeit big, but still… blind and deaf? So what? Sure, it stunk, but he felt like he could handle this.

"Great!" Daniel said confidently. "Let's do it!"

Skylar looked like she was about to say something, but Vosco gave her a stern look and shook his head.

"Great attitude, Daniel," Vosco said, carefully choosing his words. "Do me a favor and keep that confidence, okay?"

Daniel looked across the swamp for any sign of a crocodile. Nothing. Were they joking? It seemed as though Vosco and Skylar were in on *something* at Daniel's expense.

"Okay?" Vosco asked more loudly and sharply. Why was he so emphatic about Daniel's attitude?

"Okay..." Daniel started, "Why—"

"Let's go now," Vosco interjected.

Skylar was eyeing Daniel with concern.

They were moving at a good pace along the stone path when a loud, blood-curdling shriek broke the silence. Every hair on Daniel's body stood up.

"What in the world was that?" he asked.

"Just a crocodile," said Vosco, studying Daniel.

The sound of a large splash boomed closer to them, and another shriek echoed even closer still.

"Daniel," Vosco said. "Daniel, take a deep breath—you're attracting them."

"Me?!" Daniel wanted to yell, though his iPad still spoke in the same measured voice. "I haven't done anything!"

"Yes, you have. They sense your fear."

Daniel's eyes met Vosco's, his brow furrowed.

"How do you know that?" Daniel asked.

"That crocodile is getting closer and closer. It's deaf and blind, but the one thing it can sense is fear. That's how it hunts and kills its prey," Vosco spoke quietly and quickly, trying to relay as much information as possible. "Daniel, I need you to stop being afraid."

"Stop being—?" Daniel couldn't even finish typing his sentence. "I can't control that! It's an instinct!"

Daniel looked up just in time to see a massive crocodile rising out of the water. It was swimming slowly, but moving directly towards him. It was large enough to be a Mack truck.

"Yes, you *can* Daniel!" Skylar yelled, with either enthusiasm or frustration; he couldn't tell.

Another supersonic shriek shook the path.

"Just keep walking. Ignore it, and it will vanish," Vosco said.

"Ignoring something this big is impossible. How do I ignore it when I'm afraid of it?"

"Treat your fear the same way!" Vosco said. "Ignore the fear. Pay it no attention, and it will have no power over you. It will vanish too."

Daniel felt the fear gnawing on his stomach from the inside. He tried to do what Vosco said. His mind was grasping at straws. *Crocodiles. No, the wolves. No, those are just as scary. Alcazar? My grandfather. I just met my grandfather for the first time. I thought he was dead, but he's not. He's alive and how cool is that?*

As he continued to force these unwanted thoughts away, he saw the crocodile disappear back into the murky brown water. He could feel a weight leave his chest. The more he relaxed, the further the crocodile swam away. Daniel stopped thinking so hard. He allowed his mind to go blank as he made his way down the path. He turned around again. Was it really gone? He surveyed the water's surface. There was nothing. He turned back around, but not before another crocodile slithered across the path in front of him. He was trapped.

Vosco and Skylar watched in horror as the massive crocodile lurched towards Daniel. It was within a few feet of his wheelchair.

"Just stay—"

Vosco's sentence was drowned out by the crocodile's thunderous belch.

It was so tall and wide Daniel could no longer see Vosco and Skylar behind it.

Sklyar chimed in, "The only way he will know you are there is if he senses your fear. Try singing a song. It's almost impossible to be fearful when you're singing."

*Singing? Singing? Is she being serious? I've got a five-ton crocodile in my face and she wants me to sing a song?*

The crocodile lunged forward. His massive body hit the ground so hard it almost knocked Daniel's chair over. He panicked. He couldn't help it. This was too much. Skylar and Vosco watched helplessly as the crocodile opened its massive jaws. They could no longer see Daniel.

"Daniel? Are you still there? SING!" Skylar shouted. Suddenly, Daniel's iPad began blasting a tune...

*Never smile at a crocodile*
*No, you can't get friendly with a crocodile*

*Don't be taken in by his welcome grin*
*He's imagining how well you'd fit within his skin...*
*Never smile at a crocodile*
*Never tip your hat and stop to talk awhile*
*Never run, walk away, say good-night, not good-day*
*Clear the aisle but never smile at Mister Crocodile...*

Vosco looked at Skylar in disbelief.

"Is his iPad singing *Never Smile at a Crocodile*?"

Skylar shrugged her shoulders. She had never heard the song from *Peter Pan* before. Meanwhile the crocodile appeared to be wildly confused. Its jaws were still open, but now it seemed hesitant to close them. It slowly inched closer to Daniel. The iPad continued to blare its music. Then the crocodile paused, closed its mouth, and slithered back into the swamp as if nothing had happened. Daniel took a deep breath as he looked at Skylar and Vosco.

"Please get me out of this place."

# 12 THE BRIBE

"Please get me out of this place," the president said in despair.

His head was down. He felt defeated. This job was running him ragged. He was talking to his personal assistant, Mary. She seemed to be his only confidante at this point, or at least the only person who seemed to listen and support him.

A lot had occurred over the past eighteen hours in the White House. The president had watched helplessly as riots spread across the nation. Countless top-level politicians and high-ranking officials had disappeared. Many had taken Kore up on his offer. Other senators and state representatives took sudden leaves of absence or family vacations. No one wanted to be associated with politics in America. Even leaders from other countries had publicly renounced the president. They said America was falling apart. They said the president was in over his head. He was going down as the worst president in the history of the United States. He went from being one of the most powerful leaders in the free world to one of the most hated men in the entire world. The global stock market had its largest single day drop in history.

"I'm losing my mind being stuck here," he told Mary as he ran his fingers through his greasy hair. "I haven't been outside in days. I can't sleep. I don't think I've showered in two days. I'm so burnt out it's not even funny. Why didn't they advertise that being president is the worst job ever created?"

She had never worked this hard in her life either. She wished he would slow down for a minute to acknowledge that. He didn't seem to notice any of the sacrifices she had made over the last two days since Kore hacked the White House. But it was her job to serve the president, and she intended to stick by his side as long as he was the POTUS. When she first landed the job of being his personal assistant, her friends were so envious. She was a single 38-year old woman, who had dreamed of working in the White House since she was a little girl. It didn't hurt that the president was handsome. However, he seemed way too focused on his job to ever notice her.

"Have you seen this yet?" he asked her. He was waving a sheet of paper in his hands.

"What is it, sir?" she asked.

Whatever it was, she knew it couldn't be good. Nothing good had occurred in the past two days. She gasped as she read it. The text was written in bold red font. It looked like something out of the *Billy the Kid* western movies she used to watch with her dad as a little girl.

## REWARD
## $20,000,000 in Gold Coins

### Will be paid for by Kore's Renegade Army
### For the apprehension
### DEAD OR ALIVE
### of
### Jay McFarland
### The President of The United States
### Wanted for treason against the United States of America

Jay watched her read it. Her hand instinctively moved over her mouth in complete shock.

"Is this for real?" she asked.

He nodded his head yes. "Don't get any ideas," he replied sarcastically.

She gave him a concerned look.

"Mr. President, are you going to be okay?"

He hadn't even had time to think about getting murdered. He felt pretty safe inside the White House, but he wasn't so sure any more.

Jay replied, "I'm not sure. The country is in chaos… not to mention there's a reward out for my head. Truthfully speaking, I've never been so confused and scared in my entire life."

"What are you going to do?" asked Mary.

He looked up at her. He had never noticed how blue her eyes were against her sandy blonde hair.

"What do you think I should do?" he asked. He'd never considered asking Mary for advice. At this point, he'd take advice from anyone.

"I'm… ummm, I'm not really sure. I haven't really thought about it. Can I ask what options you are considering?"

Jay looked down at another piece of paper on his desk. It was a copy of the message from Kore. It was the same message that all the political leaders and high-ranking officials had received yesterday. He handed it to her.

"Here's what I'm considering."

She held it in her hand.

*Dear elected official,*

*The piece of paper you hold in your hands is a voucher for a one-way ticket to a new life. Your dream retirement. A private island with only the most elite and wealthy people in the world. A life of abundance, no stress, no crowds, no traffic, and no more politics.*

*This voucher entitles you to the following:*

- *Private flight to a secluded island*
- *A full acre of beautiful oceanfront property with a fully furnished villa for you and your immediate family members, which has already been purchased on your behalf*
- *Private chef to cook all of your meals*
- *Private butler to cater to your every need*
- *Free health care from some of the top physicians in the world, who will also be living on the island*
- *Enough money in a private account to ensure you never run out*
- *Concierge agents who will take care of you every step of the way*

*This voucher is good for the next 48 hours.*

*After that, it will expire and you will be considered an enemy of the new world order.*

*Sincerely,*

*Kore*

*Contact us here to begin your booking: support@koresarmy.com*

She dropped the sheet on his desk. "Wouldn't this be giving up?" she asked innocently.

Her answer threw him off. He didn't expect it. Most assistants simply gave him lip service. They found it easier to nod in agreement rather than risking a future job promotion.

He thought about her reply. *Is it really giving up if the vast majority of the country wants me gone? Is it really giving up if I get to live my dream retirement?* He wasn't sure anymore. He wasn't sure of anything. All he knew was that he had less than two days left to make a decision. He would either flee or be hunted down like an enemy of the state. In the meantime, it was clear that Kore was going to keep making it tougher for him to remain president.

He ignored her question for a bit longer as he processed it all. He finally spoke. "Hey Mary, is Paul Glazer, the head of cyber-security, still around? Or did he disappear too?"

She scanned her laptop for his name. "He's still here. He's over in the Pentagon right now," reported Mary.

"Please ring him and have him report here as soon as possible. Get me on the phone with the press. We're going to bring this Kore guy onto my own turf... and then talk."

"What are you going to do?

He looked her in the eyes. She could see a gleam of confidence in his face.

"We're going to televise a debate between Kore and I. It's the one arena in which I know I can beat anyone. It's how I got to be president in the first place. I'm going to publicly reveal who Kore really is: a socialist terrorist."

Mary wasn't sold on this. The entire country was basically eating out of Kore's hands right now. Some were even calling him the Messiah, who finally came to rid the world from capitalism and corruption.

"Do you think that's a wise idea?" she questioned.

"Right now, it's my only idea."

# 13 MAGIC MIRROR

*I can hardly breathe!* Daniel thought.

He began spitting up orange sand.

The three of them had just descended down the second Fall of Faith after his near-death experience with the crocodiles. This free-fall took twice as long as the first. Daniel thought he was going to vomit, but he finally felt his wheels come to rest on the invisible floor below him.

A short time later he found himself in what appeared to be a small sand storm. It engulfed him momentarily before moving on its merry way.

"Welcome to the desert," said Skylar. "This is the third and final level of the middle grounds. This is where we're given the task of finding the magic mirror, which leads to Alcazar. What you just swallowed was part of a dust devil. It's basically a mini sand and dust storm, but it sure can make it tough to see if it gets in your eyes."

Daniel wiped his glasses clean with the bottom of his shirt and scanned the area. All he could see was orange sand for miles and miles in all directions. There were no clouds, trees, or animals. The barren desert appeared untouched, interrupted only by the occasional tiny sandstorms, which dissolved almost as quickly as they formed.

"Yep, the desert loves creating these sandstorms because it is an instant deterrent. Nobody like sand and dust in their eyes," said Vosco. "As soon as you start feeling comfortable, that's when the scorpion appears."

Daniel recalled his grandfather mentioning a scorpion.

"This is not a normal scorpion," Skylar said sarcastically. "This thing is the size of a jeep. It has two massive tails with needle-like stingers powerful enough to kill a human."

Vosco glared at Skylar.

"Great," Daniel said. "How do I avoid the scorpion? The desert seems big enough to do that if there's only one scorpion..."

Vosco and Skylar looked at each other.

"Well, here's the catch. The only way the magic mirror will appear is if you face the scorpion," Vosco said quietly.

"So... I can't avoid it?" Daniel asked.

"You can..." Vosco said, "but it means you'll never get past this level."

Daniel sighed.

"So, it will sense my fear and attack me blah blah blah."

"Not exactly," Vosco said. "The scorpion will *not* appear if you feel afraid. It senses your fear the same way the crocodiles do. However, unlike the crocodiles, it will not engage with you unless you are fearless. That's how you challenge it to a fight.

Daniel felt his anger rising.

"I need to just magically lose my fear because I *want* this giant scorpion to fight me?"

"Well..." Vosco said. "Yes."

"I don't want to fight this scorpion!" Daniel exclaimed.

"Fighting the scorpion is the only way the magic mirror will appear."

"Why can't these challenges be normal?!" Daniel asked. "Why do they all seem to be psychological games?!"

"Daniel," Skylar said gently. "Fear is part of life. It's natural. These middle grounds give you many opportunities to face your fears and overcome them. Don't waste those opportunities."

He stared at Skylar. He felt like she was being genuine. He began to calm down.

"What if I become afraid during the fight?" Daniel asked.

"The scorpion will go into hiding and become even harder to challenge in a fight," Vosco replied.

"You have to remain fearless no matter what is happening. The scorpion won't fight you if you're afraid..." Skylar said.

"It sounds more like the fight is with fear itself rather than with a giant scorpion," Daniel said, sarcastically.

"Yep," Vosco and Skylar said in unison.

Daniel had not been expecting that response.

"Okay," he said. "I can do it."

Vosco and Skylar scanned the desert. There was no sign of the scorpion.

"You're still afraid," Skylar said.

"Yeah, I know Skylar!" Daniel's robotic voice from his iPad interrupted. "I know! It isn't here yet obviously. Give me a minute to get my mind under control."

Daniel closed his eyes. Remembering Skylar's advice, he began humming softly to himself. Immediately, he could feel his body relax and his mood lighten. He felt calm, but not fearless. Singing wasn't his superpower—hacking was. He imagined himself at his computer. He was no longer disabled behind that screen. He was more capable than anyone. He felt powerful...

"There it is," Vosco whispered, breaking the silence.

Daniel opened his eyes slowly, but he couldn't make it out very clearly. His glasses were still filthy despite having attempted to clean them moments ago. All he could see was what looked like a moving sand dune with two massive tails. He took his glasses off. He cleaned the dirt-caked lenses with his t-shirt as fast as his hands could move.

"Fifty yards in front of you at two o'clock," Vosco informed him.

Daniel's heart began to race as he put his glasses back on, so he started taking deep breaths. Vosco wasn't kidding. He could see the giant scorpion and its two stingers as clear as day. The stingers looked like daggers as they glistened in the bright desert sun. The scorpion had sensed Daniel's heart racing and began to retreat in the direction from which it came.

*Ahhhh!* Daniel screamed and dropped his face to his knees. *My eyes! I can't see anything!* He covered both of his eyes with his hands in order to stop any more sand from coming in. They felt like they were on fire. He was starting to panic.

Skylar and Vosco held their heads down and closed their eyes. A small dust devil momentarily engulfed them. It died down almost as quickly as it came.

When the dust cleared, they found themselves alone again. The scorpion was nowhere in sight. Daniel let out a sigh of relief.

As soon as he exhaled, it was back. Daniel continued to breathe deeply. The giant arachnid thundered through the desert sand swinging its tails from side to side. It was making a beeline towards Daniel, who was still picking sand out of his eyes and mouth. The scorpion came to rest within a few feet of Daniel with a loud thud. Vosco and Skylar split off to the side leaving him alone in its shadow.

"Daniel, stay calm," reassured Vosco. "Don't panic. Take some deep breaths."

Daniel attempted to slow his breathing and calm himself down.

It took everything he had not to scream. The scorpion towered over him. He watched the large tails coil up behind it. He tried to imagine it was all a computer game. *I'll win this by hacking,* he thought to himself. He took a deep breath and closed his eyes for another moment. There he was back in front of his computer screen.

"This would be a good time to move!" yelled Vosco.

Daniel whipped his wheelchair around and took off. The scorpion unleashed both tails, which smashed into the sand only inches behind Daniel's wheelchair.

He glanced behind him to see the scorpion in hot pursuit. He pushed his joystick down as far as it would go, but the sand was slowing him down. The scorpion had caught up to him. Daniel looked up at its face. He challenged him with his eyes. He veered off to the right just in time to avoid being smashed by its deadly stingers. He moved his chair quickly to the other side. The scorpion slammed its tails down again. The second tail made contact with the side of his wheelchair, almost puncturing his right tire.

The scorpion didn't seem fazed. Daniel wished he could run away. He just wanted to go home. He didn't belong here. Who was he kidding? He wasn't the chosen one. Fear and doubt began to fill his head. He pushed it away.

Daniel turned left. The scorpion anticipated his next move. It swung its tail sideways, hoping to knock over Daniel's wheelchair. The tail made contact with his chair, but it wasn't enough to flip it over.

Within seconds he was enveloped by another dust devil. He closed his eyes and mouth as the orange dust swirled around him. The image of his grandfather appeared in his mind. Time seemed to stand still. His grandfather's face became clearer and clearer. Daniel could see his smile. He looked proud. He could see his grandfather moving his lips. He was trying to say something, but Daniel couldn't hear him. Then he remembered the last words his grandfather had said to him before he disappeared into the fountain: *If you're going to face your fears, then you might as well face 'em head on.*

This scorpion was more than just a fear. It was a death sentence. This wasn't something Daniel could just wish away. Or was it? He opened his eyes. The dust had cleared. The scorpion was still there. It was real. This wasn't just something in his head. The scorpion coiled its tails back again.

This time Daniel didn't move. Instead, he whipped his chair around and glared at it. It didn't falter.

Daniel's fingers glided across his iPad. He hit enter.

"I am not afraid of you."

Daniel could see the scorpion recoil as if in pain. *Interesting*, he thought. Daniel hit the enter button again.

"I am not afraid of you."

The scorpion screamed. He could feel the power shift. Its body became weaker. Daniel could feel the sand moving beneath his wheelchair. He looked over at Skylar and Vosco. They were watching with eager anticipation.

The scorpion thrashed around as a giant sinkhole opened up, taking down the massive predator and tons of sand with it. Seconds later, the scorpion had completely disappeared. There was nothing left but a crater-sized hole.

Skylar and Vosco walked over to Daniel.

"Congratulations, Daniel. You defeated the scorpion and found the magic mirror," Vosco said while motioning to the gaping hole in front of them.

"I don't see a mirror," Daniel replied on his iPad.

"Go to the edge and look down," said Skylar. "You can't miss it."

Daniel wasn't sure if she was being serious. She had been nothing but sarcastic and skeptical since he met her. Was this a trick?

Daniel slowly wheeled up to the edge of the hole. It was a solid twenty feet across. It felt like the sand supporting him would give out at any moment and he would tumble into the sinkhole itself.

"Closer!" Skylar yelled.

The closer Daniel got to the edge, the deeper the hole appeared. He couldn't see the bottom. It was just a deep, dark, massive crater.

He pulled his wheelchair all the way up to the edge. He angled it sideways so he could glance down over the side of his chair. He looked down nervously expecting the scorpion to jump out and attack at any moment. Then he saw it. His reflection glistened up from the giant mirror below. He could see the sand in his hair and the dirt caked across his face. Looking into the mirror, he thought he looked brave for the first time in his life.

There was a faint fog at the center of the mirror, which didn't seem to fade. A message was scribbled across it as if someone was writing on the car window in the middle of winter. The words read:

**Alcazar. Open only to those who can find the net. Leap.**

As Daniel continued to stare into the mirror, the sky's reflection began to ripple as if the glass were water. The mirror started reflecting not what was above it, but what was below it. Daniel mouth gaped open at the city below him.

*Okay,* he thought. *It sounds like this is just some sort of puzzle. I've always been able to find Waldo. How different could this be? Find the net... and then leap. Leaping might be a stretch for me. Maybe "rolling" into it would work too...*

Daniel's eyes swept over the twenty-foot mirror. Even though he was far above the city of Alcazar, he could really make out incredible detail. He saw porch swings and alleyways, park benches, and trees. His heart leapt excitedly every time he thought he'd caught a glimpse of a net. Upon closer inspection it always turned out to be either an awning or a chain linked fence.

He turned to face Vosco and Skylar. They were still off in the distance.

"Can you guys help me look for the net?" he inquired.

They looked at each other and then back at Daniel.

"We can't see what you see, Daniel," Vosco said gingerly. "The magic mirror doesn't reflect the same thing for everyone. A single person is complex enough. Creating a personal entryway into Alcazar is a big enough job in itself. The mirror becomes easily overwhelmed."

"Well," Daniel started, "Isn't the net in the same place every time? Couldn't you just direct me by memory without looking at it?"

Vosco and Skylar were silent for a moment.

"What net?" asked Skylar.

What Vosco had been trying to say suddenly dawned on Daniel. Everyone saw something different in the mirror, including the message. It was as if the mirror knew how to challenge him.

"No matter what the mirror says, Daniel," Vosco continued. "I have full faith you can figure it out on your own. Don't forget who you are."

*Faith.* That's exactly what the mirror was asking of Daniel. It's what he struggled with during the Falls of Faith. It's what he had struggled with his entire life. Without faith, it's easy to be afraid of everything. Daniel had always been afraid of everything.

"Ever heard of Narcissus?" Skylar said as she walked up to his side.

"Huh?" Daniel asked, caught off guard.

"In ancient mythology it's said he died staring at his own reflection in the river. Here, we say he died staring at it in the mirror."

"What are you trying to say?" Daniel asked.

"Just… don't take too long. You could spend forever trying to figure out what to do and end up like them…"

Skylar tilted her head to the side. Daniel followed her gaze. Along the sides of the sink hole were hundreds, if not thousands, of bones. Human bones. Daniel's stomach jumped lurched.

"The mirror shows people a reflection of themselves, which they may not have seen before," Skylar continued. "Some people become hypnotized by that image instead of entering Alcazar."

Daniel peeped over the side of the sinkhole and glanced back at his reflection. He could still see his face, although the cityscape remained behind it. He was sure about one thing: something about him did look braver… stronger… better. He liked this Daniel. He wanted to be this Daniel. He took a deep breath as his eyes began meandering along the curves and edges of the cityscape below. Where was this net? It felt as though he'd been looking for far too long.

*Find the net. Find the net. Find the net. Have faith and I'll find the net. Then leap—*

Daniel's thoughts screeched to a halt. Was it possible there was no physical net? At least… not yet? Perhaps this wasn't about having faith that he'd find the net. This was about having faith in taking a leap into the net. *Except… how does that saying go? Leap and the net will appear.*

It felt as though he had fallen into his own body. He felt heavy. It wasn't the sensation of being dragged down. He felt grounded… connected. It was as if he was tuned into something much bigger than himself. This was how he felt when he was hacking. It was confidence.

*Leap and the net will appear.* He didn't need to find the net and then leap. He would find the net by leaping first. The net would appear wherever he leapt. The mirror was too wise to give Daniel a simple challenge. The real challenge was having faith. That was Daniel's test.

*And wherever I leap,* he thought, *I'll be leaping into my own reflection. Maybe*

*I'll become that version of myself... the brave Daniel.*

He looked back at Vosco and Skylar, who hadn't moved an inch. They watched him intently, as if this was some great experiment. He was their chosen one. He could see the hope in their eyes. He suddenly felt emotional. He'd never gotten this reassurance from his father, nor would he. Daniel wasn't going to let them down.

He looked at the cityscape below. He thought, *maybe this will feel like skydiving...*

He jammed the wheelchair joystick forwards. He felt the ground disintegrate beneath him as he flew off the edge. The terror on his face became clearer as he fell towards his reflection in the mirror. Though not literal in the least, it did feel as though a net had caught him in mid-air. His fall slowed. The sensation of weightlessness left his stomach. Seconds later he entered the portal to Alcazar.

# 14 ALCAZAR

The sky was full of wispy, dark clouds. They looked more sooty than white. It was neither sunny nor cloudy. It was just brownish gray for as far as the eye could see. It was rather dim. Daniel's first thought was that the place looked depressing.

"Welcome to Alcazar," Vosco said as he waved his arm across the land below them. He had entered just behind Daniel.

"This is Plato's Peak," said Skylar, who'd arrived shortly after Vosco. "It's one of two twin mountain peaks, which surround Alcazar. The other peak is where Maku lives. You'll be able to see it when that cloud clears."

A moment later the clouds passed. Daniel's jaw dropped. It was like nothing he had ever seen in his life. From up here, it looked as if someone had taken a large paint brush and painted the entire landscape black. It felt like death; as if someone had burned all of the greenery from the land. There were hardly any trees or shrubs. The ground was mostly barren with a withered tree or bush here or there.

He could see a large city in the valley below. It was the same city he'd seen through the mirror before he leapt. It was filled with endless rows of homes and small buildings, yet there was hardly any activity. He could count the number of people he saw on one hand. No one was outside.

"Where is everybody?" Daniel asked.

Skylar and Vosco were silent for a second, and then Vosco took the lead.

"This is your future."

Daniel looked confused.

"This is what America and the rest of the world will look like if Kore wins. Your world will go from an industrious and beautiful place to a dark and depressing land, where no one has freedom. The nation of Alcazar used to be a vibrant, booming, and abundant place. We worked hard. We spent most of our time outdoors. We were happy, and we were free. Of course, it wasn't perfect, but it was nothing like this."

"It was that desire for perfection, which led to our downfall. Kore used this to his advantage. He did everything he could to convince our people that they would be happier by letting the government take care of their every need. Wealth and abundance were bad. Our lives would be better if everyone was the same. It turns out, it was just the opposite."

"Today everything is free. We get free rent, free utilities, free health care, free Internet... even the food is free. We are all salaried by Kore's government. It sounds great on paper, right? Well guess what happens when the government gives you everything for free? They OWN you. We have no control over our lives. We have zero freedom. Everyone stays inside from fear that we'll get a knock on the door from Kore's army saying we broke one of their rules. They confiscate anything they want without explanation. There is zero incentive to work or create anything of value."

"They also took over the underground sewer and electricity systems as their headquarters. They sneak around underneath us and enter our homes and buildings without notice. At night you can sometimes hear them beneath your floorboards."

"Isn't that... illegal?" Daniel interjected.

"Illegal by what law?" Vosco asked. "The law, which was made by the very people spying on their residents?"

Daniel didn't have a response.

"We even have a curfew. No one can be outside after dinner," Vosco continued. "If they do catch you, Kore's police have a right to shoot you on the spot without asking any questions. They have hidden cameras in every area imaginable, and they monitor every conversation. Privacy doesn't exist in Kore's world."

"How many people live down there?" Daniel asked while pointing below.

"There are somewhere around sixty thousand citizens. There used to be well over one hundred thousand before the civil war. Since we aren't living as long now due to our living conditions, the number keeps shrinking every year," replied Vosco.

"How many of the sixty thousand are the good guys? People like you?"

"There are about seven thousand of us left. Occasionally we'll convert someone, but it's been really tough now that Kore has everything under surveillance. We used to be able to sneak off into the parks for meetings, but now even the parks are off limits. It's tough to keep a movement going when we are being watched. The good news is that there are a few dozen of us, who all live next to each other. We have frequent 'Flea' meetings at our friend Sledge's house," said Vosco.

"Flea meetings?"

Skylar interjected, "When Kore and his army realized that seven thousand of us would never convert to his ways, he tried everything he could to annihilate us. When he realized he couldn't get rid of us he started referring to us as *the fleas*. At first, we didn't like the name. Let's be honest, being called a flea isn't exactly flattering. However, over time we came to embrace it. We might be small, but we aren't going away."

"We're constantly finding ways to get under his skin," laughed Vosco.

"Hey guys," interrupted Skylar. "We'll have plenty of time to show Daniel everything once we get to town. In the meantime, we've got to get him over to the fountain before curfew."

"*Another* fountain?" Daniel asked on his iPad.

"Did you ever hear about the story of Ponce de Leon and numerous other explorers searching for the fountain of youth?" asked Vosco.

Daniel nodded. He had learned about the quest for the fountain of youth in school.

"Well, there was a reason they were looking near St. Augustine… because it was there. It was literally right under their noses… here in Alcazar."

"It's real? The fountain of youth?" Daniel asked.

"See that little body of water down there where the three trees are? That's it. It possesses magical powers to heal, rejuvenate, and even add years to your life. It's how we cure illnesses around here. We don't have hospitals or doctors. We need to get there before Skylar loses any more blood from her leg," Vosco said.

"I'm surprised Kore has left something as good as this fountain untouched…" Daniel mused.

"Oh, far from untouched," Vosco replied. "Kore and his people monitor the fountain as they do everything else. They use it as much as they want, but it's completely off limits to The Fleas."

"Wait…" Daniel started, "Then where are we going?"

"There's a small spring about half a mile away from the fountain. Kore and his army never discovered that the two are connected underground. In fact, they've avoided it. It looks stagnant," replied Skylar.

Daniel looked toward the fountain. It looked like any ordinary stream of water. He was skeptical.

"Let's go," said Skylar, gripping her leg.

Daniel glanced down at her wound. She wasn't complaining much, but it looked bad.

They had made it down the winding path from the top of the peak to the bottom. It took a little bit longer than usual due to Daniel's wheelchair, but they finally made it. They were on high alert as they were now near the perimeter of town where Kore's guards frequently monitored for trespassers. The spring was only a quarter mile away.

There weren't any disabled people in Alcazar. Nobody was in a wheelchair. Vosco and Skylar knew that Daniel would draw attention, so they felt it was important to be strategic about it. Surely nobody would assume he was the chosen one. Like Skylar, most would assume he *couldn't be*. If nothing else, the wheelchair was a nice disguise. Still, it would draw attention, and they had to be prepared.

They made it safely to the small spring without any sign of Kore's police. The area was completely hidden by trees and shrubs. The water was much darker than Daniel had imagined the fountain of youth to be. He couldn't see the bottom. It looked like it had more green algae than magical healing powers. No wonder they thought it was a cesspool.

Daniel looked to his right to see Skylar had already climbed in, undeterred by the thick, almost furry layer of algae sitting on the water's surface. He watched her fully submerge her leg in the water and rest for a minute. When she pulled her leg out Daniel's mouth fell open. Her skin was perfectly smooth without even a scratch. As he leaned forward to examine her leg more closely, he felt his wheelchair begin to tip. It was too late. The wheelchair had flipped over and he was thrown into the "cesspool" at his feet.

Daniel couldn't swim. Within seconds he was swallowing mouthfuls of algae. He unbuckled the wheelchair strap at his waist as fast as he could. He was now free from his heavy wheelchair, but he could feel his body sinking as his arms flailed wildly about him. He was panicking. His head bobbed up and down. Why weren't they helping him?

"WHAT ARE YOU DOING?! HELP ME!" Daniel screamed between mouthfuls of water. He didn't have his iPad, which had slipped out of the side of his wheelchair and landed on the ground next to the spring.

He had just spoken for the first time in his life. The shock of it momentarily distracted him from the fact that he was on the verge of drowning.

"Daniel!" yelled Vosco.

Daniel's mind was in full survival mode—he couldn't begin to process what had just happened.

"DANIEL!" Vosco repeated.

Just before he went under for what could have been the very last time, his eyes found Vosco...

"TRY STANDING UP."

*Standing up?* He had the impulse to straighten out his legs. For the first time in his life, his legs listened. The bottom of the spring was just under his feet. He stood up, his chin just above the water's surface. Daniel looked at Vosco and then Skylar.

"I'm standing!" he yelled excitedly.

Shocked by the unfamiliar sound of his own voice, his hand flew over his mouth. His eyes practically popped out of his head. He could talk. He could stand. He could do things he dreamed he'd never be able to do, and it was all happening at once.

"Did you hear that?" Daniel squealed. "Did you hear *that*? I can talk!"

He looked up at the tree tops and let out a joyful hoot. It didn't stop at just one. Daniel filled the air with his voice as he laughed and howled with joy. He moved his arms with ease and precision. He slapped the water's surface with his palms like a wild bird learning how to flap its wings for the first time. Faster and faster. Water was splashing everywhere. This moment, in this magic green cesspool, was the most fun he'd ever had in his entire life. He brought his hands to his face, but stopped halfway as he examined their new appearance. His hands had been deformed his entire life. Many kids laughed and called them claws because he couldn't straighten his fingers. Now they were straight... perfect... like those of an able-bodied person. He could use them.

Daniel slid his fingers over his face. Even that felt different. His skin felt tighter. His droopy lip was no longer drooping. He couldn't see himself, but he could feel his face in a way he couldn't before. He felt its curves and edges and noticed how chiseled it was beneath his fingertips. He felt handsome for the first time in his life... without even seeing his face.

He then looked down at his legs. He couldn't see them through the green, murky water. He tried to move them. He stumbled forward. The years of being picked on and called names were now distant memories. He was new. He felt like he could do anything. He started to sob.

"Daniel?" a soft voice broke his focus, as tears of happiness continued to stream down his face.

Daniel turned to Skylar. He always felt his disability was the only thing holding him back from doing something in life. Now it was gone. This was the moment he'd been waiting for his entire life.

"Daniel, are you okay?" Skylar asked softly. Daniel looked her directly in the eyes.

"I'm better than I have ever been, Skylar," he said, savoring the words in his mouth. "No more chair!!!" he screamed.

Vosco and Skylar were grinning in awe of the magic, which had just unfolded before them.

"Daniel," Vosco said. "I had no idea this was possible... we've never had a disabled person in Alcazar. Disability isn't a disease..."

"Mine was an injury," Daniel said, beaming.

"Ah," Vosco said, nodding. "Incredible. I've never witnessed a transformation like this..."

Daniel took a few small steps forward. Vosco mused aloud.

"We continue to learn about this fountain every day. Just as the fountain learns about us."

Daniel turned around.

"Huh?"

"Some hypothesize that the fountain is intelligent. It has a conscience. It can see deeply within us, which gives it the power to heal us from the inside out."

Daniel was only half paying attention. Each step took him deeper into the fountain of youth. His chin disappeared into the dark green water.

"It gets deep pretty quickly. Be careful," Vosco said somewhat fatherly.

Vosco began to rummage through all of Daniel's gadgets. He carefully stuffed his iPad, laptop, phone, and other accessories into his backpack. Daniel noticed him scrounging around in his stuff.

"What are you doing?" Daniel asked.

"I'm packing all of your gear into this backpack so we can sneak you into town. We're going to have to dump your chair here."

"Dump my chair?" Daniel replied, his fluid movement through the water coming to an abrupt halt.

"Kore has tabs on every person, computer, phone, and IP address in Alcazar. Nothing is hidden from him; not even a wheelchair. He doesn't like surprises, so we've got to dump it here."

Daniel looked down at the water again. Then a small, coy smile spread across his face. He shrugged his shoulders and went back to splashing water. He didn't care about the dumb chair anymore. He didn't care about Kore either. He'd just been given everything he'd ever wanted. He jumped and then allowed his body to be fully submerged. Vosco stopped what he was doing. He sprinted to the edge of the spring. Skylar even took a step forward searching for signs of Daniel under the water. Before either of them could do anything else, Daniel's head popped up. His legs were touching the bottom again and he was grinning ear to ear.

He put his hand on his face. His glasses had been knocked off, but it didn't matter. He didn't need them. He was seeing better than ever before.

"This is the best day of my life!" he exclaimed.

Skylar and Vosco watched as Daniel did another awkward mini-swan dive. He was still fully clothed.

When he emerged, he was standing in a shallower part of the spring. He threw his hands out front in order to steady himself.

"What in the world are you doing?" Skylar asked, trying not to laugh. Daniel was attempting to run his arms back and forth in a mechanical motion.

"I've wanted to do this my entire life! It's called the robot."

Skylar rolled her eyes. He continued his robotic dance. It was his first robot, but far from his last. Suddenly, Daniel froze, as a thought dawned on him.

"How long does this last?" he asked.

"The fountain's powers?" asked Vosco.

Daniel nodded.

"You'll be a walking and talking young man for as long as you are down here. It should work in the middle grounds as well. After that, it's uncharted territory. It's possible that it will wear off as you get closer to the Earth's surface. It will certainly be gone once you pass through the fountain into America."

"Well, then it's official. I'm never leaving Alcazar!!!" he screamed. "I'm a new man!

Vosco heard it first. A jeep was coming their way. Kore's men must have heard him yelling. He clicked the power on Daniel's wheelchair and hit the joystick into gear. It jolted right into the water, sinking to the bottom just a few feet away from Daniel.

"What should I do?" Daniel asked with a panicked look on his face.

"Stay in the water. Get as low as you can over by those reeds in the deep end. When they come to interrogate us, go under water and stay hidden for as long as you can. They won't think to search the water because they think nobody would dare get in it."

The jeep was getting closer. Vosco tossed the backpack over his shoulder. He and Skylar took a couple steps away from the pond, hoping to avoid attracting any more attention to it. A large dust cloud continued to spread towards them even after the jeep had stopped. Two men in black military suits jumped out. They both carried semi-automatic rifles.

"You two!" the driver of the jeep barked. "Where have you been today? We've been monitoring your homes and noticed you're not honoring your normal routine. What was all of the screaming about?"

Vosco cleared his throat, his eyes on the ground. He spoke very differently in a meek voice.

"It was such a nice day we decided to take a hike. It got pretty warm, so we found some shade under the trees and took a rest. As soon as we sat down, we saw two nasty water snakes. They looked poisonous. That's why we screamed. We were about to head back home when we heard you coming."

The two men peered closely at the small, dark spring. Vosco and

Skylar turned around too, praying that Daniel was not visible. They didn't see any sign of him.

"Snakes?" said one guard. "I hate snakes. Let's get out of here! You guys are coming with us. We'll escort you home."

"That's okay, officer," said Skylar with a cute smile. She was hoping she could charm her way out of this. "We'd really prefer to walk back ourselves."

"Not a chance. Get in the back of the jeep now—before we change our minds and take you to jail. You are too close to the Fountain of Youth."

Skylar looked at Vosco to see if he had any plans for an escape. He gave her a defeated look. They hopped into the back of the jeep. The two remained silent the entire drive back to the main village. They both knew they'd never hear the end of this when they arrived at Sledge's house.

***

"You lost him? The chosen one! Are you serious?!" cried Sledge, trying not to lose his temper in front of everyone.

The other faces in the room openly displayed their dismay. The large group of community leaders were all huddled around a table in the hidden basement below Sledge's home. Sledge had personally dug out the place. With the help of the resident computer hacker, conveniently nicknamed Keypad, they made sure it was completely soundproof and undetectable by Kore's army. Finally, Gloria used her wind manipulating superpowers in order to ventilate the room.

The leaders, sixteen in all, spent the rest of the afternoon brainstorming ideas to sneak out of the village and rescue Daniel. No one seemed to agree on any given plan. They were ready to take a break when there was a loud knock at the door.

"Are you expecting somebody?" asked Vosco.

Sledge shook his head. It was almost curfew time. No one was usually in the streets at this hour except Kore's men. The group slowly tiptoed out of the hidden basement. They shut the trap door behind them. It was covered by a thick carpet followed by a heavy wooden table, which completely concealed any signs of a passageway. They positioned themselves around Sledge's living room and kitchen as though they were having a social event.

Sledge peeked through the door. It was Horst and his wife, Madeline. They were two of the elders in the community. They frequently took walks in the evening just before curfew. Kore's men had learned to leave them alone, since they appeared too old to be up to no good. For the most part they were just that. They certainly wanted Kore and his evil empire gone, but they didn't have the energy to fight like they used to. Sledge opened the door.

"Hey Sledge," Horst whispered. "Don't look now, but there's a strange young man hiding in the bushes across the street. I've never seen him before. I'm guessing he might be a spy for Kore."

"Stay right here," he told Horst. Sledge motioned for Vosco to come to the door.

"What's going on, Horst?" Vosco asked.

Horst explained what he had just told Sledge. Horst described what the young man was wearing. It sounded like Daniel. But how could he have made it all the way into town without being captured?

"Where is he exactly?" Vosco asked Horst, looking over his shoulder into the street.

The instant Horst pointed to the bush across the street, Vosco knew it was him. He'd recognize that mop of hair anywhere. How in the world did he make it here? He turned around to tell the rest of the crew inside.

"It's Daniel. He's hiding in a bush across the street."

"Well, signal him over before Kore's men start showing up," said Evan.

Vosco let out a whistle. It was enough to get Daniel's attention. He quickly recognized Vosco standing in the doorway across the street. Vosco signaled for him to come. Daniel slowly pushed the shrubbery aside and darted across the street, running as fast as his new legs would go.

Inside the house the leaders were pushing each other out of the way in order to get a peek at him through the front windows. They had been waiting years for 'the one' to finally appear. When they laid eyes on him the disappointment was palpable. The pale, skinny kid in a filthy white t-shirt and jeans was jogging *very* awkwardly across the street.

"That's him?" asked Sledge. "That's our savior? He sure doesn't look like it. He runs like he's never jogged a day in his life." He scratched his temple. "I know it's not all about size, but he's a wee bit scrawny for someone who's supposed to free the nation."

The others in the room agreed.

"You think he looks bad now?" Skylar blurted out. "You should have seen him earlier today before we got him cleaned up—"

Before she could say another word, Vosco flashed her a look, which made her become as quiet as the rest of the room.

# 15 THE SETUP

Kore looked down at the message and laughed. It had been sent by the president's office.

"Did you see this?" Kore asked his right-hand man, Khan. "The president wants to debate me. That's all he's got? Taking over America is going to be easier than we thought. He's falling right into our trap. Once we have America secured, we'll move on to China... then Europe. Before you know it, we'll have control over the entire world."

Kore grinned. He was stroking a small globe in his hand. He found himself doing this for hours at a time. He was dreaming of the day it would all be his. Kore and Khan stood across the room from each other in Kore's underground office. They had built their entire fortress under the city so they could keep an eye and ear on their citizens. It wasn't uncommon for them to pop up out of manholes to remind citizens that they were being watched.

Kore's office was dark, just like his shoulder-length jet black hair and his dark black uniform, which he wore every day. No one had seen him in anything else but a black button-down shirt, black military pants, and black boots. His boots had extra thick soles to make him appear taller than his short frame would suggest. For an unattractive man, who had zero fashion sense, he was incredibly vain.

His office was mostly barren. There were only two pictures on the walls. One was a photo of his very first computer. Sticker-clad and scuffed, the machine appeared to have been loved. It was the one he'd learned to write code with back when he was locked in his parent's basement. There were no pictures of family or friends.

The other was a large map of the world. Little red pins poked out all over the place. There was a hodge-podge of hand written notes by Kore as well. This was his war room, where he spent most of his time. His days were consumed with plotting and fantasizing about taking over the world.

His bedroom was down the hall. No one had ever been allowed in there. It consisted of a simple cot, a pillow, and a tower of books. He had accumulated old military strategy books and psychology books over the years. He read a few books each week, and was probably one of the most well-versed people on those subjects.

Kahn, Kore's right-hand man, had been wanting to talk to his boss all week. He believed there was an easier way to attack America. However, he had been nervous to share his thoughts, since most people who disagreed with Kore were never seen again.

"Sir, why don't we just hack into America's nuclear bombs and detonate them all? I mean, do we really need to rule over all these worthless humans instead of just killing them—"

"Listen closely, Khan!" interrupted Kore. He placed his globe down on the table and looked him right in the eyes. "Let's get two things straight. One, we need the people to do the work we don't want to do ourselves. Two, there is no *we*... this is *my army*. This is *my* land to conquer. These are *my* people to control. This will be *my* world, not yours. I suggest you either get on board with the plan or start looking for a new job. Now get out of here and start preparing the troops for war. Close the door behind you."

Kahn stormed out of his office. Kore ignored him. He placed the little globe back in his hand. He stared down at America. He had been waiting his entire life for this moment. He was doing this for all of the years he had been picked on and exiled from Alcazar because he was different. He had convinced himself that getting rid of capitalism and corrupt governments was for the greater good. According to legend, God had created Alcazar first, not America. So why did they get all of the money, luxuries, and freedom? Kore wanted it for himself. Like so many other corrupt leaders before him, he felt certain that he was the good guy. He was doing this for the people.

There was a knock on his door. Kore didn't like interruptions. "Who is it?" he yelled towards the door.

"Sir, I'm incredibly sorry to bother you. It's me, Dagney. I've got an update on the debate from the president of the United States."

Dagney was Kore's personal assistant. The two had been friends ever since they were young boys growing up in Alcazar. Dagney had been born with a cleft lip and large ears. He was incredibly frail and weak. Even after multiple trips to the fountain of youth, his irregular lip refused to heal. The two had bonded at a young age because they were both considered outcasts. Back when they were both seven years old, a couple of bullies were giving Dagney an ultimate wedgie. They were holding him up in the air by his underwear as he squirmed. Kore ran over and kicked one of the boys as hard as he could. They immediately dropped Dagney, but they took their anger out on Kore. After the fight finally broke up, Kore ended up with a broken nose and two broken ribs. However, he had gained his first and only friend. The two had been inseparable since. Dagney would always have Kore's back.

"Come on in," Kore replied.

Kore always liked his interactions with Dagney. He liked that he did whatever Kore said. He never questioned him or talked back. *Why can't everyone be like him?* thought Kore.

Dagney came in. He handed Kore a new memo, which had just come in from the president.

"It looks like he wants to do the debate tomorrow evening. He wants it to be live-streamed to the entire world."

Kore smiled. "Let them know I'll be ready. I've got to say, this president is a bigger problem than I thought he'd be. I would have bet anything that he would have been the first to take my offer. If he wants to be the last man standing, then I have no problem publicly humiliating him."

Dagney smiled back. He loved watching Kore take down people like the president. These politicians and business leaders made a living picking on the small guys. Dagney couldn't wait to see this debate.

"Sir, is there anything else I can do to serve you?"

Kore paused for a moment, and then turned to face him, his expression suddenly curious.

"Yes. Street cameras picked up a strange young man running across the street. It appears we don't have him in our database. Ironically, an hour before the footage from the hidden camera was taken, a citizen reported what they said looked like a human—not a Mogan—hiding behind their home. Get the recording from the surveillance team and track down where he was seen last. Start interrogating every home in that area. If it's a human, I want him found immediately."

Dagney nodded. "Yes, sir."

He was walking out of the office, when Kore stopped him.

"I just changed my mind. Let the people bring the human to us."

Dagney scratched his chin.

"What do you mean, sir?"

"Take over every news station and Internet news feed in all of Alcazar and offer a $10,000,000 reward if anyone can deliver the human to me."

Dagney's face lit up.

"We'll let the villagers do the dirty work for us."

# 16 ALLIES & ENEMIES

Everyone in the house was silent. None of the sixteen Flea leaders in the room said a word.

Although they weren't exactly sure what to expect from the "chosen one," they were certain it wasn't what just walked through the door. Everyone stared at him uncomfortably. It didn't bother Daniel. He was used to getting stared at his entire life. Of course, this time, it wasn't because he had an electric wheelchair which screamed, *I'm different!*

Vosco broke the silence. He gently grabbed Daniel's arm. "Come meet everybody."

Sledge received the first introduction. It was his house. Daniel looked up. Then he looked up even higher. The beast of a man standing in front of him was one of the tallest people he had ever seen. He must have been close to eight feet. He was a solid wall of muscle with a thick, dark-brown beard. He looked like a lumberjack. He had a massive smile. Even his teeth were big. They looked like Chiclets.

"Daniel, this is Sledge."

"Nice to meet you," Daniel said as he extended his hand to Sledge for a handshake.

"You might not want to—" someone from the back of the room tried to warn him.

"AHHHHHHHH!!!!" Daniel looked down where his hand used to be. It had completely disappeared inside the largest hand in history. Daniel tried to free his hand, but it was caught in Sledge's vice-like grip.

"Sledge, can you stop shaking Daniel's hand?" his wife asked nicely.

"Of course," he replied. His face turned a bright shade of red.

"Sorry, I was so excited to meet you. I forgot my manners," he said with a smile.

"Can I guess why they call you Sledge?" Daniel said while trying to shake the feeling back into his hand. "Is it because anyone who shakes your hand feels like it was smashed by a sledgehammer?"

The biggest, most boisterous laugh he had ever heard came rushing towards him with such force, Daniel nearly fell over. The entire house shook. Apparently, everything about Sledge was big.

"Close, but no cigar," he answered. "They call me Sledge because of this."

Everyone in the house stepped back. Sledge placed both of his massive hands in front of him, slightly above waist height. Vosco used his arm to pull Daniel back.

His hands began to shape shift. Sledgehammers appeared where his hands used to be. There was one on each hand. Sledge raised them up above his head and started pumping his fists in the air.

A voice from the back of the room started to chant, "Sledge… Sledge… Sledge…" Within seconds the entire room was shouting it. "Sledge, Sledge, Sledge."

The villagers in the house cheered as Sledge moved his sledgehammer hands at impossible speeds. The energetic crowd finally died down as his hands morphed back to normal. He gave Daniel a fist bump. "It's great to have you on board, Dan the man," he said. "We've all been really excited to meet you. As you can tell, my special power is breaking things with my sledgehammers. If you need something pounded, busted up, or broken down, just let me know. I'm at your service."

"Thanks, Sledge," said Daniel. He was incredibly grateful that Sledge was on their team and not the other one.

Vosco led Daniel around to meet the other leaders and learn about their superpowers. There was Rodney, who could shoot flames from his hands. Eric could make himself completely invisible. Evan could turn into a small beetle and crawl into the smallest of spaces undetected. Ian could freeze anything with his ice-cold powers. Then there was Whiz, who could whip up tornadoes by twisting his body like a spinning top. Thunderclap was a rail-thin man with a funny bowl cut hair-do, who could create rain, thunder, and lightning. There were the twin brothers, Jerry and Terry, who both could turn into hawks and fly. Oh, and finally, there was a real special character named

Scooter. He could turn into a skunk and put out a toxic smell from his rear—as in the worst thing you have ever smelled in your life.

Scooter was the first to ask Daniel a question.

"Hey Daniel, what's it like up there in the other world?"

Everyone quieted to hear Daniel's response. He thought for a second.

"There are certainly some advantages to living up there. We've got things like cool fast cars, Chinese food, Netflix, public libraries, and 9,000 channels on TV."

"Who was the last person you destroyed?" asked Thunderclap, disinterested in what Daniel had just said.

"Destroyed?" he asked. "I'm not sure what you mean..."

"You know, like some bad guy you took down, beat up, or flattened out," interjected Rodney.

Everyone leaned in. All eyes were on Daniel. For a brief moment he considered telling them the truth. He was a crippled young teenager, who could barely make it through a day in high school without someone picking on him, belittling him, or calling him 'retarded.' He spent most of his waking hours in fear. He just couldn't do it. These people believed he was the ONE—the chosen one. If he told them the truth, he'd be a nobody again. He decided to tell the biggest, bold-faced lie of his entire life...

"Well, not many people mess with me up there. Fortunately for them, I don't get into many fights. There was this one guy—his name was Brad. He was a real bully. One day he decided to mess with the wrong person... me. He was coming down a hallway in school pushing everyone out of his way. I was the only person brave enough to stand up to him. He attempted to push me over, but before he could lay a hand on me, I punched him right in the nose. The force of my punch knocked him down so hard he had trouble getting back up. Blood poured from his nose. He gave me one quick look through teary eyes and ran away as fast as he could. It certainly wasn't the only nose I've broken, but it sure was a memorable one..."

The place erupted in cheers. There was renewed energy in the room. They loved the story. They loved Daniel. They began to believe in him. For the first time since meeting him, they thought he really could be the one. Vosco and Skylar still had their doubts.

Daniel quickly changed the subject. "What's the latest with this Kore guy I keep hearing about?"

The place fell silent. No one wanted to speak up. Finally, one man rose to his feet. He was the only man with white hair in the group. He looked wise... distinguished. Everyone turned around to listen to him speak.

"Daniel," he said with a slow almost southern-like draw. "First and foremost, welcome to Alcazar. I suspect everyone else has introduced themselves already, but I only arrived moments ago. I've heard many wonderful things about you. My friends call me Mac. I was a dear friend of your grandfather and grandmother while they were here. I can still recall how proud your mom and dad were that you were on the way. Your mother was especially excited. She was such a beautiful and loving woman."

Daniel felt warm inside. It was so meaningful to hear this from someone who knew his family. Mac continued.

"Kore and his army have completely taken over Alcazar. They control everything about our lives. Kore got bored just controlling us. He craved more, so he decided to take over America. Kore is one of the best computer hackers in the world, and he knew the best way to do it was through the Internet. It provides him with a massive audience, which is looking for free handouts and entitlements. He knows his audience incredibly well. He's a sharp man. He knows politics and psychology better than anyone. He attacked America at the perfect time, and he'll eventually get control of it if your president can't find a way to stop him. It will be scary if he really does have the ability to shut down the entire power grid. He's been trying to control and harness electricity for years. Either way, Kore won't stop until he controls it all."

Mac finished. Everyone was quiet, waiting for someone to speak next.

"So, what's the plan? How do we stop him?" Daniel asked him.

"We're hoping you hold some of the answers. It's certainly going to take someone who can match his computer hacking skills and is bold enough to challenge him..."

Mac was interrupted by a loud knock on the front.

"Who's that?" whispered Ian, pointing at the door. More hard knocks followed.

"Open up. It's the police. We have a warrant to search your house."

"Get Daniel into the basement fast!" Sledge cried. "I'll hold off the goons for as long as I can."

"We'll be back to get you before the sun rises in the morning," whispered Vosco to Daniel as he reached for the trap door. "There's someone else you need to meet... and we're going to need to climb a mountain to meet him."

Daniel nodded. Vosco shut the trap door and covered it up with the carpet and table. He could hear Sledge talking to Kore's men up front.

"We've had a report of a possible human refugee coming up to this house. We need to search it now."

"A refugee?" Sledge asked, pretending he had no idea what they were talking about. "Who approved a warrant? You aren't coming in my house unless you can show me something."

The two policemen looked at each other. They had heard many rumors about this Sledge guy. No one wanted to risk fighting this giant. The officers noticed quite a few other people in the house. They weren't going to take any chances. The officer on the right hit a button on his radio.

"This is Officer Hardwick. I'm here at 187 Main Street. We've got an issue over here. I need some backup A-S-A-P."

Sledge took a step closer to the two men. He towered over them. They quickly took a step back. One officer drew his gun.

"Don't come any closer or we'll be forced to take action," the officer warned.

Sledge was fuming. He started to wish he had knocked these two out before they called in for back-up. Now it was too late. Of course, some street camera probably would have picked it up anyways. He knew Daniel had to be hidden by now, so he made the quick decision to let them in and pretend they had nothing to hide.

"Gents, I apologize for the lack of hospitality," he said in his most gentle voice. "Please do come in. Search anything you need. We have nothing to hide. I happen to have some of my closest friends over for a small gathering, but we haven't seen anyone or let anyone in."

Sledge motioned for them to come in. As he did, two more officers pulled up in a green military jeep. The four came in the house with their weapons drawn. They told everyone to keep their hands up and not to move as they inspected the place. They looked in every cabinet, pantry, nook, and cranny. They searched under beds, boxes, and anything else which looked like a potential hiding place.

"I told you, officers, we don't have any human here," said Sledge.

One of Kore's officers was standing right next to the table, which covered the underground hideaway. Daniel could hear the wood softly crack above him from the weight of the man. *Did they find the trap door?* Daniel thought. It was so dark down there he couldn't tell. All he could hear were the sounds of footsteps above his head. He wanted to turn on the light so badly, but Vosco had instructed him to keep the lights off. He heard the footsteps fade away.

"You haven't seen the last of us," said one officer. "We know there is a human nearby and we will find him," he grumbled. He gave Sledge the evil eye and the four men walked out. Sledge's wife shut the door behind them.

"That was a close one," he whispered to the group. "The bad news is that they will be back tomorrow. That's a given. The big question is with how many more officers and police dogs to sniff him out?"

Vosco nodded. "Skylar and I will be taking him to see Maku early in the morning. We'll be by early so the house will be clear when Kore's men show up. Let's pray Maku gives Daniel the blueprint to take Kore down."

"What if he doesn't?" asked Evan, always the pessimist—or *realist*, as he preferred to be called.

"He will," chimed in Rodney. "Daniel's the chosen one. He has to be—or else we're all goners…"

# 17 MAKU THE MAGU

Daniel's body hurt in ways he'd never imagined possible.

He felt like he had just run an ultramarathon. Every single muscle and joint in his body was aching. He never imagined that having working legs could be this painful. Vosco and Skylar had told him the hardest part was getting out of the village undetected. The truth was, sneaking out of the village paled in comparison to the trek up the mountain.

"Guys, I'm not sure I can hike any farther. I can barely move my legs. Can we rest?" Daniel was sitting on a rock, which had made its home in the middle of the trail. They were so high up they were almost at cloud level.

"No. We've got to do this now. Time is running out. Besides, we're getting close. Maku's cave is not much farther," replied Vosco.

They continued their hike up the mountain. Daniel couldn't believe how narrow the trail was getting. There were times when he was literally hugging the mountain to avoid falling to his death. Occasionally the path ended, leaving a gaping hole with nothing but hundreds of feet of sharp rock below. He was forced to climb up old tree roots in order to bypass these chasms. Once he had to take a running leap over a crevice. Daniel barely cleared it. If Vosco hadn't grabbed his hand on the landing, he might have slipped off the ledge completely.

"This Maku guy better be worth it," grumbled Daniel in-between breaths. "If I can ask him for anything, it might have to be a shortcut down this mountain. How much farther?"

"Dead ahead." Vosco pointed up above. "The top opens up to a nice flat area, where Maku's cave resides. He'll be waiting for us right next to his bonsai tree."

"Does he know we are coming?" asked Daniel.

"Maku the magu knows everything," replied Skylar.

They were right. The top was nice, but mostly because it meant no more climbing. Daniel looked around. The only living thing up there was a single bonsai tree. It was massive—at least two stories tall. Next to it was the fattest, ugliest looking creature Daniel had ever seen. Its eyes were closed. It appeared to be deep in meditation.

"Is that him? The magu?" whispered Daniel.

Skylar nodded.

If a manatee, an elephant, and a walrus all somehow yielded offspring together, Maku was it. He had four elephant-like legs, the blubbery body of a large manatee, and big, white tusks protruding from his whiskery face. He sat on his rear end with his two back legs splayed across the ground in an attempt to support his massive weight. The front of his body was propped up by his two stubby front legs. They watched as his eyes slowly opened. He squinted as if he was unaccustomed to the light.

"I've been expecting you, Daniel," said Maku. Daniel looked at his friends. He didn't know what to say. They both kept staring forward.

"Good afternoon, Maku," said Vosco.

Maku ignored his greeting. Vosco was empty-handed, and the magu had no patience for visitors who did not come bearing gifts. He looked at Daniel.

"It appears as though you are already ruffling some feathers in this land, young man."

"What—what do you mean?" stuttered Daniel.

"Kore and a couple of his henchmen were here last night. Kore wanted to know all about a human who had entered Alcazar," replied Maku.

The three of them stood there nervously, not sure if whether they had permission to ask questions.

"Would you like to know what I told them?" asked the magu as he shifted his massive body a bit closer.

"Yes. I mean, no? Well, I guess so," he stumbled, looking to Vosco and Skylar for approval. Was it okay to want to know more?

"Well, I normally don't reveal my secrets to others, but I'm willing to do it just this one time," he replied with a grin on his face.

"Really? Wow. Thank you, Mr... Um... Maku," Daniel replied nervously.

"Are you sure you want to know what I told them?" he asked again.

"Yes. That would be incredibly kind of you," replied Skylar, trying but failing to contain her excitement.

"Then I'll reveal precisely what I told them. I told them... the TRUTH!"

Maku burst out in hysterical laughter. His flabby body was shaking as though an earthquake had hit a big bowl of *Jell-O*. Daniel looked over at Skylar and Vosco. He wondered if Maku was ever going to stop laughing. Finally, his giggles slowed down and he straightened up.

"I assume you didn't come up here for comic relief. How can I help the three of you today?"

"You told us to find the chosen one in America. Well, we found him—at least, we're pretty certain it's him," said Vosco as he realized he was digging himself into a hole with Daniel standing right there.

Maku looked at the three of them through his big bulging gray eyes.

"Aha. So, you are doubting that this Daniel character is really the chosen one. Is that correct?"

The three of them froze, afraid to admit that they had doubted Maku's guidance.

"Yes. That's correct." said Skylar boldly. "We're not sure he's the one."

Daniel looked at her coldly.

"Mmmm... well, then."

Maku shifted his gargantuan body on all fours. He moved towards his cave.

Daniel watched in amazement as the giant magu moved with unimaginable speed. He was like one of those 400-pound NFL linemen, who could shock the crowd with their agility on the field. After what seemed like mere seconds, he was completely gone and out of sight.

"What do I do now?" Daniel whispered to his companions.

"Follow him," said Skylar.

Daniel ventured into the cave after Maku. Once inside, he felt queasy. The place smelled horrible. It was a damp, musty odor—as though someone had left clothes in the washing machine to mildew. The magu motioned for him to take a seat in a stone chair. It was directly across from Maku's mound—a rock formation, which rose from the bottom of the cave and plateaued just a few feet above. It gave him a better vantage point, as though from a throne.

Daniel looked around. It was tough to believe anyone could live here. It was a total mess. There was stuff everywhere. It looked like the place belonged to a bunch of hoarders. There was an entire wall of trinkets, gizmos, toys, and junk piled three stories high. There were towers of gold coins, crowns, statues, and even a miniature bronze airplane, which was suspended from the ceiling. He had never seen anything like it.

Daniel caught Maku's eye.

"Do you like my collection?" His face was beaming. Daniel could tell he was incredibly proud of his things.

He turned around and pretended to admire it. "Yes, it's quite impressive." He hoped that was the right thing to say.

Maku grinned. "I've been a collector since I was a kid. It's my passion. It makes me happy."

The magu scanned Daniel's face.

"You're judging me. I'm supposed to be some spiritual guru and here I am, a self-proclaimed lover of things money can buy. Do you think this collection is outrageous, unnecessary, and over the top?"

Daniel sat there expressionless. He prayed that Maku couldn't read his mind because that had been exactly what he was thinking.

He started talking again. "Let me share something with you, Daniel. It's scary sometimes when you're alone. It's tough when you have no real friends. Everyone who comes to visit just wants something from you. As soon as they get it, they leave and never return. Do you know what it's like to spend the majority of your life in isolation? Do you know what it feels like when no one understands you? Do you know what it feels like not to be loved?"

Daniel nodded. This he did know. They had something in common.

"I've never met my parents. Villagers from Alcazar found me up here in this cave when I was young. I was alone, hungry, and scared. I thought I was going to die, but I was too big and heavy to move down the mountain."

"Have you *ever* left this mountaintop?" Daniel asked.

"Not once, "Maku replied. "The people of Alcazar didn't know what to think of me. I didn't look like anyone or anything in our world. Some said I was a gift from God—a prophet. Some said my parents left me there to die because I was too ugly. People started coming here just to look at 'the freak up on the mountain.' Do you know what that's like?"

Daniel found himself nodding.

"Look, I know what I look like, and that's not my gift. My gift is seeing into the future. Once the people of Alcazar realized what I could do, they started bringing me presents in return for my predictions. They brought me food, gold, trinkets, toys, art, and much more."

"In gratitude?" Daniel asked.

"Yes. What is gratitude rooted in, Daniel?" Maku asked.

"I'm not sure what you mean," Daniel stumbled.

"Every emotion is rooted in one of two things: love or fear. Which one does gratitude come from?"

Daniel paused. The way Maku phrased this almost sounded like a riddle. Was it? The answer seemed obvious.

"Love?" Daniel asked slowly.

Maku smiled.

Daniel looked around the cave and realized these gifts of gratitude were far more than trinkets. They represented love. Now he understood why he had saved every one of them. Daniel looked back at Maku. His eyes glistened enough to make Daniel wonder if he was close to tears. Maku inhaled deeply.

"Daniel, now you know why I'm here. I want to know why you are here?"

"Well…" Daniel started. "I'm not sure. A week ago, I was a kid in a wheelchair just trying to get through life. Then a frog and an owl came knocking on my door and the world seemed to fall into chaos. My dad died the same day I found out my grandfather was still alive. Now there's some bad hacker dude trying to take over America by shutting down the power grid. I guess I'm a bit confused on what I'm doing here…"

"Just ask the question!" interrupted the magu in a burst of frustration. "All of this exposition… it's like you're apologizing for asking something you haven't even asked! If you want to know something, just ask it."

The calm and sensitive Maku from earlier was gone. Daniel had a blank stare. He wasn't sure what to say.

"Just ask it," Maku demanded.

"Am I the chosen one or not?"

Maku started rubbing his fat chin with his elephant sized hand.

"Aha! The real search for truth comes out. Let me ask *you* a question, Daniel. Do you *believe* that you are the chosen one?"

"I'm not sure. Vosco told me I am. I certainly don't feel like it."

"Well then, I'm afraid I can't help you," replied Maku.

"What do you mean you can't help me? I thought you were supposed to know everything!"

Maku raised his eyebrows. He stared down at him like a parent whose child is out of line. Daniel felt embarrassed.

The magu spoke up, "Daniel, I've got an answer for you, but I'm not sure you are ready to hear it."

"I've made it this far. I think I can handle anything at this point."

Maku spoke a single word.

"No."

Daniel looked puzzled.

"No? What does that mean? No? As in no, you aren't going to tell me?"

Maku interrupted, "No, you fool! You are *not* the one. You are not the chosen one. Period. End of story."

Daniel was caught off guard. He'd expected to come here for validation and confirmation, not this. Immediately he began to think of his dad. Was he a loser? Is *that* what this was confirming? What would Vosco think? What would the people of Alcazar think?

"But… Vosco and Skylar said…"

"Receive what I SAID!" the magu bellowed back in a booming voice.

Daniel shouted back in anger, "Then how do you explain the fact that I made it through the three middle grounds alive? Huh? Explain why Vosco and Skylar sought me out! Wasn't that based on your recommendation? Huh, Mr. Know-It-All?"

Maku was getting angry. His fat face became tight.

"Your grandfather failed and so will you. You're simply not the man I thought you'd be. Get out of Alcazar while you can. If not, you'll be forced to leave in shame."

Daniel was sick to his stomach. He knew he'd be forced back home if anyone found out he wasn't the chosen one. He'd lose his new body. He'd be back in a wheelchair. He'd be a nobody again. Tears were gathering in his eyes. He looked up at Maku.

"Are you one hundred percent certain? Is there any chance I might be the chosen one? It seems crazy to think I was dragged down here only to be told I'm the wrong guy."

Maku stared right through him. He was eyeing something shiny. Based on its location on top of one of the towers, it was likely a newer addition to his collection. For a moment, Maku appeared to be lost in thought. Daniel wondered if he hadn't heard what he'd just asked.

"Hey! Walrus face! Any chance you're wrong?" Daniel asked boldly.

Before he could start his next sentence, the magu lunged forward at him. The ground trembled. Daniel took a quick step backwards, but he was already inches away from his nose. His two white tusks framed Daniel's head, and he could smell his horrible breath.

"Listen closely to me, young man." Daniel felt a drop of saliva land on his cheek. "I'm going to make things incredibly clear to you before I kick you off my mountain. One, I'm never wrong. Two, you are not the chosen one. Three, you'd best head back home to America while you're still alive."

Without another word Daniel slowly backed away. He turned around and walked calmly out of the cave. Vosco saw him coming out and excitedly ran over to him. He grabbed Daniel's shoulders and looked him right in the eye.

"Daniel. We're going to start an attack today."

"An attack?"

"Well, more of a strategic operation," Vosco said. "I'll brief you as soon as we're back at headquarters. We can't do it without the chosen one."

"But is he really the chosen one?" Skylar interjected. "What did Maku say?"

"He said exactly what he already told us when he sent us out to find Daniel," Vosco responded impatiently to Skylar. "Don't you recall the entire reason we traveled to America? I think Maku would have come out here and told us if he'd been wrong. Are you happy now?"

Vosco slapped Daniel on the back, a big grin plastered across his face.

"But I'm—"

"We don't want to hear it, Daniel!" Vosco interrupted. "Accept it already, okay?!"

Skylar rolled her eyes, clearly not sharing in Vosco's sentiment.

"We're this far in, and he's still complaining and doubting and..." Skylar trailed off.

Daniel opened his mouth to speak again, but this time he couldn't seem to find his voice. He couldn't bring himself to confess what he had just learned from Maku.

Daniel trailed behind Skylar and Vosco as they headed down the mountain back to the village. When they reached their headquarters at Sledge's house, it was obvious everyone had been chatting enthusiastically about him for hours. Here he was, arriving to catch the tail end of it. The Fleas rushed to greet him. Not a single person actually asked him how the meeting went with Maku. They were too busy dreaming aloud about what would happen now that their chosen one had arrived. Although he was able-bodied for the first in his life, he felt more disabled than ever before. His body ached and his voice was failing him. Daniel swallowed hard and quickly gathered himself together. He wasn't about to let down an entire nation of people... even if it meant living a lie.

# 18 THE TRAITOR

There was a secret path through the backside of town. It was completely covered with dead vines and debris, which had been purposely collected to keep it hidden from the villagers. It appeared so overgrown no one would have given that area a second thought. The path led towards the back entrance of Kore's underground headquarters.

Terry and his twin brother, Jerry, were two of the engineers summoned many years ago to help construct the underground labyrinth, which extended underneath Alcazar. The path and the back entrance had been created for convenience when the headquarters were being built. Terry and Jerry's final task had been to permanently seal up the back entrance with rocks, dirt, and debris from the excavation site. It had been seventeen years, but they still knew exactly where the back entrance was. It was a long shot, but it was their only hope of making it into Kore's compound undetected.

The plan was to break into the main control room and destroy as much of it as they could. Without his computers, Kore was powerless. His used the web to control Alcazar's money, communicate with his army, spy on the people, and hack organizations and governments in order to aid his bid for global domination. If his computer network was shut down, he'd cease to exist.

Eight of the Fleas has been designated to go on this mission. All were men, who had served with Vosco in the civil war with the exception of Skylar. They were confident. For the first time in decades, they believed they had a fighting chance. They were going into battle with the chosen one...

Daniel felt sick, but being admired and appreciated was filling a void, which had lived within him for as long as he could remember. Everything was based on a lie. He felt trapped. If he told them the truth, he'd go right back to being the forgotten kid in a wheelchair. He promised himself he would tell them at some point, but now was not the time. They needed to believe in him just as much as he needed to believe in himself.

On the walk to the headquarters, Whiz, who could whip up tornados with a wave of his hands, sidled up next to Daniel.

"Hey Daniel," he said, his quiet voice testing the waters of conversation. "I just want to let you know it's an honor to get to serve next to you. I've been waiting for this moment for years."

Daniel gave him a weak smile. He wished he could tell him the truth.

"There's also something else I want to tell you," Whiz continued.

Daniel didn't say a word. He kept walking, hoping Whiz wasn't going to ask about his meeting with Maku.

"I don't know how to say this, so I'll just come right out with it... Maku told me I'll end up dying in order to save the chosen one."

Daniel's heart skipped a beat. *I've got to tell him the truth.*

"At first, I didn't know how to take it... I mean, it's not easy hearing you're going to die. I just wanted to let you know that after meeting you yesterday, I'm finally at peace with it. I've got your back whenever you need it."

He tried not to vomit. He was in way over his head now.

The two continued to walk in awkward silence for a few minutes. Daniel was trying to think of the right words to say. He finally looked over at Whiz and spoke.

"Let's both hope Maku was wrong."

They stopped as they came around the next bend. Standing before them was the back entrance, which was sealed with solid rock.

"Now what?" asked Vosco. "It's so thick, we'd need dynamite to get through." There was mumbling amongst the group. They all looked at Daniel.

"Perhaps I can help," bellowed a loud voice from behind him. It was Sledge. He was ready to destroy the indestructible.

"Stand back, and watch out for falling rocks."

Everyone backed up a solid fifty feet, and waited for the show to begin. Sledge slid on his safety glasses and warmed up his fists, the way a boxer warms up for a fight. His sledgehammer fists punched the air faster and faster until they were moving so quickly, they were nothing more than a blur. Seconds later, the ground began to shake as rock went flying.

Sledge's two hammers were moving at full speed, busting off pieces of rock as large as Daniel. Sparks flew, rocks tumbled, and dust was clouding the air. Sledge was no longer visible, but you could hear the sound of his sledgehammers pounding away.

Then it stopped abruptly. Everyone looked at each other through the dusty air, wondering what had happened.

"Sledge, how does it look?" someone called out.

No response.

"Sledge, can you hear us?"

With all of the dust, nobody could see more than a foot in front of them. Still no response.

"Come on guys, let's see what is going on," said Vosco.

The group slowly inched forward. Finally, a voice shouted out, "I found him!" Everyone gathered together. Sledge was on the ground. His eyes were closed and both of his hands were smoking as if they had caught fire.

Evan immediately unscrewed the cap of his canteen and splashed water on Sledge's face and hands. He opened his eyes. He attempted to sit up straight, but he couldn't.

"Hey guys, you've got to come see this," said Jerry. The smoke and dust were slowly clearing. "The wall is completely gone… it's like it was never even there!"

They stared in disbelief. There was a gaping car-sized hole where the wall of rock used to be. They let the dust settle a little more, while Thunderclap and Evan attended to Sledge. Once he was back on his feet, they all gathered around the hole, waiting for their next order from Vosco.

"Terry? Jerry? Do you remember the quickest way to Kore's computer command center from here?" asked Vosco.

Jerry quickly chimed in. "Once we go through this back entrance, there will be a fork in the cave. We need to go right. That will take us down a series of paths, which will eventually lead to the area where Kore's mainframe is located, and then—"

Jerry was cut off by his twin brother, Terry.

"No, we need to go left at the fork. If we go right, we'll have to pass by their ammunition room, which is always guarded. Your way is too risky."

"Risky?" replied Jerry. "Going left will take us directly into the main eating hall, where we're sure to run into someone. Not to mention, we'd have to go right through the front door of the control center, which seems like a really bad idea."

The two argued for a while longer, unable to come to an agreement. Finally, Vosco jumped in.

"Guys, I'm tired of this bickering. Just pick the quickest way, and let's go for it. We can't sit here all day."

Everyone agreed to go left. It was the shortest route. They looked at Daniel for approval. He nodded innocently. All he could do was pray his laptop could hack into Kore's mainframe quickly in there. Everyone was counting on him. He was terrified.

They made their way into the headquarters. The only sound was the quiet pattering of their feet on the cold stone floor. Torches hung from the walls, illuminating the dark hallway.

Everyone had their weapon drawn in front of them. They each carried a gun and a knife. Sledge wielded a massive wooden bat, which he couldn't wait to use. They were ready for anyone or anything that might be in their path.

After a short walk through the musty underground tunnel, they came to a fork in the path. It was just as Terry and Jerry had described. The right side was pitch black without torches lighting the way. The group agreed it was just another sign they were supposed to go left.

They descended downwards, and after a few sharp turns, they found themselves in Kore's dining hall. The ceiling was vaulted like a cathedral but without the ornate decorations. The rocks had been carved out by explosives. It was completely desolate except for two yellow eyes peering down on them from the chandelier above.

"What's that?" cried Skylar pointing up at the light fixture. "I just saw something with yellow eyes looking at us. It darted into a hole in the ceiling."

"Well, it's not there now," replied Thunderclap. "It was probably just a rodent."

"I don't know, guys. I don't like the looks of this. It's too quiet. Where is everyone?"

"Perhaps he sent his troops up through the middle grounds

already?" Rodney offered.

"No," replied Vosco. He was whispering to keep his voice down. "I saw on the news that Kore is going to have some debate with the president tonight. Apparently, the president only has a day and a half left to hand things over to Kore, or he'll shut down their power grid."

"Yeah," Scooter chimed in. "They were trying to convince us on the news that taking down America is a good thing for Alcazar. What a joke! I guess that's what you get when he controls the news stations around here."

"Let's keep moving," said Terry. "We don't have time to waste. If that animal was part of their team, we'd better get moving before it alerts their troops."

They moved through the dining hall quickly, trying to get out of the open space.

They followed Terry down a dimly lit path. As they descended, it became darker and darker. Daniel could feel a sharp pinch in his upper chest. He recognized the feeling. It was the beginning of an anxiety attack. His body was telling him something was wrong.

"Why is it so dark down here?" whispered Vosco.

"We're almost at the main computer control area. Kore likes to keep this area dark and quiet so he can concentrate while he codes," Terry replied.

There was another large opening up ahead. The tunnel led them into a circular room with a high vaulted ceiling. They tiptoed quietly. Daniel's mouth dropped open when he saw the control center. It was a hacker's dream. Computer screens were everywhere. There was a 92-inch main screen, where Kore did most of his coding. He had never seen so much computer processing power in one room. Behind it he could see a server room, which went on for days. *There's enough capacity to keep Google running in here,* he thought.

Vosco looked around. Something didn't seem right. Why wasn't anyone here manning this critical station? He tried to flag down Sledge, but it was too late.

"Good afternoon, Vosco," an icy voice said. "We've been expecting you."

The eight of them swung their bodies around to face Kore, who was standing before a small army of men. They all had automatic weapons pointed in their direction. Daniel tried to remain hidden behind Sledge's large frame, but Kore took a step over to inspect who was present. He felt the blood drain out of his face as Kore looked him right in the eyes. His eyes lingered on him for a minute.

"Drop your weapons now!" demanded Kore, as he aimed his pistol directly at Vosco's head. "I have you outnumbered by ten-to-one and each of you has a gun pointed at your face. It will not end well if you try to fight."

They slowly dropped their weapons to the ground. They felt helpless. Even Sledge knew a losing battle when he saw one. The sound of his wooden bat hitting the hard rock floor echoed across the room.

Kore immediately walked over to Terry. Everyone's eyes followed. *What was going on?* Kore raised his gun to Terry's temple. The stainless-steel gun was just inches from his forehead. He began to sweat. His Adam's apple practically burst as he tried to swallow.

Kore let him sweat it out for a few more seconds. The he dropped the gun by his side and smiled at Terry. There was a communal sigh of relief.

"I only need one thing from your dismal looking group," said Kore, looking back at Daniel. "Thank you for bringing me the human, Terry."

Vosco turned to Terry, shaking with anger.

"Terry? You did this?" he asked.

Terry didn't respond, but everyone could see the guilt on his face. His shoulders slumped. He had given in to the reward.

"You traitor!" yelled his brother from behind. "How could you do this?"

"Oh, shut up. It doesn't matter," spat Kore. "I was going to find the human anyways. All he did was speed up the process. Now get Terry out of here and give him his money, so I can deal with these maggots."

"You told me you wouldn't hurt any of my friends if I gave you Daniel!" yelled Terry as two guards ushered him out of the room.

"I changed my mind," said Kore as he watched his men drag him out by his arms.

Kore's attention settled back on Daniel the way a lion focuses on its prey. He slowly paced around him, not saying a word. Daniel kept staring down at his feet. Kore continued to pace. Daniel finally had the courage to look him in the eyes. They looked as though they belonged to a serpent. His big, black pupils gave Daniel the chills.

"This is the human you poor villagers have been hiding from me?

Kore looked Daniel up and down. "He sure doesn't look like someone to die for."

Kore laughed. His men followed suit.

"Guys, seriously… this can't be your new hero. Look at him. He's a weak teenager. Your chosen one looks like he should be at home popping pimples. He can't be that great if he led you into this predicament."

His men kept laughing.

Kore walked up to Vosco. "What happened, Vosco? You couldn't find anyone better?"

He looked at his men. "If this is the best America has to offer, then maybe we don't even need to shut down their power grid."

The place erupted in more laughter. Daniel's fear transformed into fury. He could handle the name calling, but he couldn't get used to the laughter.

Kore moved in front of Daniel.

"Boy," he said coolly. "Why are you here?"

Daniel remained silent.

Kore raised his hand and pointed the gun at Daniel's head.

"Answer me now—or you die."

He was about to lie, but his grandfather's words rang out in his head once more: *If you're going to face your fears, then you might as well face 'em head on.*

"I'm here to hack into your computer system."

The entire room was swallowed by silence. The answer caught Kore off guard as well. Everyone waited for him to respond.

He turned to his small army of men. They still had their weapons drawn. "Do you hear that, guys? The little boy here believes he was sent to hack into my system."

His men busted out into laughter once again. Daniel felt humiliated. *Why did I say that?* He instantly wished he could take it back.

Kore motioned for his men to pipe down. He moved even closer to Daniel. They were about the same height. Kore was so close he could feel his breath. It felt cold, like a reptile.

"Want to play a little game?" he asked Daniel.

He stood frozen. He wasn't sure what to say. Kore became impatient.

"I said, WOULD YOU LIKE TO PLAY A LITTLE GAME?" he shouted, spit hitting Daniel's face.

He nodded his head, while using his t-shirt sleeve to wipe the spit off his cheek.

"Here's the game," said Kore. "I'm going to give you seven minutes to hack into my system. Seven. One minute for each of you. If you somehow miraculously hack into it, then we'll give you and the rest of your Fleas a small head start, before we come and hunt you down. Sounds fair doesn't it?"

His men chuckled.

"And if you *can't* hack into the system within seven minutes, then you all die. No shocker there." Kore smiled. He was delighted with himself. "Of course, there is always option three—don't play the game at all and we can just kill you now. It's your call. I'm fine either way."

Vosco felt as though he were dying inside. How could he have let this happen? Why did he risk the lives of his men around someone he barely even knew? He had never even seen Daniel use a computer. Even if he was good, surely no one could hack into Kore's system in seven minutes. He wanted to tell all of his men he was sorry. He never meant for it to end like this. He looked over at Skylar. She was crying. Thunderclap, Evan, Whiz, Rodney, Jerry, and Sledge all had their heads bowed to the ground. They were praying for a miracle.

Three of Kore's bodyguards pulled Daniel aside. They inspected the contents of his backpack. The first thing they found was his laptop. Kore grabbed it and shoved it into Daniel's face.

"Is this your weapon of choice? Is this what's going to save you?"

Daniel nodded. He couldn't talk.

"Just to show you I'm a nice guy, here's the WiFi password," Kore said with a laugh.

He opened up Daniel's laptop and connected it to their network. He motioned for Daniel to take a seat at a small table in the corner. Kore gently put the computer down.

The main 92-inch monitor was hooked up to Daniel's laptop so everyone in the room could watch what was happening. Kore typed on his electronic wrist watch.

"Ready, set, go!" Your seven minutes have begun." He smiled at his men. He hadn't had this much fun in a long time.

The entire room watched as Daniel started searching for any obvious back doors into the network. He attempted three different penetration tests. He quickly realized Kore was too smart to leave any access points vulnerable. However, he had gained some quick intel on how he had set everything up. Daniel had spent the last ten years of his life hacking into websites, but this was by far the toughest one.

Vosco, Skylar, and the rest of the group watched with anticipation. None of them knew much about hacking. All they saw was Daniel blazing through new windows and typing furiously.

There was another fire wall. Daniel kept hitting dead ends.

"Three minutes left," yelled Kore. Daniel took a deep breath. He was out of options. He had a couple crawlers running trying to detect any access points and passwords, but that could take hours. He only had one shot left. It was a Trojan horse that he had spent two years perfecting back at home. It was built to work even if nobody clicked on the malicious virus. It was his final Hail Mary. He opened up a new window. The room watched as code went flying across the screen.

Kore dropped his gun on the table. He stepped closer to the screen. He couldn't believe it. He had never seen code so perfect... so clean. He watched hungrily as Daniel continued to stroke out line after line of code. Kore could sense he was onto something, but he found himself hypnotized by the computer screen.

Daniel was in his zone. Everything around him faded away as he funneled his energy into the hack. He knew it would take a couple more minutes to complete. He continued to type as quickly as his fingers would allow.

As Kore watched impatiently, he remembered something Maku had told him: a young man from another world would humiliate him. Could this be the one? Kore glanced at his watch. There was one minute left. Daniel was almost done. The ultimate Trojan horse was about to be launched on his network. He only needed a few more lines of code.

"Kill him," whispered Kore.

"Sir, he has thirty seconds left," replied the guard next to him, loud enough for his friends to hear.

"KILL HIM NOW!" howled Kore.

The guard aimed his rifle at Daniel's head. Before he could pull the trigger, Kore and his entire army were in the midst of a violent tornado. A thunderous shot echoed across the room, but the bullet didn't reach Daniel. Whiz had jumped into the line of fire.

"Get out now!" Whiz screamed. He was holding his chest with his left hand as a circle of dark blood grew on his shirt. His right arm was outstretched firmly, his palm pointing directly at Kore and his men. He was using every ounce of energy he had to create a monster tornado.

"GO!" he screamed.

"We can't leave you here!" Vosco yelled back.

Sledge grabbed Vosco and picked him up. "We'll never have a chance to escape like this again. We can make a plan to come back and get him once we're back in the village," lied Sledge. He knew they'd never see Whiz again.

Everyone ran for the door. Out of the corner of his eye Daniel watched as one of Kore's men was picked up by the wind and tossed against the rocky wall like a ragdoll. They ran through the dark tunnels, retracing their steps, and somehow made it to the back entrance. They emptied into the forest, dodging trees and branches, as they raced to the village. Eleven minutes later, the storm had died down.

The Fleas had escaped, except for Whiz. Kore's men began to collect themselves. They were badly beaten. A few had bloody noses. The guard Daniel had seen flying through the air still lay on his back. He was out cold. The rest of the men were dazed. They began to inspect the area. Besides a few cracked monitors, the network was untouched. Daniel never had a chance to engage his virus.

"Well, well, well… what do we have here?" Khan asked, a smirk on his face.

He reached down to grab the laptop, which lay on the ground. It was Daniel's; his secret weapon. Kore smiled. All of Daniel's short codes and pre-saved HTMLs were now at his fingertips. He couldn't wait to see what was on the hard drive. Strangely, he reminded Kore of himself. He couldn't help but remember the delight he felt watching Daniel in is element. He was fast, agile, and fearless in front of a computer. He knew the minute he saw Daniel's coding skills that this was the boy Maku had predicted. He needed to be destroyed.

"Sir," said Kahn, interrupting his leader's thoughts. "What was that virus he coded on the computer? I've never seen anything like it."

Kore was silent for a brief moment.

"It was… fine." Kore stopped himself from saying *brilliant.* "Even if he had deployed it, all it would have done was shut down a small portion of our systems. It wouldn't have impacted the impending power grid shutdown or the electrical project I've been working on."

Kahn smiled. "What do you want us to do next?"

"Bring me that boy dead or alive. Even if it means killing every villager in Alcazar."

# 19 THE SPEECH

"Maybe I wasn't such a great mentor after all," Jack said under his breath. "I sure never prepared him for this."

He was shaking his head while watching the news. The country was falling apart. The last thirty minutes had been one vicious attack on the president after another. Even his own party had completely turned on him. There were countless websites and political bloggers demanding impeachment.

Jack was living in his son's trailer home. He had stuck around to take care of his property after his death. Mark didn't have much of anything, so the entire process was pretty quick. By the time he looked into getting a bus ride back to California, all the major highways were closed due to the nationwide riots. Hardly anyone was working thanks to Kore. It looked like he would be staying in St. Augustine for the foreseeable future. He wondered how Daniel was doing in Alcazar. From what Jack could see on the news, he guessed they hadn't slowed Kore down one bit. Jack was itching to go down there and help...

Earlier that day, Kore had made an announcement over the Internet that the president had challenged him to a debate. It would take place that evening. He also urged every American eighteen or older to register for their free online bank account, so he could start depositing money into their accounts. It practically shut down the Internet. People were already posting screenshots on social media of money being wired into their accounts. This fueled the fire even more. Free money was just too hard to resist. No one wanted to miss out.

President Jay McFarland watched his trusted board of advisors dwindle to half of what it was. Then it became half of that. None of the career politicians wanted to be associated with Jay when the ball dropped. They were more worried about getting reelected than sticking around and fighting for their country.

Perhaps they were right—from the looks of it, there was simply no way to win this battle. What Kore lacked in manpower, he made up for in his ability to manipulate his followers. Most Americans were already sold. He was like the kid in high school running for class president with a promise to deliver ice cream for lunch every day— while his opponent promised broccoli. It was no wonder the number one selling t-shirt on *Amazon* was now 'Kore For President.'

To make matters worse, the president's wealthy supporters had pulled away as well. Due to all of the fear and uncertainty, the stock market had collapsed. In the last two days alone, the Dow Jones Index was down twenty-six percent—the biggest two-day drop ever. A quarter of the world's wealth had essentially vanished into thin air. Investors were pulling their money out as fast as they could. It was a true run on the bank. It might have been even worse if they didn't shut down the markets early to stop the bleeding. People cancelled their real estate deals at breakneck speed causing another crash. The world was living in fear. The future scared them more than the present or past.

Mary handed Jay the latest press release. The president glanced at the headline.

### "Tonight's Debate: The President's Final Curtain Call"

*For once, the news is right,* he thought. *Maybe I should just take the offer and disappear.*

He paced around the room. A few of his trusted advisors were still there. He had spent more hours in the Situation Room than any other president in history over a three-day period. He desperately needed a shower and a shave, but there was a new fire to put out every five minutes. Public transportation had come to a complete halt. Flights were cancelled nationwide. Entire cities were on fire due to rioting. There weren't enough police and firefighters to contain the chaos.

Jay still pondered how he, supposedly the most powerful man in the country, had now become one of the weakest. Just thirty days ago, he had everything imaginable at his disposal. He had an endless number of cheerleaders at his back, the largest economy in the world, and the largest military in the world. He looked up at his team, who were all working quietly on their laptops.

"Did it ever feel this helpless in the past?" Jay asked Admiral Hardy, the oldest member of his cabinet still around. The admiral, although a bit irritable and old school at times, was still the kind of guy you wanted on your team when things got tough. The country didn't seem to make men like him anymore; men who still believed it was an honor to fight until the end—even while your ship is sinking. It gave Jay a slight feeling of hope seeing the admiral come in every morning.

"Well, this is certainly unlike anything I've ever seen," replied the Admiral. "This Kore guy seems to be a Hitler and Lenin hybrid—a cold-blooded, socialist, communist killer. He is the kind of man, who won't stop at anything to gain control. What's really scary is how well he knows exactly what to say to American people to get them on his side. It's like he's reading their minds. He knows every weakness and fear they have. He tells them exactly what they want to hear. He's better than any politician I've ever seen—and I've seen a ton of them over the years. I just hope it's not too late when we finally find a way to stop him."

Jay looked over at Bruce Cromwell, Secretary of Defense. He was shocked Bruce was still around. He always had the feeling Bruce didn't like him.

"Bruce, what's the latest on the power grid? Can he really shut down the entire thing?"

"Yes and no. Although a big chunk of the interconnected power system grid is all tied together via the Internet, it would be impossible to shut the entire thing down without the help from real people at each of the main locations. We've already sent in trusted agents to each area. They are armed and have been told to do whatever it takes to keep the power on."

"Sir," interrupted Darren Daley, the National Security Advisor to the President. "Do you really think this debate with Kore tonight is a wise choice? I mean, you aren't exactly the most popular guy right now. Heck, you're not even the underdog. I just don't see how this will do anything but result in public humiliation for you and the rest of us in this room."

The president noticed everyone nodding in agreement. Mary seemed to be the only one with an ounce of support left in her eyes. He paced around the room. No one said a word. They all just wanted this to end.

The president stopped pacing. He had made up his mind. He was sick and tired of being pushed around by this terrorist.

"I've got to face this guy tonight. We all have to face Kore."

Everyone looked up. Jay stood up in front of the room and arched his back. His two-day old white shirt hadn't seen a tie since yesterday. His sleeves were rolled up. His face showed signs of determination.

"I can't let this terrorist continue to interrupt our lives and brainwash *our country* with his fear tactics. We've got to fight back. Is this not the same country, which fought tooth and nail against England to gain its freedom? Is this not the same nation, which birthed the Declaration of Independence and the United States Constitution? Are we not the same people, who learned how to fly and land on the moon? Of course we are! We're Americans. We were born fighters. It's time to fight back. I plan on exposing him to the world tonight. I'm going to do everything in my power to make such a fool of him that even the rats in the sewers won't want anything to do with him."

\*\*\*

Eric, the Flea who could become instantly invisible, was beside himself. He was pacing back and forth in the secret room under Sledge's house. He was belligerent. He had just lost his best friend. The crew had only shortly arrived, and already there was chaos inside of Sledge's basement.

Besides Terry, the traitor who would never show his face in town again, Whiz was the only person who didn't make it back alive. To make matters worse, Eric blamed Daniel for his death.

"It was you!" Eric yelled pointing at Daniel. "Kore was aiming for you! You were supposed to die back there—not Whiz!" he screamed at Daniel.

The room fell silent. People were tending to their bumps and bruises. They all looked up. Daniel could feel his face turning red. He was flustered and at a loss for words. He wished someone else would speak up. He looked over at Vosco, but Vosco looked deflated. He had lost yet another man in battle—something he'd sworn would never happen again. He wanted to throw in the towel and give up.

Thunderclap finally came to the rescue.

"Eric," he said gently. "I understand how you must be feeling right now—we're all hurt by this—but blaming Daniel isn't going to bring Whiz back. We're all on the same team here. The only way that we have another chance at stopping Kore is to work together."

Eric stood there looking angry and bewildered. He was scared. It was one thing to experience hell on Earth with your best friend at your side. It was entirely different to have to go through it all alone. Eric gave Daniel one last dirty look and slumped into the chair at the back of the room.

"We've all had a long day," said Sledge. "Everyone needs some rest before we make another run at it later this evening."

"Have you guys gone mad?!" replied Eric from the back, shooting up out of his chair. "Didn't you see what happened back there? We lost one of our best friends. What are we trying to prove? How many more people do you want to lose, Vosco?"

Vosco looked up. The pain in his eyes was obvious.

Eric sat back down in his chair with his arms folded. "We are outnumbered by the thousands. That back entrance is certainly being sealed back up as we speak. Besides, your so called 'chosen one' doesn't even have his laptop anymore..."

The entire group was quiet.

Eric stood up. The more he talked, the angrier he became.

"How do we even know he's the chosen one? Huh? Did anyone confirm it with Maku? Aren't there seven billion people up above? It seems like there is a high probability that you and Skylar could have grabbed the wrong human. Things weren't great before he arrived, but now they are worse. Not only did we lose Whiz, but now we are all marked. We're going to have to spend the rest of our lives hiding in fear."

Daniel felt like the entire room was spinning. Deep down, he wanted to come clean. He didn't want to keep this lie going. If he told them the truth, there was no way they would ever trust him again. He couldn't go back to his old life—the constant teasing, harassment, and uncomfortable staring. He had finally ditched his wheelchair, and he wasn't going to go back.

"Maku told me I'm the one," he lied.

Everyone looked at him without saying anything.

"He also told me that there's something looming over this village, which is far worse than Kore. It's what has been holding you back from being happy and prosperous."

Now he had their ears. The entire room listened attentively. They were on the edge of their seats.

"FEAR. You all live in complete fear. The worst part is that you brought it upon yourself. Yes, Kore is a part of it, but who created Kore? YOU ALL DID!"

Daniel was suddenly shouting. He hadn't realized what he'd been feeling until this moment.

"When Kore was young, he only had a few friends. You all outnumbered him a thousand to one. You labeled him as different, and this allowed him to grow more different. You alienated him because you were afraid of someone DIFFERENT. Then it was too late. Alone, unloved, and feared, he grew into the monster you created."

Daniel was sweating. His face was bright red and his muscles were tight. Was he talking about Kore or himself?

"The truth is, having a 'chosen one' is a scapegoat so you don't have to take responsibility for anything. If your chosen one succeeds, then you're safe. If he fails, then you can blame him for having to continue to live in FEAR!!! You are all too afraid to fix this yourselves!"

No one spoke. Daniel couldn't stop talking.

"Am I right? Huh? Am I right?" Daniel yelled. "Why was today the very first time in almost fifteen years that any of you have ever set foot in his underground fortress? Oh, and NOW you're 'marked'? What were the Fleas doing before I arrived?!"

Daniel lowered his voice.

"I know what it's like to live in fear. In fact, I've spent the majority of my life in fear—just like you. Every day I was afraid of people laughing at me. I was afraid to go into public places because people would stare at me and talk behind my back. I was afraid to approach adults because they would treat me like a baby. I was afraid to approach young kids because they would ask why I was 'retarded.' I was afraid to try anything new… to take chances. Lastly, I was afraid to love because everyone who had ever cared for me seemed to die… including my own mom and dad. I know fear better than almost anyone, and I could smell it coming from this village a mile away."

Daniel wiped a tear trickling down his face.

"You know what? I also discovered another little secret today. Do you want to know what it was?"

A few people in the room managed nods.

"I can beat Kore at his own game."

The room straightened almost in unison.

"Something crazy happened when I found myself only a few feet from Kore. It was like a spirit entered my body. I should have been scared, but I wasn't. He was pointing a gun at my head, yet I wasn't afraid. In fact, I felt more confident than I've ever felt because I felt *his* fear. I could smell it on him. As soon as I felt it, I knew I was doing something right. I've created a weapon, and I'm not afraid to use it."

"Friends, it's time we face our fears. It's time we stop blaming each other and making excuses. It's time we take a stand... a stand for what's right. It's time we actually go after the things we want. I'm tired of living a life full of regrets. I don't know about you, but I'm not going to sit here while they go kill more innocent people. I don't want that hanging over my head. Even in the face of death, I'll know I did what I could. I'm headed back down there tonight to release my virus into his system. Time is running out. Who's with me?"

No one said a word.

Daniel paced around the room. He looked at each one of them, praying someone would join him. All he needed was one person, but no one budged.

The men looked around at each other, wondering if anyone was crazy enough to follow him. No one came forward. Daniel wondered if he was willing to do this by himself.

"I'm out," said Eric. "This is ludicrous. I don't want any part of it." He crossed his arms and gave everyone a stern look.

"Ditto," another voice said.

It was Skylar. She stood up to walk out. "You know how protective my mom is. I already lied to her about where I was today. I'm not going to do it again. I'm headed home."

Daniel watched her slowly walk up the steps. She shut the door to the hidden room behind her. She was gone. He was stunned. He'd known that Skylar didn't like him, but after all they had been through the past two days, he thought for sure he could count on her. He began to feel defeated.

"Well, I'm in," came a voice from the back.

Everyone looked back to see Jerry raising his arm up high.

"I owe you guys for my double-crossing brother. I intend on making it up to you tenfold. Like Daniel, I refuse to keep living in fear. Let's do this."

"You can count on me, too," said another voice. It was

Thunderclap.

"I've got your back, Daniel," came the voice of Sledge.

Daniel smiled at Sledge. One by one the remaining members agreed to join the crusade: Rodney, the flame thrower; Keypad, the tech guy; Evan, the beetle; Ian, the freezer; Scooter, the skunk. Eric, however, still sat there with his arms crossed.

There was a violent knock at the door.

Then another.

"Are you expecting anyone?" Vosco asked Sledge in a hushed tone.

"No. It could be Skylar changing her mind. Just in case it's not, get your weapons ready."

Sledge put his ear to the door. He heard a familiar voice—his wife's.

"Sledge, it's me. Sorry to interrupt, but you and Daniel have got to see this."

"Hang tight, guys. Keep your weapons ready. It could be some kind of trap."

Daniel and Sledge slowly walked up the stairs and into the living room. They shut the trap door and walked towards Sledge's wife. She appeared to be alone. She guided them to the front door. On the doorstep there was a gigantic, majestic bald eagle. It had something in its mouth.

Daniel had only one thought: Jack.

The lines of Jack's bald eagle tattoo were carved into his memory. He remembered retracing them on the bus as he unknowingly observed his grandfather for the first time. He had no idea how Jack did it, but he knew this was his way of helping. After all, no one else knew Daniel was here, and nobody else would think to send such a powerful American symbol.

Sledge took the item excitingly and they made their way back down into the basement.

"Wait until you see this everyone."

He held up a document, which continued to unroll onto the ground. There was no mistaking what it was: a detailed map of Kore's entire underground system, including all the secret rooms and hidden passages.

Vosco looked over at Daniel with a grin.

*He must be the one.*

# 20 THE GREAT DEBATE

It was one hour until showtime.

The president was in his green room. He was sweating bullets. He had just given his pep talk to the team not too long ago, but for the first time in his political career, his confidence was dwindling. He wasn't sure why, but over the last few hours he was wondering if he had made a huge mistake challenging Kore to a debate.

The White House was as empty as it had been in decades. Everyone seemed to want as much distance from the president as possible. Many went home to watch the debate with their families. Both the House and the Senate voted themselves a leave of absence and shut down for the day. Jay had to completely turn off all social media. There wasn't a single media outlet in the country, who had his back. He still had a devout following, but it consisted of the small business owners and ultra-conservative voters who wanted nothing to do with socialism. America, for the most part, wanted Jay gone.

Meanwhile, miles below in Alcazar, Daniel had just seen his face on TV for the first time. The Fleas had been planning their attack and dissecting the secret map, when Sledge's wife alerted them that to something urgent. Daniel wondered if another mysterious bald eagle had arrived—nobody yet had been able to explain how or why that had happened. When they surfaced into the living room, Daniel's jaw dropped. His image was plastered on the TV screen. The excitement of seeing himself on TV didn't overpower the panic he felt when he saw the headline below.

## WANTED: HUMAN FUGITIVE. $10,000,000 REWARD.

They continued to watch as the news video showed each of them sneaking around Kore's underground headquarters. Their entire break-in had been captured on film. The segment portrayed them to be terrorists, who were armed, dangerous, and out to hurt the people of Alcazar. It ended with a blurb about how each of them was wanted for treason.

Vosco felt sick to his stomach as he imagined how the conversation was going over at Skylar's house with her overly-protective mother. He was certain she was bawling her eyes out knowing her daughter was a wanted fugitive.

The team, led by Vosco, Daniel, and Sledge, all agreed that the best plan was to launch the attack right before the debate was scheduled to go live. They knew Kore's entire army would be watching it. Every citizen in Alcazar would be glued to their TV or device. It was the one time Kore might have his guard down. He'd never expect them back the same day.

Looking at the map, there were far more secret tunnels and rooms than they ever could have imagined. The tunnels were connected to manholes throughout the city, which explained a lot. It was always baffling how Kore's men would appear in the street out of nowhere at just the right time. Now it all made sense. The group agreed that they would need to split up into two groups. There were two manholes in the right location for their attack.

One of the manholes opened up above a tunnel near Kore's main control center. It was one of the original tunnels, which had been abandoned before it was ever completed. It ended only a few feet away from the main control room. Daniel, Sledge, and Thunderclap were going to go that route. Even if it was a dead end, they were hoping Sledge could create a new entrance from there.

Vosco would take Evan, Jerry, Keypad, Rodney, Jerry, Ian, and Scooter with him. He would lead them into a nearby manhole, which was connected to a corridor where all traffic in and out of the control room passed. The plan was to let Daniel, Sledge, and Thunderclap go first. Once inside, the rest of the team would prevent additional soldiers from entering. They had to buy enough time for Daniel to shut down Kore's system. The mission would only be a success if he could hack into the mainframe and prevent the power grid from being shut down. Daniel was confident his Trojan horse virus would work.

Vosco looked down at his watch.

"We've got an hour before showtime. Let's go."

The group crept off into the dark night. The two manholes were about a mile down the street. Vosco had snuck around the village at night many times before, but he could never recall his heart beating so fast.

"This way," whispered Sledge. They knew they were getting close when Sledge spoke up. "This one is yours, Vosco."

Vosco nodded and gave a signal for his team to stop. "See you down there. Be safe."

In another forty feet was the next manhole. Sledge had no problems popping the steel cover off with his mighty hands. Daniel and Thunderclap watched in awe as Sledge picked it up and placed it gently on the ground. He pointed for Daniel to lead the way.

Daniel clambered down into the tunnel. It was pitch black. He felt his way down the dark, musty stairwell. When his feet touched bottom, he turned on his headlight. There was a small passage ahead, but it was quite obviously a dead end. Daniel shined his beam on the map. According to the map, there shouldn't have been a dead end there. Sledge and Thunderclap caught up to him.

"What's that?" whispered Sledge, as he pointed to an area on the wall with a small indention. "Shine your light back in that area. I could have sworn I saw something."

Daniel saw it too. It was a small circular button, which was concealed within the wall. It was dark green, and blended in perfectly with the moldy rock. He pushed the button. The fear of the unknown sent a chill through his body. At first nothing happened. Daniel wondered if it had set off an alarm for Kore. He turned around to face Thunderclap and Sledge. They just shrugged their shoulders.

"Hit it again," said Sledge. Before Daniel could it a second time, the wall in front of them began to shift. The three of them watched as the wall opened up into a secret passage. Daniel's light bounced off the walls. There was another set of smooth stone steps, which appeared to lead further downward. Old brass lamps hung from the walls. Daniel paused to look down at his map. This passageway should take them right behind Kore's main control center. He gave Sledge and Thunderclap a nod. They continued down the spiral staircase.

Meanwhile, Vosco and his team had all descended into the nearby manhole. They found themselves in a holding room, which was directly above the corridor to the control center. The room was barren and perfectly square. There was a small door with a handle on the floor, which would put them exactly where they wanted to be. It was tight, but there was just enough room for the eight of them. As long as Scooter didn't let any odors out, they would be okay. The plan was to drop into the corridor when they received a text from Daniel or Sledge—or if they heard any commotion.

Daniel, Thunderclap, and Sledge had reached the bottom of the stairs. It was still pitch black. Daniel moved his head lamp around slowly. They appeared to be standing in a large room, which was completely empty. According to the map, they were just a couple feet away from Kore's main control center.

"It's nothing but a dead end," whispered Daniel, frowning at the wall in front of him.

"I don't know," said Thunderclap. "Remember the hidden button earlier? I'm willing to bet there's another one down here on somewhere."

"What was that?" Daniel whispered in a petrified voice. He shined the light at Thunderclap and Sledge. They didn't hear anything. The three of them remained silent.

This time they all heard it. Voices were coming from the spiral staircase behind them. It was two men talking. They were coming their way. Sledge pointed to the back, left corner. Daniel turned off his light and the three of them quietly shuffled over there. They stood with their backs against the wall, praying the men coming down the staircase didn't see them.

The voices seemed closer now. Daniel recognized one voice immediately. It was Kore. His heart started beating faster. Daniel watched as a small flashlight beam flooded the dark room. Kore and his companion were at the bottom of the stairs. Daniel could hear every word of their conversation.

"It looks like it was another false alarm. Nobody was out in the streets after curfew," said the soldier.

Kore grunted. "I was really hoping it was the boy. I had to go and see for myself. I'm sure he'll be brought to me very soon. I can feel it."

"What do you want us to do with him if we find him?" asked the guard.

"Kill him, and then bring me his body."

The color drained from Daniel's face. He hadn't realized he wanted him dead. Kore and his soldier walked up to the wall in and pressed a hidden button. A large door swung open, creaking as it moved. Light from the control room engulfed the staircase behind it. None of them spoke. Daniel's heart was now hammering against his chest.

The light was only inches away from exposing them, when the door finally came to a stop. The three of them took a deep breath.

"Sir, do you want me to close this door?" asked his guard.

Kore glanced at the door. The shadow line made it impossible for Kore to see them, even though the three of them could see directly into the room. Daniel looked down. He couldn't bear to look at Kore in the eyes.

"Just keep it open for now. I'm going to head back up there and get some fresh air once the debate is over," replied Kore.

He took a seat next to one of his engineers and his personal assistant, Dagney. They were discussing the debate, which was set to start in thirty-five minutes. Kore was already mic'd and ready to go. He just needed to bounce some last-minute debate ideas off of Dagney.

Daniel had an idea. The only thing which separated them from Kore was a twenty-foot shadow. He had a clear shot at hacking into Kore's system from here. Daniel still had his network password after he had secretly shared it with all of his devices earlier. He whispered something into Sledge's ear. Sledge nodded his head and shifted his large body in front of Daniel.

He turned on his iPad and lowered the display brightness as much as it would go. His plan was to hack into the computer system and find a way to start Live streaming Kore's discussion with Dagney. The small, red light on Kore's microphone receiver was on, and he knew exactly how to hack into the audio.

He just prayed enough people were already plugged into the Live stream to hear Kore's incriminating discussion with Dagney.

Daniel started typing away on his iPad. His heart was racing. He was in his element. Before he tried to humiliate Kore on camera, he needed to release the Trojan horse on his computer system...

\*\*\*

## The White House Green Room: 11 Minutes Before The Live Debate

Jay's heart was racing as if he'd been sprinting. He should have been in his element by now. After all, he was about to enter his comfort zone: debating. He tried his best to take deep breaths to get ahold of the anxiety. He had never been so nervous in his life. His life and entire career depended on this debate.

There was a loud knock on the door to the green room. He practically jumped. Before he could say a word, the door swung open and crashed against the back wall.

"You've got to see this!"

It was Mary. She was holding her phone. Her hands were shaking with excitement. Something was playing on her device. There were two men talking to each other. The camera seemed a bit far away, but you could hear every word.

"Getting away with this has been too easy," one laughed.

"Well, sir, with all due respect… the American people are sheep."

The black-haired man slapped his friend on the back, nearly choking on his laughter.

"They're idiots—all of them!" he exclaimed.

"They are far too easy to manipulate," the other added.

"Give me a challenge, someone, *please*," the black-haired one begged, rolling his eyes.

The conversation was excruciating to watch. Mary and the president cringed as the man in all black made death threats to all Americans, who didn't align themselves with his dictatorship.

Text popped up on the screen, identifying the person talking. All it said was KORE.

The president slowly lifted a finger and pointed at the man with jet black hair on the screen.

"That's him? That's Kore? He looks like a witch."

No one had seen him before, but the voice was impossible to forget. It was him. Mary nodded.

"He's definitely not the most attractive guy. You won't believe what he said a few minutes ago. He called us everything from puppets to beggars to roaches. He even said he's planning on turning us into his slaves once he takes over!"

"How did this happen? Who's filming this?"

Mary wasn't listening to him. She was trying to pay attention to what Kore was saying. He was belittling the poor.

"Ninety percent of Americans are useless! They deserve what they have coming!" spat Kore.

"Is this being recorded?" asked the president.

Mary gave him an impatient look.

"Of course. It's the Internet. Everything is recorded. There are over 500 million people watching this live right now. By tomorrow morning, billions will have seen this."

"Mary. Cancel the debate. As soon as he's done humiliating himself, I'm going live to the public to announce that we're taking back our country."

She nodded. He grabbed her wrist gently. She could tell he wanted to tell her something important.

"You've got to promise me one thing."

She looked back at him and nodded. She'd do anything for the president.

"You've got to promise me that you'll go along with my story."

Mary looked confused. "What do you mean? What story?"

"Listen, Mary, I've got to take full credit for whole hidden camera deal. It's the only way I can earn back the trust of the American people. It's the only way they'll follow me as their leader again. They've got to believe that I planned this. Didn't everyone tell me the other day that my job is telling the American people what they want to hear?"

He felt guilty the second it came out of his mouth.

"Let me get this straight. You plan on lying to them in order to earn their trust?" She replied skeptically. She had never seen him lie. Was he just like all of the other politicians? Her affection towards him was waning.

"It's not like that. I mean—it's not what it looks like. Mary, if we tell the public we have no idea who did this, then they won't know who to believe anymore. Someone has to take credit for this, and I can't think of anyone who needs it more right now than me... than us. I can't lose this job."

Mary was about to challenge the president, when she noticed Kore had stopped talking. They looked down at the screen. The view started shaking a bit, as if the person filming was suddenly scrambling to hide the camera. The man next to Kore pointed directly at the camera. The entire nation watched as he walked quietly in that direction.

Kore walked into the dark room with two armed guards flanking him. America—and most of the world—watched with uncertain anticipation. It was reality TV on steroids. Who was behind the camera? Who set him up? Everyone was dying to know.

Daniel tried to keep the iPad steady, but each step Kore took made his hands shake. He was only ten feet away when one of the men flipped a light switch. The space lit up like a hospital operating room. Daniel kept on filming as his hands trembled.

"You'll die for this!" was the last thing the public saw before Kore's body engulfed the screen. Then everything went blank.

# 21 UNDERGROUND WAR

"That's our sign," whispered Vosco.

The eight of them were still crammed into the small room above the corridor. They were secretly happy to hear the loud crash followed by a bunch of yelling from below. Scooter's odors practically had them gagging.

"Let's go."

Vosco lifted open the hatch, which led directly into the corridor near the control center. He peeked down to make sure the coast was clear. A soldier was running by and noticed the open hatch. Before he could pull out his pistol, Vosco leapt through the air and kicked the man in the face. The impact knocked him out cold.

The rest of the team jumped down from their hiding spot. Ian started looking for a place to hide the soldier's body. Before he could do anything, they heard footsteps running their way—lots of them. Around the corner came at least ten armed guards.

Vosco and his team fled down the corridor towards the main control center. They came to an abrupt stop. A thick steel door blocked their way. A bullet whizzed by them and ricocheted off the walls.

"No more shots!" echoed a voice from behind them. It was the leader of the guards. "That ricochet almost killed us. Wait until we get closer."

Vosco yelled frantically, "Look for a button. FAST!"

"Found one!" shouted Jerry as he mashed the button down as quickly as he could. A second steel door slammed shut behind them. Now, they were trapped.

153

"What do we do now?" asked Rodney. "Not even my flames can put a dent in this steel."

"Keep looking for another button. There has to be a way to open this door so we can get to Daniel, Sledge, and Thunderclap. Make sure no one presses the button that opens up the back side—or we're dead."

They scoured the walls for any sign of a button. Each of them took turns using their special powers to open the door. Rodney tried to heat up the steel. Keypad tried to hack into a lock system with no luck. Ian tried to freeze the bottom of the door to no avail. Finally, Evan turned into a beetle and attempted to slide under the door.

"You thought you could sneak back in and make me look bad?" Kore spoke softly.

He had the three of them cornered with an armed guard on either side of him. Dagney had left the control room to get help.

"That fat slob of a prophet was right after all. You did embarrass me. Well done. Now it's my turn. I'm going to take immense pleasure in killing you."

Kore's face was far from amused. His expression was deadly serious. In fact, the intensity of his gaze made Daniel break eye contact.

"Look at me, boy!" he screamed. Daniel hesitantly gazed upwards to find a sly smile on Kore's dark face. "I want you to remember my face when I break you with my new electromagnetic gun. The exciting news is that you'll be the first one to try it out."

Kore pulled something out of his belt holster. It looked like a pistol with four intertwined titanium barrels. He pointed the gun at Daniel's chest. It felt like slow motion as Kore pulled the trigger. Was this how it was all going to end?

Electric waves shot out of the four muzzles and stabbed Daniel. His body went limp. Electricity jolted through his body, as though he had been struck by lightning.

Suddenly, he felt his body flying through the air. He heard screams. He landed with a thud on the ground. It felt like his back was broken. He opened his eyes just in time to see Kore's fist coming towards face. His punch broke Daniel's nose. He was barely conscious. He tried to open his eyes, but he couldn't. The warm stickiness behind his head told him that he was bleeding rather profusely.

More screams were coming from behind him. He didn't have enough energy to turn his head. He opened his eye in time to see

Sledge's massive body come thundering down next to him. The limestone floor practically cracked beneath him. Daniel watched as Kore picked Sledge up again with his electromagnetic gun. He slammed him to the ground once more in order to finish him off. Sledge's body went limp. A trickle of blood crept down his lip.

"Sledge... I'm sorry," was all Daniel could muster.

He tried to move his arm to wipe away a tear, but he couldn't. He felt paralyzed. It reminded him of his old body in his old chair.

Something else flew across the room. It was Thunderclap. Daniel watched as his friend was being tossed around like a rag doll. *We're all moments away from dying,* he thought. The two bodyguards watched as Kore used his gun over and over again.

Daniel closed his eyes. He couldn't bear to watch anymore. He wondered if his Trojan horse virus had worked before Kore had shattered his iPad against the wall. Where was Vosco and his team when they needed them?

Thunderclap's body hit the ground one final time. Kore dropped his special electricity gun and crouched down beside Daniel. Through his swollen eyelids, Daniel could make out a dark face covered in small, black whiskers. He could see Kore's pointed brown teeth. He smelled like sweat and blood. Daniel's heart was pounding against his bruised ribs. Kore pulled out his normal gun. Daniel heard him engage a fresh bullet. He gently touched the barrel to Daniel's face. This was it. This was how it was going to end. Daniel closed his eyes. He waited for the gun shot.

There was a short pause.

Daniel peeked through his right eye. Was he dead already? No. Kore was swatting violently at his neck. There was a tiny, blue beetle. Kore jumped up, dropping his gun. It was like watching a child trying to dodge a bee. He continued to slap his neck and back, but the beetle was too fast for him. As soon as it pinched him, it was already somewhere else, pinching him again.

"Don't just stand there! Help me, you idiots!" Kore screamed to his two men. They looked puzzled. He continued to dance around the room. Kore finally grabbed the beetle from his neck and threw it. It lay motionless on its hard-shelled back.

"Squash it! I'm going to finish off the boy!"

Daniel had begun to get some feeling back in his body. His fingers and toes were tingling. It was the same feeling you get when your foot falls asleep. He tried to clench his fist. It worked. He still didn't have full mobility in his arm. He saw Kore walking towards him. *Please work for me this one last time.*

Kore knelt back down next to Daniel. A tiny drop of sweat rolled off his forehead onto Daniel's chest. Kore grabbed the gun he had dropped earlier. He checked the chamber. It was still loaded. He placed the barrel up against Daniel's forehead. Daniel tried to move his legs. Nothing. His arms wouldn't move either. He closed his eyes and waited for death, but in its place came a loud thud. He could no longer feel Kore's presence over him. Sledge had woken up beside him and thrust his colossal legs out. They made direct contact with Kore's stomach and launched him into the air. There was a loud snap as he landed directly on his neck.

The two guards in the corner heard it too. They were still trying to chase down the beetle, which had sprung back to life. They were shocked to see their fearless leader on the floor... paralyzed.

One of the guards felt a tap on his shoulder. He turned around and was met by Evan's fist in his face. Evan had shape-shifted back into his normal body. He laid out the first guard with one heavy punch. The second guard turned around, only to be met with an identical punch to the face.

Evan saw his three comrades still struggling to get up. Only Daniel had his eyes open. Evan ran over to the big steel door, which he had snuck under earlier. He quickly located the button on the wall and tapped it with his hand. The door slid upwards, disappearing into the ceiling. Vosco and the rest of his team ran in, hitting the button one more time to shut the door behind him. The first thing they noticed was Kore. He hadn't moved since he hit the floor, and he appeared to be dead. Blood was pooling around his jet-black hair as if it were some hellish version of a halo. Vosco ran over to check his pulse. Nothing. He turned around and gave his team a look that said it all. The plan had worked. Kore was gone. Daniel must be the one. They rushed over to pick up Daniel and Thunderclap as carefully as they could. It was going to take three of them to carry Sledge.

"We've got to get out of here," Vosco said as he pointed to the spiral staircase. "Kore's entire army must know about this by now."

They struggled to get the three limp bodies up the stairs. After bumbling up the narrow staircase and back through the small tunnel, they finally made it to one of the manholes.

Vosco reached up to move the manhole cover, but stopped when he heard something in the street directly above it. The sound was muffled. He tilted his head up and placed his ear near one of the tiny holes. He whispered to the rest of the team.

"It's Kore's men. There are at least two of them. They know about the attack. They're armed and waiting on us. Any ideas?"

Just then, the voices above went quiet. Vosco held his finger over his lips to signal silence, worried they'd heard his voice. Nobody expected to hear what followed. It sounded like an animal attack in the street above. There was a screech followed by a loud scream. Then there was a gunshot and a thud right above the manhole. Feet shuffled. There was a struggle as someone tried to hold their ground. Then there was another thud. Vosco looked at his team. Even in the dark room, he could see the whites of their eyes glistening with terror. What was going on up there?

The manhole cover started to move. Everyone started backing up as quickly as they could. Vosco pointed his gun up, ready to shoot. A head popped over the manhole.

"Vosco, don't shoot! It's me!"

"Eric?" Vosco recognized the voice.

The light from outside was blinding, making his face hard to recognize.

"Yes! Skylar and I came to help. I made myself invisible and took out one guard while Skylar took on the other. I wish you could have seen the nose dive she just executed. She was like a fighter jet. The coast is clear for now. Let's get you guys home before more guards show up."

They carefully moved the three injured Fleas out of the manhole. Sledge barely fit. Daniel came up last. He caught his breath for a moment. His ribs were broken and his head was throbbing, but he was relieved to be above ground and far away from Kore. Skylar leaned down unexpectedly and kissed Daniel on his puffy cheek. Nobody had ever kissed him before.

"Daniel, thank you for helping me get over my fears. Your courage inspired me to tell my mother the truth about what I really want out of life. That's why I'm here—to fight for justice," she said.

"I thought you hated me," he said through his swollen lips as his eyes became tearful.

She laughed.

157

"I did. Don't make me change my mind again..."

# 22 CELEBRATION

The celebrations rang out across America.

Shortly after Kore's hidden camera performance, the president had gone live announcing Kore's defeat. He replayed the entire hidden video with his own commentary, reiterating all of the reasons why America will never allow a socialist terrorist to take over the country. The president took full credit. This baffled even his closest advisors, but they didn't really care. Everyone was ready for the country to get back to normal.

The riots began to fizzle out and lose momentum—minus a few areas still demanding a new world order. Most people still didn't like or trust the president. It was one of those instances in politics where they settled on the best of the worst...

The stock market announced it would re-open the following morning, which lead to the largest pre-open upswings in history. The world was less fearful. Other world leaders sent congratulatory messages to the president. They needed the stability of America.

President McFarland did his best to dodge any questions regarding the hidden camera. He kept saying that it was classified information. He reiterated that America was now safe from a hostage takeover and any type of power disruption. The main headline across the Internet that evening was:

**President's Clandestine Operation Defeats Kore**

Jay had completely shrugged off the white lie as he chugged down his third glass of champagne. Tonight was a well-deserved celebration. Besides, who would ever know the difference?

The cheers and laughter in the White House continued well into the night. Everyone was in great spirits. Members of the cabinet, who had vanished, were coming out of the woodworks to celebrate. They laughed about some of their co-workers, who had taken Kore's offer to leave the country. Was their paradise now officially over?

Secretary of Defense Bruce Cromwell was the only one who wasn't happy. He pulled Mary aside, pouring her a drink. Bruce never did care for the president. He thought he was like a slick used car salesman, who would say anything to get what he wanted. He had never been caught in a lie, but this felt different. Something wasn't sitting well with Bruce. Yes, he was glad to have some normalcy again, but he was also offended that he had been left out of the operation.

"Mary, you never left the president's side throughout this nightmare. Tell me… what really happened with Kore?" he asked in an inquisitive tone.

They were well out of earshot of the rest of the party, and he wasn't one for playing games. Mary seemed to value transparency, so he wasn't going to beat around the bush.

Mary was caught off guard by his question.

"What do you mean? You saw it for yourself, didn't you? Kore was caught on hidden camera—"

"Not that," interrupted Bruce. "I'm talking about *how* did it all happen? Why was I left out?"

She stared at him blankly. Her champagne buzz made it even more difficult to keep up her front. Bruce pulled himself in closer. She could smell his cologne.

"I'm the secretary of defense." He glanced around really quick to make sure no one could hear them. "I have to know what's going on here. Tell me the truth."

Mary's heart was torn. The champagne got the best of her as she whispered in his ear.

"Jay has no idea how it all happened—but please Bruce—you can't tell anyone I told you, or I'll never trust you with anything again."

Bruce gave her a wink. He gently grabbed her right shoulder with his left hand. "Thank you, Mary. Your secret is safe with me."

The two rejoined the party and the celebration continued.

Alcazar had reason to celebrate as well. Cheers, laughter, and thunderous loud music could be heard coming from loudspeakers. It wasn't the end of the war, but it was the first win for the Fleas. It was time to celebrate. News had spread that Kore was dead, which meant it was only a matter of time before the war ended.

People weren't afraid to use their powers anymore. Madeline, Horst's wife, who had the ability to fly, was hanging up bright blue streamers on the streetlights. Families were outside in the streets without fear of a curfew. There was a sense of newfound freedom in the air. It was like the first day of spring after a brutally long winter. Kore's police had all but disappeared.

Daniel peered out of the front window of Sledge's house. He smiled at all of the laughter and dancing outside. He was a hero for the first time in his life. It felt good. *I could live here forever*, he thought. He walked back into Sledge's room to check on him.

"Thanks for saving me back there, buddy," he said to Sledge.

Sledge flashed the best smile he could manage. He had multiple fractures, a few broken ribs, and a back that was screaming in pain, but he was going to make it. He was a fighter. The three of them, Daniel, Sledge, and Thunderclap, agreed to head to the fountain to heal at day break.

"You did great down there, Daniel."

Vosco appeared behind them. "Both of you did. I'm sorry it took us so long to get to you."

"Who would have thought a beetle could save the day?" replied Daniel. They all laughed.

"Daniel," said Vosco. "Did your Trojan horse hack have time to initiate before Kore discovered you?"

"Yes. I'm certain of it. The iPad didn't have the kind of power I'm used to with my laptop, but I saw it engage and start to corrupt Kore's system. With him dead, I'm not sure there's anyone that who *can* repair it."

"Good," replied Vosco. "The last thing we need is to lose any momentum. Our force is the strongest it's been since the Civil War. People are coming back to our side in droves. They believe again. They believe in you... the chosen one."

Daniel blushed as he remembered Maku's prediction.

"What's next for you, Daniel?" asked Vosco.

"What do you mean?"

"Are you going to stay in Alcazar?"

"Yes! I mean… Um… sure, if you'll let me." He couldn't imagine going back to America. Even with all of the pain he was feeling, it beat being in that wheelchair any day of the week.

Vosco gave him a big smile.

"I'm proud to have you on the team. Now go get some sleep. Tomorrow is going to be a big day. We're going to have a parade in the streets—and you're the guest of honor."

Daniel's head hit the pillow hard. He thought about everything, which had occurred over the last few days. He thought about his grandfather, and even his dad. Deep down he missed them both. He wished they could see him now. He wondered if the world above knew what happened tonight. Were they celebrating too? Did they know he was a hero? Did Maku? Clearly the magu had been wrong…

# 23 TRUTH HURTS

The president's deep sleep abruptly ended when his emergency phone started ringing off the hook. He clumsily reached over to grab it from the nightstand.

"What?" he paused. "Huh?" Another long pause. "Okay. I'll be down as quickly as I can."

Jay practically leapt out of bed and ran into the shower. He had just been told that massive power outages were being reported across the nation overnight. How could this be happening? His security staff had reported that the power grid was practically impenetrable after all of the steps they had taken the last week. Plus, he hadn't had any contact with the infamous Kore since the hidden camera ordeal last night.

The president hopped out of the shower, threw on a suit, and combed some gel through his damp hair as he looked at his reflection in the mirror. He flashed himself a quick smile and ran downstairs to the Situation Room, where his staff was waiting.

Far below the Earth's surface, Daniel also woke up frazzled. Two people were standing over his bed with their arms crossed. He rubbed the sleep out of his eyes. It was Vosco and Skylar. They didn't look happy to see him. In fact, they looked ticked off.

"He's still alive," was all Vosco said. His smile was gone from the night before.

"Who? What?" Daniel asked, incredibly confused.

Skylar practically lunged at his face.

"Kore!" she screamed. "He's still alive! Not only that, but your virus didn't work. He's in the process of shutting down the entire power grid in America right now."

Daniel didn't believe it. He had seen the Trojan horse initiate. He had watched Kore break his neck. He was dead. This couldn't be happening. It wasn't possible.

A mixture of anger, shame, and fear welled up inside of him. He looked up at Skylar. Her eyes were now full of tears. Vosco had a look of disgust on his face. Their feelings towards Daniel were clear, and Daniel didn't blame them. He had broken their trust. He now wished he had told them the truth.

"The rest of the village is outside," said Vosco. "Get dressed and meet us in the street."

Vosco and Skylar walked out of the room. Daniel sat there in bed. He was afraid of what was to come next. It was the first time he had wanted to run back to America.

He walked slowly through the house, hoping to run into Sledge, but his home was empty. He opened the front door to a barrage of people in the street.

"You owe us an explanation!" yelled someone in the back of the crowd.

"How is Kore still alive?" exclaimed another citizen. "You claimed he was dead!"

Daniel locked eyes for brief moments with Eric and Evan. Concern was clearly stamped on their faces. They looked hurt and defeated. He searched the crowd for Sledge, but he didn't see him. Daniel took a deep breath.

"How do we know that Kore is still alive?" he asked innocently.

As soon as the question left his lips, he spotted Sledge. He was seated in a chair and wouldn't look up at Daniel. Scooter handed him a sheet of paper.

"The entire nation of Alcazar received this an hour ago," he said. Daniel began to read:

*Dear citizens of Alcazar,*

*It is with deep regret that I have to report an unfortunate incident, which occurred last night.*

*Some members of our community decided to unlawfully break into Alcazar headquarters in an attempt to sabotage our Internet system and commit murder. I was personally attacked by these evil men and left to die. It is only by a miracle that*

*I am alive today. However, due to the injuries inflicted upon me, I now find myself in a wheelchair for the time being. My right-hand man, Khan, will take over certain parts of my job while I recover.*

*The traitors have been identified, and we've issued warrants out for their arrests. There will be no trial. Each of them will be executed.*

*These proceedings will move forward unless the human's body is delivered to me—or I'm given proof that he has left this land forever. You have until 11 am today. Otherwise I will execute the nine rebels, their family members, and the boy. We will not tolerate terrorism, traitors, or humans in Alcazar.*

*Finally, I am pleased to announce that our takeover of America is still going as planned. The first round of power outages has already begun. We will soon have full control of their country, making ours the most powerful in the world.*

*Thank you for the continued support to take back what is rightfully ours as the first people God put on this Earth.*

*Yours truly,*

*Kore*

Daniel couldn't believe what he was reading. He wished this was a bad dream. He felt as though someone had forced a brick down his throat. Something didn't seem right. Why was Kore in a wheelchair? Even if he'd been injured, couldn't he just visit the fountain and be healed? He looked away, trying not to make eye contact with anyone. A sarcastic voice broke the silence.

"Some chosen one you are."

It was Skylar. Daniel looked up at her. He could still see the hurt in her eyes. He looked out across the sea of faces staring blankly at him. He felt for them. He knew the feeling of being helpless. He had spent his entire life hoping and praying that someone would come along and save him from his mundane life. He could see himself in the crowd. He couldn't lie anymore.

"I'm not the chosen one," he confessed.

The gasps were audible. People went from somewhat hopeful to fearful and devastated. He saw a few people burst into tears. Some put their arms around their families as if to shield them from the truth, while others shook their heads in disappointment. Daniel felt horrible. He wanted to run away forever.

"I wanted to tell you the truth—I really did—" he continued.

"You thought it would be better to lie to us?" Tears were now flowing down Skylar's face. "You thought it was a good idea to lead us into a war we couldn't win? We lost a good friend because of you. You're nothing but an imposter! We should have left you back home in your wheelchair!"

She stormed off. Her mother, a quiet but stern-looking woman, followed behind her in dismay.

"I knew we shouldn't have ever trusted a human!" yelled someone from the back of the crowd.

Everyone was staring at him. He looked down at his toes, trying to avoid their incredulous faces. The next question was barely audible.

"Wheelchair?" asked Ian. "Why did she say that?"

Daniel slowly looked up.

"Oh, it's nothing. Just something from my past. Guys, can't we focus on what's important right now? If Kore is really alive, we've got to stop him. This isn't over. I know I might not be the chosen one, but I can help you. I can help stop him—"

Mac, the town elder, interrupted him.

"Daniel, I speak for everyone when I say it's best that you go back to your country immediately. It's not safe for you here. Half the town wants to turn you in for the ransom money. Our only chance at receiving a lesser punishment and saving our friends is if we banish you. Now go. You've got one hour to get out of Alcazar."

Daniel looked around. They wanted him gone. He could see Sledge shaking in his seat. He was crying. He had lost a friend. Daniel wanted to go hug him and tell him he was sorry, but he knew he couldn't. The sound of the door behind him opening made him turn around. It was Sledge's wife. She was holding his backpack. It was time to go home.

***

"Sit down," demanded Bruce Cromwell. "You've got some explaining to do."

The president looked around the room. He glanced at Mary. She appeared to be crying. He could tell by her face that she was scared. The hairs on the back of Jay's neck stood up. He had been caught in a lie; the bold-faced lie he had told the entire world. He sat down, a million thoughts racing through his head.

Luke Christenson, the Chief of Staff, handed a thick binder to

Bruce. It contained a list of every reported power outage across the United States. There were over three thousand in total. Some areas had complete black outs, while others were sporadic outages. The president glanced through the binder.

"This is all from the past few hours?" he asked, still praying he was dreaming.

"Yes," replied Bruce. "More reports are flooding in by the minute. The worst part is that we don't know how to stop this."

Paul Glazer, the Cyber-Intelligence Director chimed in. "The attacks are being orchestrated by some of the most complex software hacks our cyber-intelligence team has ever seen. We've got some of the best hackers in the world trying to re-engineer the sequences, but they can't even keep up with it. As soon as they stop one, three more pop up."

Jay's mind wandered a long way from the Situation Room, back to afternoons spent with his mentor, Jack Fullerton. Politics seemed like so much fun back then; the ability to lead and make a difference, and to see positive impacts in your community. People loved and respected their leaders back then. Those moments seemed too good to be true.

"Sir, what should we do next?" asked Paul.

Jay gave a noncommittal grunt. He wasn't sure about anything. His head was spinning. He felt like there was an elephant in the room. Should he tell them the truth? Should he confess that he had no idea about the hidden camera? He felt Bruce's heavy presence next to him.

"Jay, while you were sleeping off your champagne hangover, I was busy preparing these two things," Bruce said in a condescending tone. He looked down at the folder. "The first one I need you to sign immediately. It's an order to declare a national emergency. It will give us the ability to get all the first responders in place, where we need them. We've got to get the power back. Sign here."

Bruce shoved the paper in front of the president. He autographed it and slid the signed papers across the table to Mary. She grabbed them and quickly marched out of the room. Mary was relieved to have an excuse to leave. She didn't want to be in there for what she knew was going to happen next.

There was some uncomfortable silence in the room. Jay spoke first.

"Paul, Sam—any news on Kore? Where are these attacks originating from?"

"Sir," butted in Bruce. "We need to speak to you about that—about

Kore. It's been brought to our attention that you didn't have anything to do with the hidden camera situation..."

The president's face became red. He felt incredibly uncomfortable. His brain quickly explored all options he could use to get himself out of this mess, but he knew it was too late. He was caught.

"Jay," Bruce continued. "You lied to us. You lied to the entire world. Things were already getting out of control here in the White House—and to be honest, you were on your last leg. Last night you appeared to have redeemed yourself. You finally restored some peace, unity, and stability to our country. It was all a lie. I don't know how else to tell you this, but everyone here has already signed off on it."

Bruce slid a piece of paper over to Jay. He didn't even need to read it. The headline at the top of the page said everything he needed to know.

## Impeachment Trial

"I'm sorry Jay," said Sam, the vice president.

Jay stormed out of the room as everyone stared blankly.

# 24 THE RETURN HOME

All he could think about was one thing on his return home: the chair.

Would he be returning to a wheelchair for the rest of his life? Would he lose all of his freedom again? Would he lose his confidence? He dreaded even thinking about it—the weird looks people gave him. The hurtful names. Disabled Dan. Handi-Dan. Retard. His electric wheelchair was somewhere at the bottom of the fountain right now. Would he have to get a new chair? How would he be able to afford it? For a moment he considered heading back to the fountain to retrieve it—and to heal his wounds—but he knew he was out of time. It was too dangerous.

He gave Alcazar one last look before glancing over at Plato's Peak. He wondered what Maku was doing. Daniel felt bad for him. He reminded him of himself. He had no real friends, limited mobility, and everyone was always looking at him funny. At least Maku had a special gift, which everyone admired. Daniel used to think his gift was hacking, but apparently, he wasn't good at that either. His best virus didn't even work. Kore was a far superior hacker, and Daniel knew it.

He looked down at the village. He felt sorry for lying. He had caused a lot of pain in people he really cared about over the last two days. He was responsible for killing one of their friends. Skylar hated him. Sledge could barely walk anymore. Thunderclap was still confined to a bed. Daniel felt sick to his stomach. He turned around and headed through the portal back to the middle grounds. It was time to move on and forget about Alcazar.

The good news was that the desert was a cakewalk. There was no sign of the scorpion, which was strange because Daniel felt fearless. Perhaps the scorpion didn't care about challenging visitors, who were *leaving* Alcazar. In fact, there were no signs of life at all. He casually walked up the escalator, thinking about his life in the real world.

The swamp was void of life as well. There was not a single crocodile to be seen. Daniel was starting to wonder if something was wrong. Was it because he wasn't afraid anymore? Either way, he was glad to have an easy walk home. The last thing he needed was another fight. His back was still killing him from the encounter with Kore. His face was still black and blue. He wasn't sure he could endure another physical encounter.

He had just finished his ascent up the last elevator shaft. He walked through the cloud layer into the forest. It was the final stretch before going home. He started feeling afraid. He didn't want to, but all he could think about was being stuck in his wheelchair for the rest of his life. More thoughts started flooding in.

Daniel tried to shake it off. It seemed awfully quiet—too quiet. He certainly didn't remember the forest being this dark before. It was like the darkness which creeps in before a nasty rainstorm. Something wasn't right. He could feel it.

He sped up his pace and looked around for signs of trouble. He was breathing hard. He needed to get to the brick wall. It wasn't too far ahead. Daniel started to jog. He could see the brick wall ahead in the distance. Then he stopped.

"We've been waiting for your return," came a voice from behind him.

Shadows began to emerge from the darkness of the forest. Daniel felt his heart beating faster. He felt helpless, like the day he and his grandfather were cornered in the alley. Except this time, he was surrounded.

"My friends and I wanted to greet you with a little welcome party of sorts," said Natas, the wolf. He slowly walked out of the shadows and came closer to where Daniel was standing.

"Just let me go home. You'll have my word that I'll never be back here again," said Daniel.

"Oh, but Daniel, we don't want any trouble. We just want to congratulate you."

"Congratulate me? For what?"

It appeared as though the wolf was smiling.

"You were one of the first humans to get past us in many, many years. However, there's a downside to that."

"What's that?" Daniel asked, feeling frightened.

"When wolves get a second chance at someone, it usually doesn't end up well for them."

The other wolves began to snicker and hiss. They came in tighter, forming a small circle around Daniel. He could see the brick wall in front of him. If he could knock off three or four of them, he could make a run for it. He was about to take a step forward, when he felt warmth near the back of his neck. He ducked.

He looked up to see a wolf flying over him. It had barely missed his neck. The fight was on. Daniel started swinging his arms and kicking his legs. He made contact with one wolf, but it wasn't fazed. They knew they had him trapped.

Daniel swung at three more, who were snarling in front of him. It was to no avail. He was outmatched.

He felt a stinging bite on his leg. The wolf had a firm grip and wasn't letting go. He felt the blood trickling down. Daniel dropped down in pain. He saw a thick branch on the ground a few inches from his reach. He extended his arm as far as it would go. He couldn't grasp it.

The wolf's teeth dug in deeper. He heard laughter from the others. Daniel stretched his arm towards the branch one last time. He got it. In a flash he jammed the sharp stick into the wolf. It screamed in pain. The stick had gone right into its eye. It immediately let go of Daniel and ran off into the forest. The rest of the pack looked over at Natas. He was fuming.

Natas leapt through the air and landed on Daniel's chest. The impact knocked the air out of him. As Natas held him down, the other wolves tore into his arms and legs. Daniel could feel the warm blood flowing from his body. They were going to kill him. Wolf drool dripped onto Daniel's chin. Natas looked into Daniel's eyes and grinned. He was out for blood.

Daniel attempt to push him off one last time, but the blood loss had made him too weak. He was too heavy. They had won. He slipped in and out of consciousness. He closed his eyes. This was the end. He was ready to die.

The next thing he felt was the weight of the wolf being lifted off of his chest. He could feel sunlight hitting his face. His eyes were still closed. He felt warm. This must be heaven. The light became brighter— more intense. He opened his eyes. The wolves were gone, but he was still in the forest. He could see the silhouette of the trees against the light. Something was moving towards him. It was a figure so bright he couldn't bear looking at it; it was like looking into the sun. The figure moved to his left. Daniel opened one eye and saw the recognizable outline of a beautiful horse. Her perfect white mane hung down to one side. She appeared to be glowing.

The mare came closer to Daniel. As she brushed up against his messy brown hair, a bolt of magnetic energy rushed through him. He felt alive again. The horse lowered her body and tilted her head, signaling for Daniel to climb on.

He could still barely move. It felt like everything was in slow motion. He carefully climbed onto the horse's back. He finally got his arms around her neck. He lay on her back, breathing slowly. The horse was warm, but there was more than just heat radiating from her. It was an emotional warmth. It felt like love. It felt like a mother's embrace. The last thing he remembered was gripping the horse with all of his might as she headed towards the entrance to the fountain.

# 25 POWER OUTAGE

The power went out again in his son's trailer home. Jack decided he needed a good walk to clear his head. The last twenty-four hours had been crazy. He watched as the entire nation went from riots in the streets, to cheers of joy and celebration, to utter confusion and fear.

The nation's mood quickly soured when millions of people woke up without power. Of course, that didn't stop social media from blowing up with news of the impeachment. The president would be tried for lying under oath.

Bloggers and online news agencies stirred up conspiracy theories that the president was in fact, Kore. They wondered if the president and a small group of elites had set the entire thing up in order to steal money. Why else was the debate canceled? Why did so many wealthy politicians disappear? The story began to gain traction on the Internet.

Jack didn't know what to believe. He knew something wasn't right. How could Jay make such a blunder? Why did he lie to the country? Where was Daniel now? Did they fail down in Alcazar? Did Kore defeat them? Was Daniel still alive?

Jack decided to take a walk to the fountain at Hotel Alcazar. It was a few miles to the abandoned hotel. The riots had stopped. Jack casually made the walk, waving to a few people on the streets. A few waves turned into small talk. Nobody seemed to recognize him. Everyone was anxious to know what was going on. Were they ever going to get power back? Was Kore behind this? Did the president already get impeached? Everyone had an opinion. Jack could only imagine what this town had said about him twenty years ago, when he had disappeared. He laughed at the thought.

He finally arrived at the hotel. He strolled around the perimeter, looking for any signs of life. It was a ritual he had performed ever since he first started sneaking down to the hotel decades ago. The coast was clear. He headed around the back to the fountain. He was delighted to see that he had the place to himself. He figured it would be a great time to meditate and clear his mind.

Those thoughts vanished when he took a few steps closer to the fountain. There was a body in the water. It was face down. Jack's heart stopped. He could see blood swirling around in the water, making it even darker. He started to jog towards the fountain.

The body was that of a young man with short, brown hair. It looked like Daniel. At the edge of the fountain, he bent down and used his arms to flip the body over.

It was Daniel.

Jack felt like vomiting. He frantically grabbed him under the armpits and pulled him out of the fountain. *Why did I wait so long to come back here? How long has he been unconscious and underwater?*

Daniel didn't appear to be blue, so he couldn't have been under for too long. He felt for a pulse. Nothing. He looked down and winced when he saw Daniel's legs. They had been completely mauled. He knew that the wounds likely came from Natas and his pack. He quickly started performing CPR on Daniel. He wasn't going to give up.

After countless breaths and chest compressions, Jack took a break. He was exhausted. He knew he had to call an ambulance, but that also meant he would be brought in for questioning. He had been a wanted man ever since his daughter-in-law died in this same fountain seventeen years ago. They'd assume he was guilty even before trial. He would end up behind bars for life. He pulled out his phone and hit the three buttons.

He was selfishly relieved when a recorded message said that due to increased call volume from nationwide power outages, it could take up to three minutes for a 911 operator to answer. Jack hit the speakerphone button, placed his phone on the brick walkway, and went back to performing CPR on Daniel.

It was thirty-eight minutes before the ambulance arrived. Jack had continued to do CPR. At one point, Daniel had vomited up some water. Jack could have sworn he felt a slight pulse, but then it was gone again. He knew that even if his grandson made it, he'd probably suffer from massive brain damage.

Jack bent the truth slightly when the ambulance arrived. He said he was was an uncle from Ohio, so he could ride in the ambulance.

The two first responders cut off Daniel's shirt, checked his vital signs, and continued to perform CPR. There was still no sign of life. Jack closed his eyes. He prayed silently. *Lord, if you let this boy live, I promise to tell the truth once and for all—*

"We've got a heartbeat," said the female EMT.

Jack opened his eyes. He felt like he was witnessing a miracle. He saw a pulse show up on the monitor. Just as quickly it turned ugly again. Jack grimaced as he watched Daniel experience uncontrollable spasms. His body was twisting and turning against the gurney. The violent spasms got worse. The EMTs looked at each other with wide eyes. They had never seen anything like this before in a drowning victim.

Daniel's dreams were disturbing. Natas showed his teeth. Blood flooded his vision. The crocodile and scorpion came into view as well. All of the animals were attacking him simultaneously; ripping his legs to shreds while he watched. Finally, a black shadow came over him. The animals scattered. They were all afraid of whoever it was. A face appeared out of the shadows. It was Kore. He was laughing violently. Daniel looked down to see Kore's hands coming towards his throat. He grabbed Daniel with a vice-like grip. Then he felt a shock to his chest. He awoke in quick spurts, panicked, convinced there was water coming in over his head and filling his lungs. Then there was a white horse. Then there was nothing but darkness.

The power had been flickering on and off in the hospital waiting room for over an hour. Jack had spent the time fabricating a story so that he would not be arrested. He had to be here for Daniel. He had also made a promise to God. His message to Daniel kept ringing in his ears: *If you're going to face your fears, then you might as well face 'em head on.*

He saw a nurse pointing over at him. She was whispering to a doctor and two police officers. This couldn't be good. The doctor stepped forward and introduced himself. He was a middle-aged man with a bald head and a light brown goatee.

"You're with Daniel, correct?" the doctor asked.

Jack nodded his head yes. The doctor looked down at his chart.

"In one report here it says your name is Jack, and you're Daniel's grandfather. In the other report it says your name is David, and that you're his uncle. What's going on here?" asked the doctor, looking slightly confused. The cops both looks of concern on their faces.

"My name is Jack. I'm Daniel's grandfather. Sorry for any confusion. How is Daniel?" he asked nervously, trying to change the subject.

The doctor ran his right hand through his goatee. He was trying to think of the right words to say.

"Daniel isn't doing well, but he's out of his coma. I'll be honest, I have never seen anything like it in all of my years. I'm still not sure how it's possible considering how long he was underwater and everything else he's been through. He's still alive—and he's actually showing signs of brain activity. He's going to need some rest."

Jack dropped to his knees and broke down crying before the doctor could finish his sentence. His cupped his face in his hands. He didn't hear anything else the doctor was saying. In this moment, he didn't care who saw him sobbing uncontrollably. He didn't even care about the two police officers, who stood just a few feet away. His grandson had been given another chance, and Jack had been given another chance to rebuild a relationship. He had dreamed about this ever since he lost his wife, son, and daughter-in-law many years ago.

He pulled himself back up on his feet. He looked the doctor in the eye, tears still streaming down his face. "I'm sorry, doc. He's all I got left. Can I see him?"

"I'm sorry sir, but without some proof of ID, by hospital rules we can't let you back. These officers have been patiently waiting to speak with you. This could be an attempted murder case, and you are the only witness so far. I told them I wanted to deliver the good news to you before they take you away for questioning."

"Can I at least see him first? I need to make sure he's alive. I need to see it for myself."

The doctor studied Jack's face. He thought about it for a second. He nodded to the two cops. "Let him in, but only for a minute."

Daniel had his own room. The only thing in there besides his bed was a small chair, a TV on the wall, and an oversized painting of a sailboat. Daniel had his eyes closed. His chest was slowing rising and falling. His steady breaths matched the beeping machines, which surrounded his bed. Jack felt a fresh tear run down his cheek.

"What's the chance—um—that he fully recovers? Will he remember anything?"

"We're not entirely sure. As I mentioned, it's a miracle he's showing signs of brain activity at all. You know he was born with cerebral palsy. The good news is that he already knows what it's like to spend his life in a wheelchair—which is where he'll be for the rest of his life. His *normal* is a whole lot different than most people's normal. Disability is all Daniel has ever known. So, the big question will be how much memory loss, if any, did he suffer? We should know more in the next day as we run some cognitive tests—"

"Can he hear me?" Jack interrupted.

"It's possible. He's no longer in a coma, but we've got to get you going. I can't keep the police waiting any longer." The doctor nodded to the two policemen. The officers started walking towards Jack.

"Let's go, sir," said the cop as he gently grabbed his shoulder.

"Daniel! Can you hear me?!" shouted Jack as he fought to shake off the cop's grip.

The second cop saw him fighting. He grabbed Jack's left arm. The other cop grabbed his right arm. They placed his hands behind his back.

"Sir, don't make us handcuff you here in the hospital. We can make this easy, or we can make it hard. We'd prefer to let you walk out of here without your hands in cuffs."

"Yes, sir," he replied.

They let go of his hands and began to lead him out of the room. When he was a few feet from the front of the door, he turned around quickly and screamed, "DANIEL! Can you hear me? It's me—Jack!"

The cops pinned his hands behind him and applied the handcuffs. The nurses ran over to monitor the situation. One noticed that Daniel's heart monitor was beeping faster and faster. The two officers picked Jack up and began to drag him out of the room. He was digging his feet into the floor as they applied more pressure.

"DANIEL!!!"

The last thing Jack saw as he was removed from the room was a weak smile on Daniel's face.

# 26 HAIL MARY

The president had officially hit rock bottom.

He was sitting in his large leather office chair, which had not even been broken in yet. This might be one of the last times he used it. He'd been alone since he stormed out of the Situation Room.

He looked around at the paintings on the wall; Washington, Lincoln, Roosevelt, JFK... Reagan. These were the men he had looked up to and admired since he was a child. Now he was embarrassed to look into their eyes. He was a failure—a disappointment. Perhaps he'd go down as the worst president in history, or at least the quickest to be impeached. Nixon made it five years before Watergate.

Jay's biggest fear consumed his thoughts. It was the fear of returning to what he once was. He reflected back on being poor. After living with his mom, who worked multiple jobs just to make ends meet, he swore he'd never be poor again. He wanted to do something with his life. He never wanted to be like his dad, who walked out on his family. He wanted to be important, rich, and powerful. He finally had that. He'd earned it. Was he even qualified to do anything else outside of politics? It was all he knew. Would he be on the streets like his dad? Maybe he could get a book deal on how to get impeached in sixty days...

He thought back to his early days in politics. He reflected on how much he loved serving and helping others. He had quickly risen to the top because he had focused on what was right. He did everything his mentor, Jack, had taught him. He learned to listen to both the liberals and the conservatives. He became a chameleon; able to talk, listen, and sympathize with any voter. It didn't matter now. Just like his mentor, Jay appeared to be going down in flames.

The president never had much time for religion or family. After he lost his mom, he vowed to devote every waking hour to his career. That was his church. He hadn't stepped foot in an actual church in years. Right now, he wished he was there. He wished he could feel the presence of a higher power, like when he used to go to church with Jack as a kid. He closed his eyes and prayed for one last chance.

He was still praying when he was startled by a knock on the door.

"I'm busy," he replied.

The door opened. It was Mary. She softly shut the door behind her, and quietly walked up to him. She leaned up against his oak desk, unsure of what to say.

Finally, she said, "I'm sorry."

He looked up at her. "For what? You didn't do anything wrong."

"Well, that's not entirely true," she said. "I was the one who told Bruce the truth. I had been drinking too much champagne, and I let it slip. I feel horrible, sir. I'm really sorry."

They stared at each other. Jay normally would have felt betrayed, but his self-reflection made him realize who was really at fault.

"They would have found out anyway, as soon as the power grid started failing. You told the truth, which is what I should have done from the beginning."

She gave him a warm smile. Mary had been so nervous to speak with him. It meant so much that he forgave her.

"What's the latest on the power grid?" he asked, anxious to know what had transpired over past few hours.

"It's getting worse. The vice president is in way over his head. He's losing his cool because we just can't seem to keep up with Kore's attacks. Most businesses across the country are closed for the day, so many people have taken back to the streets. Riots are being reported across the country. The global stock market is floundering, and all flights are currently grounded. It doesn't look good."

He thought about how easy it was going to be for them to impeach him.

"What are Sam and Bruce going to do?"

"The latest talk is about declaring war. The problem is nobody really knows with whom. There's still no sign of Kore other than his hacks on the power grid."

"Hmmm. Any other updates? Is there a set date for my impeachment trial?"

"Not yet. The good news for you is that everyone is too busy putting out fires. It's all hands on deck."

Mary was about to walk out, when she remembered one more thing. She handed him a note.

"What's this?" Jay asked.

"The police in St. Augustine have called three times saying they have a man in custody; Jack Fullerton. He said he really needs to talk to you. He claims to have some top-secret information about how to stop Kore. Do you know who he is? The police think he's a nut job."

He looked up at her in disbelief. *It couldn't be. Is he still alive? Is he somehow behind all of this?* His hands trembled.

"Are you ok? You look like you've just seen a ghost."

"I think I have... Did the police say anything else?"

"No. The man was brought to jail today and given one phone call. He said he only wanted to speak with you."

*It's not possible*, thought Jay. Jack Fullerton? He had been missing for almost twenty years. This certainly wasn't what he had asked for in his prayer. The man was wanted for murder. *Why is he just showing up now?* It didn't make any sense.

The president looked down at the note again. There was a phone number to the St. Augustine sheriff's department scribbled in black ink. The words *Jack Fullerton* were written across the top. A part of him wanted to throw it away. Jack had already died in his mind, but another voice inside of him wouldn't let it go. Mary was shutting the door behind her.

"Hey, Mary! Come back for a minute, if you don't mind. I want there to be a witness to this phone call in case it gets weird."

He dialed the number on the note. After speaking with the prison operator, he waited for the prison guards to escort Jack from his jail cell to the telephone.

"Hello?"

His voice hadn't changed. Jay could hardly breathe.

"Hellooo?"

"Jack," was all Jay could manage.

Warmth filled the voice on the other line.

"It's great to hear your voice, Jay," Jack said.

"Is this really you?" he asked, still in disbelief.

"It's really me."

Jay had known it was him as soon as he answered. The tone of his voice... the vibrance. He still had it. Jay had so many questions to ask. A million thoughts flooded his head. He blurted out the first one, which came to mind.

"How's Mark doing? Is he still down in Florida?"

"Mark died."

There was a long moment of silence.

"I'm sorry to hear that," he replied solemnly. He instantly wished he had picked a better question. "Where have you been?" he asked, changing the subject.

"Listen, Jay," said Jack. "I can't get into that right now. I don't have much time. I need your help, and you need mine."

The president looked over at Mary. She was listening in via the speaker phone.

Jack continued, "My grandson, Daniel..." He paused. He took a second to think about how to phrase things. "He's the one who filmed Kore the night of your debate. He's been underground for the past couple of days in... well, where Kore is. I think he knows how to defeat him. I need you to pardon me and fly us to D.C. We can help you—"

Jay interrupted. "Is this Mark's son? The one in the wheelchair?"

Jack hesitated because he knew his story wasn't believable. How could a kid in a wheelchair, who can't walk or talk, secretly film the man trying to take over the world?

"Yes."

"Jack, it's really great to hear your voice, but to come out of hiding for the first time in twenty years and to call me with a story like this... it's just a bit much. I'm being impeached. I can't risk looking like a fool. No one will believe it. I don't even believe it."

Jack thought for a moment. How could he prove it? He remembered what Vosco had told him the first time he asked if Daniel was a good hacker.

"How about this," Jack said. "You grant the cops permission to escort me back to the hospital to see Daniel. We give him one hour to see if he can hack into the Pentagon missile system. If he does it, then you will pardon me and fly us to the White House. If he fails, then you can forget that we ever had this conversation."

Jay looked at Mary. She gave him a look of utter disbelief. Her expression was full of judgment. She clearly thought Jack was a nut job. Even though this whole thing seemed outrageous, the president had nothing to lose.

"Okay. You've got one hour once you get Daniel set up. After that, it's out of my hands."

"Thank you, Jay," Jack hesitated. "I'm proud of you."

Jay felt a rush of emotion. He hadn't heard anyone tell him that in years. In fact, the last person to utter those words was Jack himself, many years ago. He had been longing to feel appreciated; to feel loved. It meant even more coming from someone like Jack, who had been a father figure to him.

The nurses didn't know what to do when a group of police officers burst into the room with the same old man that they had escorted from the hospital earlier. Jack was relieved to see Daniel looking alive with his eyes open.

He spent a few minutes telling Daniel what had transpired with the president. He looked more fearful with every word that came out of his grandfather's mouth. He motioned for the nurse to bring him the hospital iPad, which he had been borrowing to speak. Daniel typed slowly. He was frustrated. His claw-like fingers were back to how they used to be. He would have given anything to be back in Alcazar. He finally hit enter.

"That missile hack occurred over two years ago," came the robotic voice from the iPad. "Certainly, they've updated all of the firewalls since my hack."

Jack could see the defeated look in his grandson's eyes. He watched as he typed as fast as his deformed fingers could go.

"Even if it works, I can't defeat Kore. He's a better coder than me. I now know that I'm not the chosen one. The whole thing was a mistake."

Jack was taken by surprise. He had just bet his life and freedom on his grandson's ability to defeat Kore. Daniel appeared to be giving up before he even started. The room fell quiet. The nurses stepped out. The four officers looked at Jack, wondering what was happening.

"Daniel, listen to me," his grandfather said. "God doesn't make mistakes. You are perfect in his eyes. He made you exactly as you are for a reason. I still don't know what transpired down there, but the fact that you're even alive right now is a miracle. With or without that chair, you are a miracle. You can defeat him. You're our only hope. You're *my* only hope."

Daniel looked back at him. The idea that he could defeat Kore seemed incredible and impossible, but he had never had someone believe in him as much as his grandfather did in this moment. The past twenty-four hours had driven all the confidence out of him. Getting banished from Alcazar, nearly drowning, and then waking up in a hospital disabled again was too much to take in.

He thought about his grandfather and his old friends down in Alcazar. He remembered the first time he met Kore. It didn't scare Daniel as much as he thought it would. Although Kore was a superior coder, he did have a weakness. It was his only chance. It was worth a shot. Furthermore, he was being given a chance to legally hack into the government's missile system with no repercussions. It was time to hack.

Jack placed the iPad on Daniel's lap. He looked down at it. He was still nervous, but willing to give it everything he had. He turned on the device and asked for it to be hard-wired in for speed. Daniel took a deep breath. Jack dialed the president via video conference on his phone. Jay watched on video as Daniel started typing. He knew there was no way this disabled kid in a hospital bed was going to be able to hack into the Pentagon's missile system.

Thirty minutes had already passed. Daniel wasn't nearly as far into the system as he had hoped. So much had changed since he last attempted to hack into the White House. Their security system had been beefed up big time. Daniel caught his reflection on the laptop screen. It was the first time he had seen his face since coming back from Alcazar. He missed the feeling of being able to walk and talk. He hated this version of himself. He couldn't do this hack in an hour… a day… or ever for that matter.

He felt a hand on his wrist. It was his grandfather. Jack could tell he was getting frustrated. His keystrokes had slowed down. A few small beads of sweat were forming on Daniel's forehead. They glistened as the sun peeked through the hospital room window. Daniel wanted to throw in the towel. He wanted to go back to the library and be alone. This was too much pressure.

"Hey Daniel," said Jack. He looked directly into his eyes. "I know you can do this. At first, I wasn't really sure, but I felt something a moment ago in this room."

Daniel stared at him, unsure what he meant. Jack took a deep breath.

"This is going to sound weird, but I feel your mom's presence. She's here, and I know she's as proud of you as I am."

Daniel's mind shifted to the white horse he had seen in his dreams. He felt love rush through him...

***

Back at the White House, Jay had all but given up. This Hail Mary attempt at saving the world was nothing more than a wild goose chase. He wasn't even paying attention to Daniel anymore. Mary had already left. He was returning e-mails and trying to focus on any last-ditch efforts to save his job. Something made him look up. He watched as Daniel stared intensely at the computer screen. He was on a mission. Jay looked at his watch. There were ninety seconds left.

Daniel had busted through multiple security levels. He was farther along than he imagined possible. His grandfather tried to remain calm. He didn't want to break his concentration. He sat still and prayed as he watched Daniel type.

Then an alert popped up on his phone in red text.

## SECURITY BREACH - US BALLISTIC MISSILE SYSTEM

Jack waved to the president. His grin took up the entire screen. The president sat in his office chair, flabbergasted. How did this kid do it? More importantly, how was he going to explain this to his staff? There was no way he could walk back into the Situation Room with a wanted fugitive and a kid in a wheelchair, and tell them that he'd found their answer. They'd laugh him out of the room.

"Let me know when we should expect the plane" Jack said. "See you soon, Jay." He hung up the video phone.

It was the proudest moment of Daniel's life. He had felt a rush of energy run through him as he envisioned his mother in the room. Goosebumps crawled up his arm and around his neck. He felt an unexplained presence in the room. Daniel had accomplished the impossible because of it.

Jack wrapped him up in a big hug. Daniel watched as he grabbed a hospital wheelchair from the corner of the room and wheeled it next to Daniel. He looked over at the nurse with a smile.

"Can we borrow this chair for a day?" asked Jack. "We're headed to Washington D.C."

# 27 CIRCUIT BREAKER

"You've got to be kidding."

Bruce Cromwell gave the president a look of disdain. He didn't like Jay. The fact that he had the audacity to interrupt their meeting to tell him this, made Bruce hate him even more. He was flying up a kid in a wheelchair to fix this problem?

"Do you hear yourself right now?" he argued. "Do you really believe that this kid made it to some underground cave in his *wheelchair* and filmed Kore on hidden camera? How is a kid in a wheelchair going to get underground in the first place? Didn't we watch Kore come up to the camera and toss it? Don't you think he would have finished this kid off? Why should anyone believe any of this?!"

"I… I don't know," Jay said as he struggled to keep his composure. "I do know that he was the one, who just hacked into our ballistic missile system—"

"He's just some disabled kid, who got lucky with one hack. That doesn't mean he knows how to stop these power grid attacks. We have an entire army of coders and hackers who can't keep up with it."

"Well, he and his grandfather should be coming through the doors at any moment. When he arrives, he'll get his own power station in the intelligence management center. We'll see firsthand what he's capable of doing."

"Keep him out of our way!" yelled Bruce.

Sam took a step closer to the president. "Jay, are you willing to risk your job for this? I mean—this is a bit crazy. Even if the impeachment is successful, your career isn't over. The public forgets things pretty quickly. If you go out like this, the people will never forgive you."

There was a knock on the door to the conference room. Everyone turned around. The door opened and everyone's mouth dropped. Even Jay was caught off guard. In front of them was a young man in a hospital wheelchair, who looked like he had been in a terrible accident. His eyes were black and blue, and both legs were in white casts. His neck was wrapped with bandages and there were numerous scratches across his face. Everyone turned back to the president. They were speechless and so was he.

Nothing could have prepared them for what came next. Anthony Clapper, the director for counterterrorism, nearly leapt out of his seat when an unexpected sound came from his own pocket. He reached in, pulled out his phone, and saw the notorious white screen. This time there was a face on camera. It was Kore.

Everyone completely forgot about Daniel. They were grabbing their phones. Kore began to speak. Even though Daniel had heard his voice numerous times, he couldn't keep his heart from racing.

Jack wheeled him up to the large computer monitor, while the staff remained glued to their phones. He knew they didn't have time to waste. Paul Glazer, the cyber-intelligence director, looked at him quizzically.

"Did you really meet this Kore guy?" he asked Daniel skeptically.

Daniel gave him a nod. Paul didn't quite believe him, but he followed the orders from the president. He logged him into the computer with full admin control.

"I'm going to be here watching you, just to make sure nothing bad happens. I'll pull up Kore on this screen, so we can all see what he's saying. This monitor over here will be yours for coding."

Daniel touched the keyboard. It was now or never.

Daniel's grandfather, Paul, and Jay all watched as Kore delivered another terrifying message. He first apologized for the hidden camera video. He claimed everything he'd said had been taken out of context. Would the American people actually buy that? He wasn't sure. He then began his rant on the rich versus the poor. He painted a scary picture of what America would look like in a few years, if there wasn't a new world order.

*You'll have to work even harder for less money... you'll always be replaceable... always a slave to the man... you are being taken advantage of by the wealthy and elite... you'll never get ahead in life... it's not fair... only the rich benefit... even if you work hard enough to make your way up the corporate ladder, they'll find a way to knock you down…*

Jay shook his head. If anyone was buying into this hogwash again, he'd be floored. This time Kore had more leverage. He had control of America's power grid already. He knew precisely what to say to gain the support of millions of people, who felt jaded by the current system.

While countless White House hackers worked on restoring the power, Daniel was on a different mission. He knew his only chance to defeat Kore was to attack his ego. Kore only played offense. He was always three steps ahead of everyone else. By the time someone solved one of his hacks, he already had two more going.

Daniel knew that Kore had a special hack, which hadn't been released yet. He had gotten a sneak peak, when he hacked into his system the other evening. In order for this to work, Daniel needed Kore to lose his temper…

Bruce pointed up at the screen as Kore spoke. He couldn't believe his eyes. *Does that say what I think it says?* Laughter echoed around the Situation Room. Text had appeared on the screen.

A big caption read, **What's that smell?** with a large red arrow pointing to his face.

Kore saw it as well. He was furious. How did someone hack into his feed? It wasn't possible. Another caption popped up with the same big red arrow.

**I'm with stupid.**

Millions of people were watching the drama unfold. It was better than watching a Jerry Springer show. Parents, kids, and even grandparents found themselves laughing. Kore couldn't hear the laughter, but he was still livid. He stopped talking.

"Apparently there's a hacker out there, who thinks he or she is pretty funny. If you're so good, why don't you show your face? Let's have a chat for the entire world to see. Then we'll see who's funny. Show yourself!"

Daniel was concentrating on finishing the code for his hack. He had to have everything ready before Kore launched his final attack. He knew he'd only get one shot. If he missed the timing, they were all screwed.

Kore resumed his speech. Every few minutes Daniel would interrupt it with another funny caption.

**I'm in love with a goat… My only friend is a horse named**

*Vlad... I pee sitting down... I'm so lonely I'd date my cousin...*

Kore was losing it. After the last sentence appeared on the screen, he slammed his fist down on the table so hard that the camera angle dropped. Everyone saw it at once: his wheelchair.

Kore was incredibly vain. He couldn't bear the thought of the world seeing him in a wheelchair. He had purposely positioned the camera to show only his head and shoulders. Now they knew the truth. The terrorist taking control of America was in a wheelchair. He repositioned the camera as fast as he could, hoping no one saw his chair. It was too late.

Daniel saw it too. He felt the energy in the room change. He overheard some snarky comments coming from the other room. They were poking fun at Kore because he was disabled. He felt a strange empathy for him. He could relate to him. He could feel his pain. He knew what it was like to be laughed at for something out of his control. Why was Kore in a wheelchair? Even if he had become paralyzed, couldn't he have just visited the Fountain of Youth?

Kore tried to recover, but anger and fear had taken control of his body. He was screaming into the camera for the hacker to show his or her face. He had been humiliated. He wanted a fight. He wanted blood.

Daniel was almost done with his hack. It was what he called a reflection virus; a custom code, which would reflect any malicious energy coming through his computer. As far as he knew, it had never been done before. He double-checked his code. If he was correct about Kore's final move, it should work. Only time would tell. He had everything ready. All he had to do was hit enter when the time was right. Daniel took a deep breath. He turned around to face his grandfather and the president with a smile.

"Show yourself, you spineless weasel!" screamed Kore into the live feed.

Seconds later, Daniel appeared on the screen. Kore was speechless. He recognized his face. Where had he seen it before? It looked like the human he'd seen in Alcazar, but his face was shaped differently. He appeared to be in a wheelchair like him. Was it the same person?

"Daniel?" Kore questioned.

He nodded at the camera. For Daniel and Kore, the world around them disappeared for a moment.

"What happened to you?" he asked. He quickly remembered he was in front of an audience and added, "You look horrible. You look like you were hit by a train."

"I was going to say the same thing about you," Daniel replied.

Laughter could be heard throughout the west wing, where the Situation Room was located. Kore didn't find it funny. The president, Jack, and Paul watched from just a few feet away.

"Ladies and gentlemen," announced Kore. "I'd like to introduce you to Daniel, a wannabe hacker, who is always in the wrong place at the wrong time. Today you will witness Daniel disappear for good. It will be my best magic trick yet—and you all get a front row seat."

Jack glanced over at Jay and Paul. What was Kore talking about? Daniel just sat there with his hands on the keyboard. He waited for Kore to make a move. Everyone was on the edge of their seat, wondering what was going to happen next.

"Hey Daniel," said Kore with new confidence. "Do you remember that electric gun I showed you, when you illegally trespassed into my headquarters?"

Daniel didn't reply. He just sat there, staring into the screen with his hands on the keyboard. His right index finger was hovering above the enter button.

"Well, it's okay. I wouldn't expect someone like you to have a good memory," Kore said, mocking Daniel. "Let me refresh it for you as a courtesy to our audience. After years and years of practice, I finally discovered how to harness electricity. My first experiment was my electric gun. As Daniel and his friends found out, the gun works very well. That's nothing compared to my biggest accomplishment. I can now transfer electricity across the Internet through your computer. If you'll give me just one second, I'll show you."

Nobody knew what was going on in the Situation Room. How could someone send an electric shock through the Internet? Daniel wasn't fazed in the least. He already knew.

Kore looked into the camera of his live feed. "Prepare to meet Electro-KORE. It is the first ever electromagnetic pulsating force, which can travel across the Internet. It is powerful enough to shock anything or anyone on the other side of the computer to the core." He laughed out loud.

Kore hit a button on his computer. It was the moment he had been waiting for. He had been perfecting it for years, but this was the first time he had tried it outside of Alcazar. He couldn't wait for the world to watch in fear as they witnessed him fry his first victim. He knew that if he could control the power grids and for that matter, power anywhere—he would finally rule the world.

At first nothing happened. Everyone wondered if his experiment had failed. Then the lights began to flicker in the Situation Room. Jack, Paul, and Jay took a few steps back. It was the last place that should lose power. It felt like the electricity was being sucked out of the room. Daniel waited for the shock. He knew it was coming. He felt something pulsing through the computer. As the keyboard began to shake, he began to wonder if he should back away, but he knew he had to be close enough to hit enter when the time came.

It hit him with so much force that his head was thrown back into his wheelchair. His glasses flew off his face. His eyes felt like they were going to pop out of his head. He imagined that this was what it felt like to grab a live power line. The world watched as the young man on camera was getting electrocuted. He was completely paralyzed. He couldn't even move his fingers. The energy was flowing through him so fast that he couldn't think. His head felt like it was going to explode.

The president screamed, "Somebody help him!"

A security guard came in behind Daniel and grabbed his wheelchair handle. The second he touched the chair, he dropped to the ground. He had been hit by a massive bolt of electricity. Another guard came and pulled his motionless friend away. Everyone in the room was afraid to get close. They could see sparks flying off of Daniel's metal wheelchair with more and more intensity each second.

Kore watched with pleasure. He continued to turn up the power. It was working even better than he had imagined. The world would see how powerful he was. He moved the dial up another notch. Daniel would be dead soon.

All Daniel needed to do was hit the enter button. He couldn't move. He wished he had told someone about his plan. Everyone in the room could smell something burning. It was flesh. The world watched on in horror. This wasn't a movie. It was a live execution.

Daniel couldn't hang on any longer. He thought about his dad and his grandfather behind him. He thought about his mother's love. The pain started to fade away. He could see a white light ahead. It was becoming brighter. He couldn't feel anything anymore… only warmth. He slipped into unconsciousness… then darkness. Another faint light appeared.

Jay couldn't take it anymore. He was the president. This was his country, and the entire world was watching a terrorist kill a young man in his home. He looked over at his old mentor, Jack. He was crying. His grandson was dying. Jay had noticed Daniel's index finger hovering above the enter key the entire time Kore had been talking. Did Daniel have a plan? Would this stop the attack?

There were no other options. His career was done. Worst case scenario, he'd die a martyr in front of the world. He went for it. He ran towards Daniel as everyone looked on in disbelief.

Jay could feel the energy against his skin the closer he got. His heart was racing. He reached over Daniel's shoulder and pressed the enter button. In an instant, he was thrown back against the wall, his head crushing through the drywall. Intense pain shot through his entire body. The impact knocked the air out of him. He struggled to get a breath. The room became blurry. He could make out the silhouette of Daniel's limp body still in the wheelchair in front of the computer. Kore's face was gone. There was only static on the screen. He closed his eyes.

# 28 HOSPITAL BEDS

Jack looked down at the two of them with concern. It had been almost twelve hours since the explosion.

He watched his grandson's chest slowly rise and fall. He looked so helpless and frail. The oxygen mask covered most of his face. It hid many of the burn marks, which ran down the left side of his cheek and mouth.

Daniel finally opened his eyes. Jay had just regained consciousness ten minutes earlier. Jack had never been so relieved in his life.

"The two of you are lucky to still be here with us."

It was the White House staff doctor talking to Daniel and Jay. They were lying next to each other in hospital gurneys. The president had been thrown almost twenty feet by the explosion. He had a cracked vertebra, bruised ribs, and a concussion. Daniel had suffered severe burns and had a minor heart attack. Jack stood there in-between them.

Jay looked over at Daniel. He looked like a mummy.

"You're pretty tough for a young man in a wheelchair," he said while grinning.

Daniel looked around for his phone. It wasn't there. He looked up at his grandfather for help.

"Your phone was in your pocket when Kore attacked you. It was so hot, it melted to your leg. The nurses had to pry it off your skin. You can use mine for now. I already downloaded your voice app."

"Is Kore still alive?" asked Jay while he waited for Jack to give Daniel a phone.

"They aren't sure. When you hit the enter button, it created some type of reflection, which sent all of the power surging back through the Internet to its origin. The system imploded. The last thing we saw was a fiery explosion, which consumed Kore before the connection went black. If he's not dead, then he's definitely hurting worse than you guys. That was a crazy amount of current. The doctors still aren't sure how Daniel survived. Their only conclusion was that the rubber tires on his wheelchair diminished the shock to his body. Had he not been in that wheelchair, he never would have lived."

Daniel let that sink in. He had always dreamed that everything would be better if only he could walk and talk like a normal person. He would finally be happy. Now, he wouldn't even be here if it wasn't for the chair. It had saved him. His eyes teared up.

"Will you get your job back?" Daniel asked.

The president smiled. He leaned over his bed to face Daniel as best he could.

"I'm not sure, Daniel. If I do, it will be because of your bravery."

Daniel and Jay both smiled. Grandpa Jack wiped away a tear, which had formed beneath his eye. He had always dreamed that someone in his family would do big things. Someone would make him proud. He finally got his wish.

Daniel suddenly remembered one last thing. He turned to Jack.

"By the way, thank you for sending that eagle with the map. We would have never gotten anywhere without it."

Jack's face crumpled in a look of confusion.

"Eagle?" he asked. "I'm not sure I know what you're talking about."

Daniel didn't expect that at all. As he searched his grandfather's face, all he could find was sincerity. If this was true, then who had sent it?

"Daniel, what do you think the chances are that Kore will come up here to get revenge if he's still alive?" asked Jay.

Daniel thought about it for a second before replying. He typed slowly while a nurse checked his vitals. "I'd say the chances are pretty high. What do you think?"

The president nodded. "Yes. If he's still alive, he'll be back. This time we'll be prepared for him, and this time I won't be afraid. I've got you on my team."

Daniel smiled. He thought about what the president had said. *On his team.* He never imagined he'd find happiness outside of the library. He had always been afraid to do anything out of his comfort zone. He believed that he'd never amount to anything in his wheelchair. If only his old friends in Alcazar could see him now. He imagined the smile on Skylar's face. He wanted her to know… perhaps because she'd been the one to doubt him the most.

The president interrupted his thoughts.

"Daniel. How hard it is to get down there where Kore lives?"

He typed on his phone. He was laughing to himself.

"That all depends on how scared you are of wolves, crocodiles, and scorpions."

Jack let out a big laugh. The president followed suit, although he wasn't exactly sure why he was laughing.

"Well, as soon as we get out of this hospital, I'd like you to take me down there. This time you'll have a small army behind you," replied the president.

Daniel imagined returning to Alcazar. His heart swelled. Strangely enough, it felt more like home than America. He'd go back. He *wanted* to go back, especially now that he was fearless. Fearlessness meant one thing to him: freedom. It was never the chair, which had trapped him. It was his fear. Now he was free; free from his fear. He turned to his grandfather once more.

"Kore was in a wheelchair…" Daniel started.

"Yes…?" Jack replied.

"Well, it's strange, isn't it?" Daniel said. "Why didn't he just visit the Fountain of Youth?"

Jack paused in thought. The president raised his eyebrows, clearly thrown off by Daniel's comment.

"What do you—" Jay slowly started to ask, before Jack interrupted him.

"Did Vosco or Skylar mention that the fountain heals you because it *knows* you?"

"They did mention something like that…" Daniel said, trying to remember. That visit to the fountain had been one of the happiest moments of his life. It was a blur. "Something about how the fountain has a consciousness?"

"Yes," Jack continued. "If the fountain is intelligent, then it has a will of its own. This means it can choose whether it wants to heal someone or not."

"So, it's possible the fountain *chose* not to heal Kore because it could… see inside him?"

"I suspect that's right," Jack said. "The fountain knew Kore's intentions. He wanted to heal for self-serving reasons. He wanted to bring great harm to others."

"But it healed me…" Daniel thought aloud.

"Yes. What does that say about you, Daniel?"

Unexpected tears filled his eyes.

"Something… good?" Daniel asked.

Jack reached out and squeezed his hand.

"Something very good," Jack replied, his gentle eyes holding Daniel's gaze. "You are full of goodness. Integrity, intelligence, and kindness all live within you. That's who you are. That's what the fountain could see."

As someone who'd been constantly judged by his outside appearance rather than who he was, it was the first time Daniel felt truly visible.

*To be continued....*

# ABOUT THE AUTHOR

Joe Simonds is a fisherman, author, friend of Jesus, husband, father, beer drinker, and a recovering Chapstick addict. He has been a story-teller for as long as he can remember. From entertaining his two younger brothers, Luke and Daniel (inspiration for The Chair), to telling fishing stories to his audience at Salt Strong, he was born to entertain.

Joe is the CEO of Salt Strong, the online fishing club, which guarantees you catch more fish. He and his brother, Luke, are changing the world for the better through fishing.

*The Chair* is Joe's fourth published book, and it's the first in a series about Daniel…

Joe lives in Florida with his wife, Loren, and their three children.

You can reach him via e-mail at joe@saltstrong.com.

P.S. – A huge thanks to the following family and friends for helping improve this book: Larry Simonds, Susan Simonds, Luke Simonds, Bruce "Almighty" Somers, Peter & Lenore Verrill, Maggie Taylor, Mary & Drew Ouzts, Kynda & Tom Ray, Carolyn Baldwin, Desiree & Billy Morris, Lauren & Peter Bretz, Brett Cox Bubba Love, Lara Delorenzo-Sims, Steve Kennedy, Kevin Respress, James Guldan, Nick Pavone, and my beautiful wife, Loren.

Made in the USA
Columbia, SC
06 March 2020